INNOCENT
MURDERER

INNOCENT MURDERER

A Cordi O'Callaghan Mystery

Suzanne F. Kingsmill

A Castle Street Mystery

DUNDURN PRESS
TORONTO

Copy Editor: Cheryl Hawley
Designer: Jennifer Scott
Printer: Webcom

Library and Archives Canada Cataloguing in Publication

Kingsmill, Suzanne
     Innocent murderer : a Cordi O'Callaghan mystery / Suzanne F. Kingsmill.

ISBN 978-1-55488-426-1

I. Title.

PS8621.I57I66 2009   C813'.6   C2009-903252-X

1 2 3 4 5   13 12 11 10 09

Conseil des Arts du Canada   Canada Council for the Arts   Canadä   ONTARIO ARTS COUNCIL CONSEIL DES ARTS DE L'ONTARIO

We acknowledge the support of the **Canada Council for the Arts** and the **Ontario Arts Council** for our publishing program. We also acknowledge the financial support of the **Government of Canada** through the **Book Publishing Industry Development Program** and **The Association for the Export of Canadian Books**, and the **Government of Ontario** through the **Ontario Book Publishers Tax Credit program**, and the **Ontario Media Development Corporation**.

Care has been taken to trace the ownership of copyright material used in this book. The author and the publisher welcome any information enabling them to rectify any references or credits in subsequent editions.

J. Kirk Howard, President

Printed and bound in Canada.
www.dundurn.com

Dundurn Press
3 Church Street, Suite 500
Toronto, Ontario, Canada
M5E 1M2

Gazelle Book Services Limited
White Cross Mills
High Town, Lancaster, England
LA1 4XS

Dundurn Press
2250 Military Road
Tonawanda, NY
U.S.A. 14150

For B.W.J.

Chapter One

"Y ou want me to spend a week in the Arctic with a convicted murderer?"

My lab technician swivelled around in her chair to face me. "Well, not exactly a murderer," said Martha, her voice lingering on the word "exactly," stretching it like molasses. She tried to stare me down, all her indecision playing over her round face like a carousel of slides flicking too fast: excitement swirled into indecision, melding with consternation, mixing with uncertainty, combining with stubbornness. I got dizzy watching the play of feelings over her face, which is beautiful when it's not so conflicted.

"Martha, how can someone be a convicted murderer but not really?" I glanced out of the window of the university zoology building where I work as a professor. Summer classes were winding down and there were only a few people walking through the grassy quadrangle below. When classes are in full swing in the fall the little patch of green is thronged with students lazing about, or playing Frisbee or catch.

When Martha didn't answer I turned back in amazement. She usually views questions as one views the next potato chip. Impossible not to devour.

"Well?"

"Really, Cordi, you've got to learn to keep your mind open. You can't always take things at face value."

I started to protest but she waved me down.

"You can be a mislabelled murderer after all."

"You mean he was wrongfully convicted?"

"Exactly! Except that it's a she. *She* was acquitted." She said it triumphantly, her words placed before me like a gourmet meal that I was supposed to jump on with relish. Even without relish it sounded like a dish with too much flavour, but I was determined to show her I could keep an open mind and not look for the negative in everything.

"What's her name?"

"Terry Spencer."

The name rang some distant bell, but I had no idea what it might be trying to tell me. Not that I cared. I was damned if I was going to let Martha talk me into something I was pretty sure I wouldn't want to do.

"So what did she not do?" I asked

"She did not kill a man. She was acquitted on the evidence."

Martha hesitated and I looked at her suspiciously, but she didn't say anything else.

"Okay, so why do you think I would want to spend a week in the Arctic with this — this acquitted lady?"

"So you can help her with her creative writing course next month." She hesitated when she saw the look of incredulity on my face. "C'mon, Cordi. It's going to be a nice, leisurely nine day cruise to see the Arctic. All you have to do is give some writing students a few good tips on how to investigate a murder. That, and some natural biology of the Arctic. It'll be a breeze."

I didn't say anything. I was too busy battling the gale force wind she called a breeze.

Martha ploughed on. "Terry teaches my creative writing course and we're all going to sort of bond and get to know each other in the Arctic while we get material for our work. You know, observe the passengers and stuff."

"But you hate the wilderness," I said.

"This is different. I don't have to live in a tent and get eaten alive. This is like being a turtle. You travel with your own room attached. No hardships!"

I stood there wondering how I could work with Martha every day and sometimes feel as though I knew so little about her. I didn't want to pursue the details of my supposed role in all this, so I changed the subject instead. "I didn't know you were taking a writing course." I was getting drawn in despite myself. "I didn't even know you wrote!"

Martha swung back to her desk, looking as if I'd hurt her feelings, and began sorting through vials of my insect specimens. I must have said it the wrong way because nothing in the words sounded offensive to me.

"I didn't mean to imply you couldn't write," I said to her accusing back. Silence. She was infuriating. When

I wanted to hear gossip she was as mute as a slug, but when I didn't care she was like a rooster at dawn.

I tried another tack. "What makes a murderer qualified to teach you guys to write, and why in the name of god would she need me?"

She turned back to look at me. "You keep forgetting that she was acquitted. She wrote a bestseller while she was incarcerated — you know, all about her time in jail and stuff like that."

"But Martha, that doesn't sound like creative writing. Are you sure you're getting your money's worth?" I added, not wanting to see her scammed. She could be so damned trusting.

"Cordi, stop jumping to such negative conclusions. She's written several works of fiction since the non-fiction book. You really should read more, you know. She's quite well-known."

"No. I want to know why you seem to have volunteered my name."

"Because I knew you wouldn't mind helping out. The person who was supposed to do it backed out late last week and Terry is desperate for a replacement."

"Maybe it'd be easier to find a replacement if you just held the course here in the city."

Martha threw me a withering look that instantly made me feel like last year's lilies. "You can't possibly bond with people here in the city. It's too impersonal and we all go home after our three hours a week. There's no time to really get to know each other, learn about each other, and get some good material for our writing. There's nothing like meeting new people in close

surroundings to get good material for a story — that's
what Ms Spencer says."

Oh brother, a touchy feely teacher imprisoning her
charges on a gimungus ship in the Arctic. And she wants
someone who's allergic to bonding to be there helping
her students bond ... or was I jumping to conclusions?

"I thought writers were a solitary lot."

"Well, yeah, they are," said Martha in a voice that
sounded like a kid being denied a lollipop.

"Why are they going on this trip then?"

"Because Terry said it would be good for our writing.
And intimated that there might even be an agent on the
trip. You know, someone who could read our work and
discover the next P.D. James."

"How big is this anti-social group?"

"There are eight of us who are going."

When I didn't say anything she smiled. "What do
you say, Cordi? The trip would be paid for. Give you a
good vacation and distract you from Patrick."

Ah, my lover, Patrick — who was thinking seriously
about going to London, England, for a prospective job
that I fervently wished would evaporate. Long distance
relationships don't usually last, and Ottawa to London
is a hell of a commute, not to mention expensive. Plus
we hadn't been able to really talk about it because he
was away in Georgia for a week, giving a paper at a sci-
entific convention.

I should have just said no to Martha — I had so much
work on my plate — but her mention of Patrick had
derailed me. "When do you need to know my answer?"

"Today."

"Today? Are you nuts? How can I decide today when I don't even know if this Spencer person is a three-headed monster from Mansonville, or a sweet old geezer from church? Not to mention the problem of my not having enough material to teach your class anything useful. When is this trip anyway?"

Martha's face suddenly started doing gymnastics again and she kept flicking her eyes in the direction of the door. Startled, I turned around to look.

Standing there was a striking woman with corn blonde hair and forget-me-not eyes — cookie cutter beautiful. She was wearing a sky blue shift, belted at her tiny waist with a silver tasselled belt.

Before I could speak she said, "I think I prefer to be the old geezer to the three-headed monster." The words came out sounding pompous and stilted.

Fortunately I don't blush but I went one better with my stammering words — they came out sounding swollen and unused. "Oh ... Uh ... Are you ...?" I turned to Martha for help, wishing I was somewhere else.

"Yup, this is your three-headed monster. Terry Spencer, meet Cordi O'Callaghan." And with a flourish of her hand, Martha ushered her in. God, but she was drop-dead gorgeous, which is about what I felt like doing I was so embarrassed.

"I'm sorry. I didn't mean...." I held out my hand, at a total loss for words. Her blond hair was so shiny you could see your reflection in it and her deep tan looked fantastic on her tiny features, accenting her plump, red, heart-shaped mouth. Thirty-five? Forty-five with a nip and tuck. About my height, five feet six inches. Her handshake was surprisingly weak, my own strong grip evaporated in sympathy and I let go quickly.

"No problem, Ms O'Callaghan." She emphasized the Ms as though it was a four-letter word. She was watching me carefully, her eyes still and hard. "At least it's in the open," she continued as I said nothing. "It's harder when people look at me and I can see them wondering if I really am a murderer."

Her eyes were fixed on me. The smile on her face made it seem like she was amused, but her gaze felt arrogant. I squirmed in discomfort, wishing I could get onto safer ground so that I could feel like I had some control over the situation.

"Would you excuse us a moment, please?" I said and grabbed Martha by the arm, hauling her out into the hall.

"What the hell is going on?" I asked as we moved down the hall together.

"Shhh, Cordi, she can hear you."

I dropped my voice to a whisper. "What's she doing here?"

Martha rubbed her hands and I watched her face as it surfed through a bunch of different emotions, finally settling on what sure looked like guilt.

"I suggested she swing by here to have a quick talk about logistics and stuff before tonight's lesson so she could confirm with the class if you were coming. She said she'd be in the area anyway and would drop by."

"Why didn't you tell me?"

"I was going to but we got involved in other stuff." She looked me in the eye. "I told her there was no way you'd be able to attend the class tonight and that if she wanted to check you out she'd have to come to you. It's kind of urgent you know."

I knew Martha well enough to know I should have paid attention to that last sentence, but I was too busy thinking about what she said just before to catch the warning signs. "Check me out? What do you mean, check me out?"

"Well, you know, to make sure you aren't a shy recluse unable to string two words together who would bomb out with the students."

"Martha, are you saying that it's not a sure thing I'd be going, even if I wanted to?"

"Well she can't hire you sight unseen, can she? And you can't accept sight unseen, so I guess this is sort of a mutual job interview." The guilt was on her face big time. She hadn't told me because she was afraid I'd have made a point of not being here when Terry came — a valid concern.

There was nothing for it but to go back in, face Terry, and make the most of the situation, but I was surprised to feel a tickle of sudden disappointment that the job wasn't yet mine for the taking. How much did that have to do with wanting to be distracted from thoughts of Patrick? Or maybe I really did want to go and see the Arctic with a bunch of people I'd never met — with a teacher who I wasn't sure I liked.

Terry was standing by the window near Martha's desk and looked up quickly as we re-entered. I glanced at the desk and wondered what she'd been reading. Then I wondered why it mattered.

"You got things straightened out between you?" she asked.

Martha mumbled something and I said nothing.

Terry smiled and I offered her Martha's chair and sat down on the counter so that I had the high ground and was able to see what she was snooping — something on the life cycle of sparrows. I smiled. Terry shook her head and instead leaned against the other counter as Martha triumphantly reclaimed her chair. I thought about getting two more chairs from the office but decided against it. The more uncomfortable we all were the less likely we'd talk forever.

"I understand from Martha," I said, "that you're looking for someone to give some lectures to your writing students on an upcoming trip?"

"That's right. You sound perfect as a replacement for this particular cruise."

Did that mean that for any other cruise I was incompetent, or that I was only competent as a replacement, or both?

"Martha tells me your lectures on gruesome murder investigations are packed. Plus you can throw in some general Arctic biology on the side."

"You realize," I said stiffly, "that my expertise is not with humans. I offer a course here at the university for entomology students who want to learn how to identify insects. To make it interesting, for part of the course we use roadkill and pigs, and move the carcasses from one habitat to another. The students have to determine where the animal actually died from the insects on the body, and how many times it was moved, if at all."

"No problem with that," she said. "You can give some of the same lectures you give your students. Humans are animals after all; just like the roadkill." She said it in a way that made my skin crawl, but when I quickly glanced up at her, her blue eyes were smiling back. "I teach Martha and twenty-three others, but only eight are coming. The cruise caters to about eighty clients from varying backgrounds, most of them belonging to naturalist clubs of one sort or another. They'd be allowed to listen to your lectures up to a maximum of forty people per session."

"You mean there are only eighty tourists on board?" This was not the sort of cruise I had imagined. I had pictured one of those mini floating cities that most luxury liners seem to be these days. This actually sounded workable. Some of the classes I teach have a lot more than eighty students in them. Things were beginning to look up. I was actually thinking I could look forward to it — until she got up to leave and my little bubble exploded.

"Thanks for taking this on," she said, offering me her hand. I couldn't remember saying that I would take it on, but she forestalled my protest saying, "God, I'm glad we found a last minute replacement for Kathy Reichs."

And then she was gone.

The alarm bells that had tinkled earlier were positively deafening now. I turned and looked suspiciously at my lab tech. "Last minute?"

"Plane leaves in three days."

I gaped at Martha. How was I supposed to organize my schedule in such a short time? And why hadn't Martha warned me she was going on holiday?

"You didn't tell me you were …"

"I did, Cordi, when I told you I was getting Leah as a replacement."

The penny dropped. I'd been distracted by my research at the time and hadn't really been listening to her. I had thought it was some holiday in the distant future. But I remembered now.

"And Kathy Reichs?"

"She's no match for you."

Yeah right, I thought.

Chapter Two

Our flight left three days later from the Ottawa airport. In that time I had managed to get the graduate student who helped me with the comparative anatomy course to stand in for me while I was gone. Martha, at least, had already lined up a lab technician to take her place and look after my animals. It was fortunate that none of my experiments needed me at the moment and Martha's replacement knew the ropes — she'd helped me out before so I trusted her.

To make the early morning flight I'd had to get up as the sun was rising with the mist to drive in from my place in the country. I'd also tried to get hold of Patrick a dozen times but he wasn't picking up and the hotel phone was no better, so I had to leave a message that I'd see him in a week. Definitely not very satisfying, especially in an age when we're all supposed to be reachable in multiple ways.

The airport was deserted except for a knot of people down near First Air. I spotted Martha right away. She was wearing a lime green jogging suit and scarlet shirt. She was bending over a huge stack of luggage, rifling through it in a barely controlled panic while a very familiar figure stood beside her, patiently holding her enormous oversized purse.

"Duncan! What are you doing here?" I called out.

I may be nearsighted but there is no mistaking Duncan. Even without his imposing stature he's impossible to miss because you can't miss his face, and you can't miss his face because you can't miss the nose on it. It overpowers everything else, even his clear blue eyes and soft smile. Duncan is a pathologist who lives a couple of hours northwest of Ottawa. He works at the university in Dumoine and is the local coroner. We'd met the summer before when I'd stumbled across a body in the wilderness.

"Cordi! Cordi! Lovely to see you. How are you my dear?" He engulfed me in a massive bear hug. The tweed of his heavy jacket tickled my nose and mouth, and I could smell the mothballs that it had been stored in.

"Are you coming to Iqaluit?" I shouted into his chest, my words muffled and deadened by his tweed.

He suddenly eased up on his bear hug and held me at arm's length, "What did you say, Cordi? God, you look good."

"What are you doing here?"

Duncan glanced down at Martha, who was still wildly rummaging through her luggage, and said, "Didn't Martha tell you? I'm a member of the writing group, so I guess that means I'm coming along too."

"You?" I asked incredulous. "When did you take up writing?"

"When Martha did," he said and winked as he looked down at Martha and his smile broadened into a grin that almost eclipsed his nose. Almost. I wondered how many of his writing mates were using that incredible nose in their stories. What a gift! Duncan certainly saw it that way. It had taught him how to be blunt and open about things. What else could he do, with a nose like that?

Martha finally emerged from her bag, triumphant over her recovery of something. "Got it!" She waved her airline ticket at me. For a moment her own anxiety infected me and I found myself reaching for my bag to reassure myself that I had all my travel documents, even though I knew I did.

"He's good, you know," said Martha as she began repacking her boots and winter coat, which had sproinged all over the airport floor.

"Who's good?" I asked.

"Duncan. He's a good writer."

I looked at Duncan in frank astonishment. I'd read some of his coroner reports and even without the horrific handwriting his prose had been lean and mean, no flowers, no padding, just the facts and nothing more. He raised his eyebrows at me and shrugged.

Martha caught sight of him and gave him a friendly swipe of her hand. "He just doesn't know he's good. But he's done a nice little mystery piece on street kids and squeegees."

"Enough already, Martha," said Duncan. "You're giving away my trade secrets. Now, where's the lineup for the baggage check in?" he asked, even though he was looking right at it.

"Back over there," said Martha. "Oooo look, there's Tracey and George. And there's Elizabeth." Martha took off like a battleship with Duncan in tow.

I hung back, not quite wanting to immerse myself in these people's lives yet. For now I just wanted to observe. I guess I was afraid of being beside someone from the writing group who would talk my ear off for the entire flight. At least on the boat I could escape. I checked my luggage and then walked back down the hall to the donut shop where I bought a donut and O.J. Then I browsed for a book in the airport bookstore before making my way to the gate.

On the plane I had managed to get a window seat, affording me some degree of privacy and comfort, as long as I didn't have to use the washroom. But the seat in front of me was full, so I would have a meal tray in my teeth. I watched with interest as Terry Spencer struggled down the aisle, carrying a very large carry-on and a brief-case. When she got to my row she stopped, consulted her ticket, and then glanced at me. I nodded but she looked away and started trying to manhandle her carry-on bag into the overhead bin. A man in the next row finally got up and helped her.

As she dumped the briefcase in the aisle seat she said to no one in particular, but everyone who was listening, "Why do airplanes always come with such tiny luggage compartments?"

I refrained from saying it was probably because they figured most people would not take all of their worldly possessions on board. She clicked open the catches on the briefcase and hauled out a huge sheaf of papers, dumping them on the middle seat. As she did so a small object in the shape of an elephant flew onto the floor at her feet. I reached to retrieve it for her, but before I could she snatched it up and shoved it in her briefcase without even looking at me. I caught the eye of a dark haired woman across the aisle, who looked at me and hastily glanced away. Her face was so pale I wondered why she didn't help it along with some makeup. Terry refastened her case, hoisted it above her head, and plopped down into her aisle seat, swooping up the papers as she went.

"Glad you could make it" she said, without looking up from her papers or sounding genuine.

I thought that was a little rude but maybe she was still planning her course and was nervous about not being ready — I know I felt that way. I went back to scrawling out some possible notes for my lectures, until a voice cut through my concentration.

"George wants a word with you."

The odd, resigned but angry tone of voice made me look up. He was standing in the aisle fidgeting with his hands. He was of medium height and build, about forty-five years old with a full head of straight jet-black hair, too dark for his age, so dyed. He had bushy, too dark eyebrows, and telltale grey stubble on a face that must have needed shaving twice a day. His face was pitted by old acne scars and his nose was the red of a man who liked to drink. His chin dropped off like a landslide from his mouth into his neck. The only part of him that didn't match his age was his body, which looked as finely tuned as a twenty-year-old's.

"They're sitting across from me so why don't we just switch."

Terry looked up and grimaced. "Can't you handle it, Owen?" The way she said it sounded more like, "What kind of a fool are you?"

"No. He wants to talk to you about his wife's writing. She's pretty upset about what you said."

"Christ, what a baby." Terry quickly glanced up at him and then looked at me and began extricating herself form her paperwork. "All I said was that it needs work," she scowled. "I could have said much worse."

As she finally stood up she looked back at me. "You two haven't met yet, have you?" she asked, as if it were the most boring thing in the world.

"Owen this is Cordi O'Callaghan. Cordi — Owen Ballantyne, my right-hand man."

I reached over and gripped his hand, then wished I hadn't. It was like getting flattened by a rolling machine, my rings mashed into my skin. He smiled at me and what should have been his chin bunched up into seven folds of skin, his smile sliding into them.

Terry stuffed her sheaf of unruly handwritten papers into Owen's hand, and in a soft, barely audible voice said "Put them in your briefcase." Then she moved forward and took Owen's seat. Owen disappeared down the aisle and returned with his briefcase. He tidied the papers but didn't put them away.

As the plane took off and reached cruising altitude I kept to myself, reading a magazine about woodworking.

But it was hard to concentrate because there was a fair amount of whispering going on in the row ahead of me.

Suddenly, the seat in front of me bucked and a woman with the most amazing curly red hair stood up, forcing her seatmate to get up to let her out. He was a heavyset man in his early forties with a tremendous shock of pure white hair. I didn't catch what he looked like because he sat down immediately. I pretended to tie my shoes and peered through the crack and watched as he took the woman's purse, a red suede eye catcher, and opened it. He looked around furtively and I backed off, but my curiosity was too much for me. I stood up and as I did so I saw him take something from the bag and slip it in his pocket. He looked up and our eyes glanced off each other as I stepped past Owen and went to the washroom. I could feel his eyes on me all the way down the aisle.

There was a lineup, of course, and I lounged against the side of one of the aisle seats. There was a man sitting in it who seemed to be nothing but a mass of hair. He was reading a paper that was about the illegal trade of wild animals. I wondered if he was a fellow lecturer. His seatmate, a diminutive blond, was reading a comic book. I had scanned back to the paper the man was reading when suddenly he looked up at me. I quickly looked away, but not before I saw the annoyance in his face. Who could blame him? All these people hovering over him as they waited impatiently in line.

When I came back the shock of white hair was gone and both seats sat empty.

I must have dozed off because the next thing I knew

was hearing Terry's voice cutting through the plane "It's just a piece of writing for god's sake."

And then a male voice saying, "Lady, you have no right...."

I couldn't hear what happened next, just a lot of muffled voices, but it was enough to catapult Owen out of his chair. He dumped the papers he'd been reading on the seat with the briefcase and they spilled onto the floor along with the case. Two of the sheets fluttered after him as he disappeared down the aisle. I picked up a manual on hot air balloons and then had to get out of my seat to retrieve all of the stuff that had fallen out of the briefcase, as well as the briefcase itself. I picked up the two sheets and put them back with the rest. They were in no particular order and as I straightened them out a handwritten phrase caught my eye; the scrawl tight and legible.

"Drenched in oil and blinded by blood she held her breath and jumped." It was about a woman fleeing a black market organ attempt, or at least I thought it was, but I didn't get to read any more because someone above me cleared their throat in a way that demanded attention. I looked up and found Owen staring at me, his face so blank that there was nothing at all I could read from it.

"I'm sorry. They fell when you left ..." I stumbled along into silence. He still stood in the aisle staring at me. I felt myself start to get hot.

"Do you always read people's private papers?"

"I didn't really read them, just glanced at them."

He reached out his hand and I gave him the papers. He sat down and replaced them in the briefcase.

"Some of the students' work," he said. "They wouldn't be keen to know some stranger was rifling through it." I couldn't tell by the closed look on his face whether he was angry or indifferent.

"Your briefcase fell."

"Nothing we can do about it. But thank you." His face was inscrutable and then he smiled this weird, tight little smile and took out his earphones.

After that little rap on the knuckles I made him get up to let me out again. Most people were watching the movie and the legs of the men in the outer seats were encroaching on the aisle as they tried to get comfortable while jammed into seats meant for their children. I manoeuvred around them and caught sight of Duncan and Martha, but they were engrossed in the movie.

When I got back to my seat Owen was gone and Terry was back, poring over her work with an air that unmistakably said, "Don't you dare interrupt me." But I had to, of course, and she grumbled about people who can't sit still but she left me alone.

I felt really fidgety and shuffled around for some papers until Terry gave me the evil eye. I was about to check out the movie when I noticed a strikingly tall woman coming down the aisle towards us, her face dwarfed by the mass of curly red hair that scattered its way all across it — the woman from the seat in front of me. She wasn't just tall, she had muscle to go along with the height. And apparently she'd been crying, because her eyes matched the colour of her hair. She stopped at her row and cleared her throat. I wondered why she didn't sit down. Her white haired seatmate had moved to the window seat. She just stood there looking forlorn until I heard a hissing voice practically throttle her with its venomous intent. "For god's sake Sally, sit down or get out of everybody's way." And she sat down beside him.

I watched the movie for a while but it didn't really grab me and the earphones weren't working very well; I had to keep hitting them to get them to work, which did not sit well with Terry. It was one of those movies strung together with very little substance and lots of gratuitous violence. The four-letter words were beeped out for the kids.

I took out my earphones and stashed them in the pocket of the seat in front of me. Then I rifled though it looking for a magazine. I noticed out of the corner of my eye that Terry was watching the movie, so I was able to wrestle some papers out of my briefcase and started thinking about my upcoming lectures. It was quiet on the plane. That charged, ethereal kind of quiet that comes with being in excess of twenty thousand feet above ground and defying gravity. That is, it *was* quiet until I gradually became aware of people whispering.

"No, please Arthur." The voice seemed deflated, stripped of any resolve, totally needy and therefore totally desperate.

A male voice, bitter and sarcastic replied, "I've had enough. I don't want you Sally." He strung out the words as if she couldn't speak English very well. "What part of that do you not understand? It's over."

The seat in front of me suddenly bucked and the white haired, heavyset man stood up and barged his way past Sally. Without looking back he strode to the front of the plane.

I heard Sally calling out, "Arthur!" and then I leaned forward and glanced through the crack between the seats. She had grabbed her hair and was rocking back and forth.

I looked over at Terry, who had taken out her earphones. Sally had started to cry, low, gentle sobs under tight control. I wondered if I should do something, but then Terry got up and barged her way in. She didn't even hesitate. She told Sally to stop crying in a tone that sounded like a schoolteacher reaming out a student. Sally's sobs stopped, whether due to the suddenness of Terry's appearance, the sharpness of the tone, or something else altogether, I don't know. But it didn't last long. I sat there, prisoner to the conversation in front of me. After all, it's pretty hard not to overhear people talking, even in a whisper, when you're just three feet away.

"He's leaving me. He's leaving me."

"For heaven's sake, pull yourself together," said Terry. "You're just a jilted woman not a mourning widow."

That made the sobs grow louder. "I need to tell my friend," she gurgled. There was a long silence.

Terry's voice dropped to a low whisper, but I could still make it out. "Don't go blabbing it around."

Sally's sobs turned staccato, as if she was trying to hold them in but was not succeeding — she already was blabbing it around. There was a long pause and then Terry finished, "Or I won't help you."

Chapter Three

"I never should have listened to you in the first place," I yelled at Martha over the crash of the rubber Zodiac bucking over a wave and skittering down into another endless trough of icy cold Arctic water. I could feel my stomach start to slither around like a drunken snake and I prayed we'd make it to the ship before it decided to embarrass me.

Right after we'd landed in Iqaluit we had been given a tour of the town. Coming from a land of trees and bushes that bring softness to the harshness of manmade things, I was struck by the lack of even a little bush. I remembered hearing about an Inuit who came to southern Ontario and felt so claustrophobic he had to go back to the land of Inukshuks, those eerie stone sentinels of the north that point the way for those who are lost.

After visiting the Art Centre and watching Inuit carving stone into works of art full of motion and whimsy, we went to the community centre where we waited for hours without being told why. I should have suspected something when I went into the washroom. A group of women who had just come off the ship were gathered around the hand dryers, trying to get their clothes dry. One woman was wearing nothing but her underwear as she shook her clothes in front of the dryer. At the time I didn't really register what that meant.

I was trussed up like a cocoon, at least from the waist up. The hood of my orange rain jacket was pulled tight around my face, practically obscuring it, but my legs were drenched because I had forgotten my rain pants. I concentrated on gluing my eyes to the horizon while everyone else stared at the rolling ship that was looming up on the starboard side. I was sitting right at the rear, beside the guy manning the boat, the illegal trade paper guy. So I'd been right — he was part of the crew, which probably meant he was also a lecturer.

I was sitting amid all of the diesel fumes, fervently wishing I was on dry land. It was so tantalizingly close, yet so far away. We'd had to trudge through two hundred yards of low tide muck to even get to the Zodiacs — which wouldn't have surprised me had I known that Iqaluit has some of the largest tidal variations in the world. The muck may not have been firm land, or even dry land, but at least it hadn't bounced and weaved and ducked and dipped.

"Oh c'mon, Cordi," Martha screamed into the wind. "There's nothing to it. We'll be there in less than fifteen minutes."

Fifteen long, lurching, wiggly minutes in a boat with eight lolloping passengers and one driver, all perched on the pontoon shaped sides. And we were going to land on a bigger boat that was equally rolling and pitching. I certainly hadn't thought I would get seasick or I never would have taken this trip. I groaned and wished there was something else to take my mind off my stomach as Martha crashed into me on the next wave.

And that's when it happened. Terry, who was now wearing a yellow Eddie Bauer Gore-Tex rain suit and sitting near the bow, suddenly lurched up and staggered towards the stern of the boat where I was sitting, her eyes boring into the space between me and the orange clad driver like a razor sharp drill. I heard the driver cursing. With one hand on the engine he used his other hand to madly wave Terry down while yelling words into the wind that she couldn't hear.

When the next wave hit, Terry seemed to leap straight at us in a slow motion blur. When the boat bucked sideways on a wave she raised her arms in a futile effort to save herself, and instead of crashing into me she was thrown onto the driver. The two of them fell heavily against the bulwark, the driver's head crashing against it with a sickening thud that I could hear above the wind.

The Zodiac began to dance and slew sideways to the waves and a sickening accordion motion gripped the boat as an icy wave broke over the starboard side. The cold of the water felt like a burn, searing my face. I saw, as if in slow motion, the now bare handle of the engine jerking spasmodically, the heaving rubber and slat wood floorboards, the wildly slewing boat broaching the waves — I leaned over and grabbed the throttle with both hands, more to calm my roiling stomach than for any altruistic reasons. The thing felt alive, like a horse straining at the reins, full of power and potential, but unable to choose a direction in which to go. I shoved it as far away from me as I could, feeling as though I was pushing the whole weight of Frobisher Bay before me. Agonizingly slowly, the boat began to turn back into the waves, to more ordered motion. I felt the handle bucking my commands, wanting to be free, jerking and straining for chaos. My back and shoulder muscles were taut with the effort of keeping the boat on the proper course.

I glanced over at the driver, hoping for rescue, but he lay sprawled on the bottom of the boat, his head and shoulders draped over the round pontoon of the port side, his face unnervingly slack and grey, or what I could see of it through his heavy beard. The closest passenger to him was trying to stop the alarming flow of blood from a deep cut on his forehead and the other passengers were gripping the handrails of the boat, white knuckled, as another wave hit us and broke over the bow.

I noticed Terry had somehow crawled her way back up to the bow to sit beside Arthur, the white haired man, and was clutching her stomach. The driver was still out cold. I was on my own. How the hell was I supposed to land the Zodiac?

"Can you drive this thing?" The voice was high and shrill in the wind, almost weightless, and the disbelief that cascaded from the words was not a confidence booster. I glanced in the direction of the voice and saw Terry, her makeup smeared by the salt water and her attempts to keep it out of her eyes.

She grabbed Arthur's arm, yelling "Jesus, Arthur. Are you fuckin' going to let her try to drive this thing? She'll kill us all."

That was a funny thing for her to say, since she was the one who had just knocked out the only person on the boat who actually knew how to drive it! Still, I saw the passengers who had heard her words glance nervously at me as Arthur said something to her that no one could hear. She looked back at me and yelled, "You'd better know what you're doing lady."

I was already wondering the same thing when Martha, who looked completely unruffled by the series of events, screamed at the whole boat. "Course she can drive this thing. She's been doing it for years. Trust me. She's the best and she's one of crew."

Neither of which was quite accurate. Martha conveniently forgot to mention that my years of experience were with much smaller Zodiacs in much smaller and warmer seas, but what the heck, a boat is a boat. And technically I was one of the crew.

I watched carefully as the Zodiac ahead of us nosed up to the side of the ship at a small metal platform and threw a rope to a crew member crouched on the wave drenched dock. I could make out metal stairs snaking up at a forty-five degree angle from the water to the deck of the ship. Passengers were drunkenly weaving their way up the stairs.

Suddenly it was our turn. I kept the Zodiac pointed into the waves as we headed for the ship, aware that seven pairs of eyes anxiously watched my every move. Only Martha seemed unconcerned. What was it about her that made her so oblivious to potential danger?

We were heading straight into the wind, parallel to the ship, which was lying at anchor. I kept the throttle at full bore until we were twenty yards away and then eased back as we shot toward the dock. At the last moment I throttled way back, and the lack of power and the strength of the wind allowed the boat to float toward the dock — theoretically. Instead, we rammed the dock from the crest of a wave and my passengers tumbled around like bingo balls. Terry crashed against Arthur, her head ramming his hard camera case. Arthur scowled as another man picked her up, just as a deckhand grabbed the bow rope of the bucking boat and secured it to the heaving metal dock.

The boat, finally secured, was now tied to the energy of the ship, which was straining at its anchor and riding the waves differently from the little Zodiac hugging its side. The male passengers struggled to get the helmsman into the arms of the crewmen and to safety. He was starting to come to and was moaning as he was carried up the gangway. One by one the passengers slid their bottoms down the side of the pontoons to the two crewmen — their bright orange slickers like beacons of safety — who held out their hands to grip each passenger by the arm and swing them to safety between waves.

When it was Terry's turn she turned and smiled. "You're one lucky, lady."

I had the unpleasant feeling that she could see into the quiet depths of my own mind where my fears roiled and laboured, and that she had known the extent of my inexperience just by watching me. But what else could I do? No one else could drive the thing. The coldness in her voice went red hot as she took the arm of a deck man and yelled, "Luke, you old bastard. How are the ladies?"

I watched the man's face break into a huge scowl and he almost threw her out of the boat as he grunted, "Welcome back, Terry," in a voice that said just the opposite. Welcome back? She'd been here before? I looked at Martha, whose turn was next, but she obviously hadn't heard the exchange.

Martha tried to swing her leg over but the design of the Zodiac and the design of her round body didn't mesh. She sat there, stranded, one leg going one way and the other leg going another, just as a wave hit and bounced her painfully on the spot. Duncan reached over and grabbed her trailing leg, hauling it over. Suddenly I was alone in the boat.

As I started to move toward the starboard side to get out, one of the crewmen looked at me, a puzzled look on his face, and then glanced behind him at another crewmember on deck. I saw some communication pass between them, but before he could turn back the other guy threw the stern line at me and pointed aft where I saw the other Zodiac being hoisted into the air, its driver standing amid decks with a bosun's chair hugging his rear. I'd seen this done many times before, but I'd never actually done it myself and was attempting to clamber out when one of the crewmen waved me off. I couldn't understand what he was trying to say, but I didn't have to. The loose bowline in his hands told all and I watched, fascinated, as he threw the line into the bottom of the boat. They obviously thought I was one of the new crew arriving with the tourists. I looked quickly at the engine, glad to see it was still going, and suddenly I was free of the ship, alone in the boat, and not sure what I was supposed to do other than get out of the way of the Zodiac coming behind me.

I swung out, heading into the wind, watching as the Zodiac ahead of me was winched on board. It danced high above my head and my stomach, already churning itself into a sickening mess, lurched at the thought of going up there, so high, so far to fall, so cold a death, but at least it would be quick, thirty to sixty seconds before rescue was useless. As I moved down the ship to where the Zodiac ahead of me was already airborne I worried about controlling both my stomach and the Zodiac at the same time.

I kept the Zodiac into the wind, the waves marching at me, slinging their crests into my eyes and blinding me, the icy water sluicing down my face and finding its way past my raingear to my skin. I was very cold; my hands almost blue and stiff like talons as they gripped the throttle. I looked up the side of the ship, which looked like a gigantic box perched on a hull, and saw Martha's neon pink rain suit. She was waving down at me as if I was arriving in the calm of dusk for a cup of tea. Beside her I could see Duncan gripping the rails of the ship, as if by brute force he could lower it down to rescue me. Terry was there too and she looked as scared as I felt. This had not been the plan when we had talked and I guess she felt responsible for the predicament I found myself in.

I looked back at the crane, its guts hidden from me by the height of the ship. It was stationed on a rear deck and its arm was now swinging back over the ship where it had just deposited the last Zodiac, back out over the water to get me. Slowly the rope with the hook and bosun's chair attached was played out and I watched as it flayed in the wind like a wild thing. What it could do to my head I decided not to imagine. Where was the hook supposed to go? I looked down at the floorboard and saw a triangular series of ropes with a large, strong, confidence-boosting ring on it. The hook would go there first and then I would secure myself into the boson's chair, in case the hook didn't hold. I wouldn't have much time to let go of the engine and secure the hook before the boat would be taken away by the wind and the waves.

I made my first approach but when I let go of the engine to grab at the hook, rusty and lethal looking, it swung out of my reach and by the time it swung back the boat had drifted too far away. The next time I aimed the boat twenty feet in front of the hook, grateful that the ship's leeward side sheltered me somewhat from the waves and the wind. I made a grab for the hook with one hand while hauling up the ring with the other and staggered as a wave nearly threw me off balance. My hands were so cold they had no feeling and seemed like clumsy hunks of meat, but I got the hook through the ring and waited for the rope to lift and hold firm. Then I lurched back to turn off the engine. I could feel the Zodiac groaning under me as the rope began to lift her and I struggled back to get into the bosun's chair.

It occurred to me that this was probably the limit of the captain's ability to hoist up the Zodiacs and that any weather more severe would be out of the question. They didn't want to lose any tourists after all, and I wondered who would bear the brunt for what was happening to me. I tried to keep my mind off the fact that I was slowly rising in the air but I kept seeing myself that first horrifying time, years ago, standing frozen on the side of a mountain pass unable to go up or down as I stared hypnotized at the wide expanse of mountain dropping away beneath me on both sides. It had happened so fast. One moment perfectly comfortable, the next a raging agoraphobic paralyzed by fear; and it had never gone away. Now I was swinging wildly in the air, attached to a ship that was rolling and pitching like a drunk in search of the can.

The Zodiac swayed in the wind, the crane bucked with the ship, and I slowly rose. The crane began turning me into the ship before it should have and I could see the rust spots on the ship's side and the water crawling down to find the sea again. Suddenly, sickeningly, the Zodiac lurched violently and the floorboards supporting my weight gave way to air. I was swinging on the bosun's chair, the Zodiac tilted upwards and swinging beneath me, its stern pointing straight down at the sea. I swung into the side of the ship. The force of impact took my breath away and I felt the Zodiac bouncing off the ship below me. I swung out again, away from the ship, and felt myself rapidly rising. I guessed that the crane operator was trying to get me high enough fast enough so that I wouldn't bash into the side of the ship again, or I fervently hoped so. I looked down, which was a mistake: the churning water mirrored my stomach. I thought I could hear people yelling and suddenly the water below me vanished and was replaced by a wildly moving deck strewn with ropes, Zodiacs, and several crewmembers struggling to control the rogue Zodiac and the spinning contraption that I had become.

I felt strong hands grabbing at me and voices asking me if I was okay. I wasn't, of course. My stomach, too long denied, surrendered at last.

Chapter Four

I woke with a start. Bad idea. My stomach lurched and I groaned. I could hear a deep rumbling in the bow of the ship, somewhere near me, in fact. It awoke some long ago memory and I knew it was the anchor chain rumbling through its tunnel, winching round its drum, coming home to lodge its anchor at the bow of the ship, snuggled in against the hull, held there by the chain, held there by the winch, held there by the brake. The ship was waking up, the almost imperceptible sound of its engine coming alive, revving up as the ship's crew took her out to sea.

I looked at the clock on the table beside my bed: 4:30 p.m. I'd only been asleep an hour. Light streamed in from the porthole and I caught some flashes of sun through the swirling fog. A good sign, I hoped. Maybe the sun would chase the wind away and with it the waves. I'd been on board less than two hours and it felt like two weeks. How was I going to get through nine days of lectures if I felt like this every time the waves acted up? I was grateful that the motion of the ship had calmed down, but it felt like I was riding a sleeping monster, breathing gently. I felt like tiptoeing to keep it asleep and prayed it didn't have nightmares.

I'd been given a cabin of my own, I guess because I was a lecturer, or female, or both. But it was a really nice cabin so they must have run out of crews' quarters for me. They couldn't bunk me in with any of male lecturers, and from what Terry had said I'd deduced that I was the only female member of the expedition crew, on this trip anyway. Except, of course, for her. I wondered where she was sleeping. The cabin was well laid out with every conceivable space being put to good use. It was actually two rooms: a tiny outer cabin leading to an even smaller bedroom. There were two beds in the bedroom along two walls, with built-in drawer space under both. The porthole was in a prime location over my bed, and you could open it and stick your head out. I gingerly got to my knees and looked out. I could see land, grim, stark, barren, colourless, and, by the motion of the ship, I figured the portside; where I found myself, had to be the worst place to be.

There was a loud knock on my door and before I could answer it flew open to reveal Martha, dressed in full expedition regalia, including the khaki pants with fifteen pockets, the Tilley hat and down vest, the regulation binocs and the fifteen pounds worth of camera and video equipment hanging off every corner of her body, and an apple in her mouth. But it was what she was carrying in her arms that was alarming. It looked like the entire contents of a pharmacy and a bookstore combined.

"Cordi. Jesus girl, you look awful." She dumped the contents of her arms onto the table under my porthole and then plopped down on the end of my bed, jerking me against the motion of the waves and causing a small revolt in my stomach.

"Thanks for the vote of confidence."

"All you have to do is get your sea legs. Nothing to it. You'll be right as rain tomorrow, but I've got lots of anti stuff to get you through the worst."

I was hoping the worst had already happened.

She got up and rummaged through her vials of pills throwing me Gravol caplets, time release, multiple strength tablets, suppositories, and drink crystals. She hauled out various coloured wristbands and stood guard while I chose a pair and put them on, their little plastic cups digging deep into my wrists like tight socks.

"That's the way it's supposed to be," said Martha as I protested and began to take them off.

"Leave 'em on, Cordi, leave 'em on. You won't notice them in five minutes, I guarantee it."

"Yeah, right. That's because my hands will be numb."

She fished out a bunch of sugary looking globs. "If you want to go natural instead of all these pills and stuff, here's the best sugared ginger in the world." She threw me her little package. I sniffed at it suspiciously and the smell made me gag.

"Guess it won't be natural," said Martha as she scooped up most of the mess and stashed it in one of the drawers under my bed. "The best medicine for you right now is to get moving, take your mind off your stomach. Come on up to the bridge. I've been told the captain wants to see you."

Five minutes later we were weaving down the hallway of my deck, four, and hauling ourselves up the narrow staircase to the bridge. We made way for a woman
coming down the stairs, who turned out to be in the
writing course. Martha introduced her to me as LuEllen.
She was one of those masculine types, short-cropped
hair, no jewellery, and wearing baggy clothing that
completely hid her figure. She was wearing a baseball
cap thrust low over her forehead and a jacket with a
hunched up scarf so that I could not see her face. But
I was more interested in what she had in her arms, or
rather arm — the sleeve of her right arm hung empty
and useless. In the arm that was there nestled a little,
white, long-, curly-haired dog, about the size of a cat.
She could have hidden it in her clothing and I wouldn't
have been the wiser, unless it yapped.

"How're you doing, LuEllen?" asked Martha, as she
munched on her apple. But LuEllen obviously was not
feeling very talkative. She just nodded at us and walked
on by, but not before the dog made an unsuccessful lunge
at Martha's apple.

"Moody," said Martha, "but she's had a few rotten
curves in her life."

I thought about the arm and wondered what the
other curves were, besides a rude dog, when we reached
the bridge through the back door.

"Are you sure we're supposed to do this?" I asked as
Martha pushed her way through a deserted map room to
the bridge proper.

"Absolutely. I've already been up snooping around
and the captain was up here and told me that the bridge

is always open to us, unless he clamps down because of bad weather or dangerous navigation."

It felt weird. The only other ship I had ever been on had not allowed anyone on the bridge except crew.

"Besides, we're here on official business."

I looked at her in surprise.

"I told you the captain asked to see you."

"What does the captain want with me?" But Martha had already stepped onto the bridge.

We emerged onto the brightness of the deck and a magnificent, foggy view of the ship. Spread out three decks below us was the bow of the ship, with its tangle of anchors and cables, and about twenty tourists hanging over the rails to look at the sea below. Just beyond the fog was Frobisher Bay, where in the late sixteenth century, Martin Frobisher led three explorations in search of the Northwest Passage and to mine gold. He struck out on both counts. The gold he found was worthless marcasite, and the strait did not lead to the mysteries of the Orient but to a huge inland sea — Hudson Bay. He struck out with the Inuit too. His uncompromising character did not sit well with them. When five of his men were captured he seized three Inuit in return and took them back to England as curiosities. They died soon after.

I could hear someone's raised voice knifing its way through the bridge. "Admit it, Jason. You damn well blew it. You're the goddamn captain of this ship and it's your responsibility to hire the right people."

I turned to stare at the source of the problem, the cadence of the voice familiar. Without her wet weather gear hiding her face I was once again astonished by how beautiful Terry was, her golden blond hair fashionably messy, her clear blue eyes and pale chocolate milk skin, her trim figure, dwarfed by the man beside her.

"I don't hire the tourist crew," he said.

"But as captain of this ship you are ultimately responsible for everyone's welfare."

"For god's sake," he said. "It was an emergency, Terry. If she hadn't taken over the boat who knows what would have happened."

"I'm not talking about O'Callaghan. She at least tried to fix the mistake."

"Then who...?"

"Don't be so dense."

"You mean Peter?"

"Yeah, I mean Peter, if that's the name of your incompetent driver. Can't even keep his own passengers under control so that we were left with a total greenhorn to bring the Zodiac home. That's got to smack of negligence."

"Wasn't it you who stood up?"

"Of course it was me, but if he'd let us know everything was okay, that the waves were manageable, I would never have panicked."

"Let it go. You're blowing it up out of all proportion."

"Oh I am, am I? I could have been killed!" She raised her hand to the side of her head. "I've got a lump the size of a golf ball on my head and it didn't just magically appear. I'm lucky I don't have a concussion and O'Callaghan is lucky she didn't drown us all. A few calming words from this Peter guy would have prevented all this, including his own injury."

I was wondering what a golf ball sized lump would do to your judgment when apparently Terry read my mind. She turned and looked right at me, her anger changing disconcertingly to sweetness and light, a dazzling smile creasing her face in all the right places. "Oh, look who we have here: Cordi O'Callaghan — heroine. Thank you so much for saving my life."

I couldn't tell from the tone of her voice whether she was being genuine or sarcastic, but Jason seemed to have no doubts. "That's enough Terry," he hissed, taking her roughly by the elbow so that she stumbled. "I won't have you disrupting my ship again. You should never have come back."

She laughed with a dry, empty sound. "Is that a threat captain?" she asked sweetly, "You're assaulting me if I'm not mistaken." She jerked her arm free.

He looked momentarily disconcerted. "Let's just say I'll be watching you."

"He'll be watching me. How sweet." She laughed again, this time a gentle chortling sound that matched the perfect contours of her beautiful face. I wished she'd been this charming with me when we first met. Then I'd be on dry land thousands of kilometres away from here.

Jason said nothing and she patted him on the arm. "Take care of those pretty little eyes of yours. You wouldn't want to strain them now would you?"

Jason's jaw was so clenched that a muscle twitched in his cheek. He looked furious, but there was also something else there — wariness? Apprehension? I couldn't be sure and it didn't last long.

I cleared my throat, rather too loudly, and Terry

turned toward me with a ready-made smile plastered on her face, as if nothing had just transpired at all. "Welcome to the bridge, Cordi. Have you met Jason?"

He was tall, very tall, but it was his thinness that stood out. There was not an ounce of fat on him and his face was long and narrow and carved by age, or weather, or both, making him look old. "You must be Cordi O'Callaghan. The one who solved the murder up in Dumoine, Quebec? Very nice work." He held out his hand. "I'm Captain Jason Poole. And you already know Terry. Welcome to the *Susanna Moodie*."

I gripped his hand and then he turned to Martha and introduced himself.

Terry looked at all of us. "I'd better get back to my stateroom so that I can finish preparing my lectures for the masses."

Jason said nothing at all and I just nodded my head as she strolled off the bridge. I inclined my head at Martha. "Martha told me you wanted to see me." I really hoped he'd be fast because I could feel the woozy feeling coming back as I watched the bow of the ship, or what I could see of it through the fog, knife its way through the water.

He smiled at me. "Your friend and several others have already told me what you did to get the passengers safely aboard. I wanted to personally thank you and apologize for the crewman's ignorance in forcing you to crane the boat on your first voyage. It won't happen again, I assure you. But I need to get to the bottom of all this."

This was embarrassing. I mumbled a few stupid words before finally finding a couple of smart ones. "How is the driver?"

"He has a concussion. The doctor says he'll be okay. But I did want to ask you your version of what happened."

He listened carefully while I went through it all. When I had finished he scratched his head. "Was Terry seasick or did she just panic the way she said?"

"I don't know. As far as I could tell she looked pretty desperate."

Jason seemed to have finished with me, judging by the interest ebbing from his eyes, but I wasn't finished with him.

"You seem to have met Terry Spencer before?" I asked, hoping for — I don't know what.

"Yeah," he hesitated and clenched his jaw. "Along with our naturalist talks we have writing courses on this ship quite often — usually creative writing, different groups, anyone can join. Terry Spencer has been before. Just between you and me she's a bit of a handful. Bright, but so demanding and arrogant that no one wants to touch her. At least, not in that way." He flung this last aside in almost accidentally and then threw his hands up in the air in self-defence. "Hey. What can I say? She IS beautiful."

Chapter Five

"Beluga whale off the starboard bow!" The intercom system woke me from a groggy, Gravol-induced sleep.

I opened one eye and looked through the porthole. I was greeted by patchy, milky white fog and floating chunks of white pack ice as far as the fog would let me see. No horizon for me to fix on, just a great white abyss. How the hell anyone could see a beluga whale in such a world of white was more than I could fathom. You were much more likely to hear the "canaries of the sea," with their squeals, whistles, and little puffs. The sea was moving us in a rolling rhythm that made me want to lie back down and sleep forever. I could hear the rumbling throb of the engine coming from deep within the ship, shuddering through its core, totally out of sync with the sea, something I wouldn't have even noticed if I hadn't felt so sick.

I glanced at the clock and groaned: 6:00 p.m. I'd

missed the crew briefing, but I could make the passenger orientation — just. Even if I didn't get any questions asked of me I had to be there. Terry had left no doubts about that. I gingerly stood up, swaying with the ship. I could do this if I didn't think too much.

One of my two rooms, the sitting room, had a window that looked out over the bow and I'd been spending a lot of time looking out of it, trying to find the horizon and stabilize my semi-circular canals. There was just one easy chair. The bedroom was even more sparse; just the beds, a table, and a lamp. No shower. No bath. Just a sink and a toilet.

I pulled on my pants and a fleece jacket and headed into the hallway, which was so narrow that an oversized person might feel somewhat claustrophobic. For me, narrow was good. I could lean on both walls. The stairs were a bit of a challenge since the ship seemed to lurch out of reach of my foot every time I was trying to find a step.

People were milling around outside the dining room, so at least I wasn't late. I poked my head inside the room. It was plain, just like my room — only the bare necessities. It had already been set up for dinner and people were sitting at tables of eight with perky red and white checkerboard tablecloths, fake flowers, and cheap cutlery — this was definitely no luxury liner. I saw that Terry was there and in a sea of strange faces I gravitated towards her. But I never made it. Someone touched me on the shoulder and I turned to see the hairy man who had been knocked out in the Zodiac.

"Cordi O'Callaghan?"

I nodded and he held out his hand "Peter Stanford. Your friend Martha pointed you out to me." I followed his gaze and saw Martha and Duncan deep in conversation. How had I missed them?

"I gather I owe you my thanks," he said.

I glanced at the bandage on his head, which was holding back some serious curls that threatened to engulf his face. He smiled as I took his hand.

"They said you were on death's door."

"Somewhat exaggerated," he said. "The doctor kicked me out of sick bay half an hour ago. Just in time for the orientation meeting."

I couldn't tell whether he was happy or irked at having to be here so I said something nice and neutral. "Have you been to many?"

"Tons. I've been lecturing on Arctic seabirds for ten years. But my current field of research is the nesting habits of gyrfalcons."

I looked at him with renewed interest. Gyrfalcons are the largest falcons in the world and nest off cliff faces that are often inaccessible. Half the time, to even see their nests you have to climb up or fly over. No wonder he was reading about illegal trade in animals. There was probably a whole chapter on gyrfalcon eggs and how they somehow manage to get themselves from Canada to Saudi Arabia on a rather regular basis. But I didn't go there. Instead, I said, "Guess you're not afraid of heights."

He laughed and was about to say something when we were called in to the meeting. He looked at me and raised his eyebrows as if to say "duty calls."

I tried to get beside Martha and Duncan but the surging crowd took me to a table of strangers. Every crew-member and every lecturer (including myself) had to give a five-minute spiel. It was interminable and I spent the whole time waiting for my turn and worrying about it. In the end my speech went smoothly enough, though the crowd was more interested in the one measly murder case I had worked on than anything else.

And then Terry got up to say her bit. She'd barely begun when someone called out, "Did you cut the ropes on the Zodiac?"

Terry searched the audience for the source of the voice and said nothing. Cut the ropes?

"Aren't you the murderer?" asked the voice. I couldn't find him. Neither could Terry.

I heard a collective intake of breath as the words hit home. It was surreal. The entire room fell quiet, and once again I was aware of it moving gently up and down with the swell of the sea.

Terry slowly turned and looked into the audience, looking for the owner of the voice. "No, I am not a murderer." Her voice was quiet, defiant. She's been here before, I thought. Handling accusations from a room full of unknown people.

I scanned the audience and found him. Peter. What I could see of his face was cold and ugly and there was a tall, dark-haired woman clamping her hand on his shoulder with a look of what can only be described as alarm. I looked more closely and was pretty sure it was the woman who'd sat across the aisle from me on the plane.

"You had a good lawyer, eh?" he asked in a suddenly good-natured voice, but the look he gave her was one of frightening focus.

She looked at him curiously. "I was acquitted. Everybody knows that."

"You had a good lawyer."

The woman beside Peter was frowning and hurriedly whispered something to him. Whatever she said worked and the fight went out of him even as Terry said, "Are you trying to accuse me...?"

I heard a chair scrape back and the booming voice of Captain Jason Poole rang through the room. "That's enough everybody." He stood there with his hands up as if he was about to do a vertical pushup. Terry started to protest but thought better of it, and Peter had melted into the background with the tall, dark-haired woman.

Poole surveyed the room. "I think this meeting is over, folks. Please direct any questions to the expedition staff and pray for good weather." He started to leave and then hesitated. "And for the record? Ms Terry Spencer was acquitted. End of story."

But of course, that wasn't the end of the story. It was only the beginning.

Over the next couple of days time kind of stood still in the swirl of fog that followed us like a besotted dog. We couldn't seem to shake it. I went looking for Martha a couple of times to try and find out more about Terry's so-called murder. What with all the racing around to pack and get ready for the trip and then feeling so sick, it had been at the bottom of my list of priorities. But since I'd missed a lot of meals and spent a lot of time in my cabin I hadn't found Martha. I gave up, figuring I'd find out soon enough.

The first day was pretty much a writeoff for any trips ashore because of the fog and the pack ice, so all of us lecturers had to work double time. I hadn't yet given a lecture to Terry's class, so I thought I'd sit in on hers in the dining room to get a feel for it before giving my bit at the end. It appeared that she had already given an assignment to the class before they arrived on board so she would have some material to deal with. The newcomers presumably would get an assignment today.

Terry had put all her stuff on one of the dining room tables near the front of the room.

She paced back and forth in front of the class and then reached over and took one of the stories from the top of the pile. "Let me read you the opening two sentences of this essay," she said, her voice the physical equivalent of someone holding their nose.

"*It was an awful day. I walked along the sidewalk thinking about depressing things and worrying that my life was moving along too quickly.*" She glared at us all. "I can't count how many times I've had to drill it into my classes to show not tell. This is a perfect example."

She waved the offending sheet of paper at us. "What kind of awful day? Was it raining, hailing, sleeting? Was the smog smothering our protagonist or maybe it was fog obscuring the author's reasoning? Now try this:

"*The rain smashed into the sidewalk like a hand slapping a face.*

"Okay. Maybe a little overdone for a first sentence, but that doesn't just tell you that it's an awful day, it shows you. It gives you an image of what's happening to make it an awful day and maybe make you wonder why your protagonist used such an analogy. And the next sentence — what depressing things is the author talking about? This is a golden opportunity to describe something depressing that perhaps links back to an important past event, maybe something like:

"*I could barely keep my leaden feet moving for all the wrenching images of dead and dying people flitting through my mind, mocking me.*

"This gives the reader some indication of the nature of this person; that they're pessimistic and prone to depression. So why is the protagonist thinking of dead and dying people? Choose any depressing thing that fits the story. It doesn't have to be dead people. And the second half of that sentence is so pedestrian. It says nothing to the reader except that life moves quickly, which everyone over the age of twenty knows already.

"Say something that has meaning to your character, maybe even something that foreshadows something to come or makes you wonder. What about:

"*Making me wonder if my life had passed me by.*

"This reinforces the depressive nature of our protagonist and sets us to wondering why she's wondering if her life has passed her by. It draws us in."

The class was silent. I watched them taking it all in. It was pretty clear that Terry had just turned a piece of challenged writing into something more interesting. I wondered who the author was and was glad that Terry had been kind and not identified him or her.

"Tracey." The name rang out like the lonely hollow sound it was. I'd thought too soon.

We all turned in unison to look at Tracey, who sat frozen in her chair. She was dressed like a grey day, somber colours that reached to her grey face and iron grey hair. Her thin, pinched features seemed to recoil back, giving the impression that her face was seriously sunken. She seemed to have shrunk into the chair, her body hunched, her arms hugging herself as if to make sure she was really there.

"Come and get your writing and at least try, on your next one, to make it seem like you're listening to me. If you can't write better than this you'll never get anywhere, and even then you can't be sure."

"You mean, even if we're good there's no guarantee?"

Terry studied the man who had spoken and said in measured tones, "In this business it helps to know someone, or be someone." There was a trace of bitterness in her words, but she shrugged them off and held out Tracey's essay.

"Isn't that how you got published?"

Terry turned to face Peter, who had slipped in unnoticed. She looked at him curiously and then laughed. "I guess you could say I became a celebrity and then published a book. But I just got lucky, or unlucky if you look at the jail time I did for something I had no control over. I just took advantage of bad luck and turned it into good luck. I do NOT recommend you take my route."

Someone in the audience yelled out "What happened?"

Terry smiled and said, "Read my book. It's all there."

I thought that was rather abrupt, but it couldn't be pleasant to always be confronted with such an unpleasant memory, to constantly be asked about it.

Terry waved Tracey's paper at her. When Tracey didn't make a move to get up — I don't think she could've if she'd tried — Terry waltzed over and dumped it in her lap then went on to her next topic, without any sign that she was aware of what she had just done to Tracey. I was very glad I had no work in that pile and looked furtively at Martha and Duncan. Duncan was frowning and Martha was biting her lower lip.

"This next needs no explanation." She walked back and forth with the poor little essay quivering in her hands, stopped in front of Martha and began to read:

"The saucer-like silent, sizzling sun shone a ray of wonderment upon the little boy, who opened his mouth and gulped it down, quenching his tears away. But be patient, gentle reader, and you shall soon find out what happens to the little ray of wonderment."

There was dead silence and then rather a few muffled giggles. I looked at Martha, watched her face hitch a ride on a roller coaster of emotions: astonishment, bewilderment, anger, realization…. But it was the last one that I'll never forget. She suddenly flung back her head and laughed with the best of us. When the laughter had died down Terry handed Martha her essay.

"Gentle reader? Where the hell did that come from?"

"*Gulliver's Travels.*" Martha didn't skip a beat. "Or perhaps you haven't heard of it?"

Terry studied her for a long time. I thought she was going to say something but she didn't. Instead she turned to the class and gave them their next assignment before asking me to give my lecture. It was just my luck that she was handing over a giggling class to me. I confess I thought that maybe she had done it on purpose, but that was uncharitable. Still — talk about daunting.

I was just about to start when someone poked their head in the door asking for Terry. She scowled but got up and went out, leaving me alone at the front of the room. I was immediately peppered with questions from people doing research for their books. I finally threw aside my notes and opened the floor, allowing them to query me about the body I had found in the wilderness the summer before. Then they grilled me for information for their own books.

"I'm researching a book where my murder victim is killed in Quebec, then moved three days later and dumped in the woods in northern Ontario. How can my protagonist know how long since death?" asked one man.

"Well, flies love dead stuff and they can find a vacated body really quickly — within seconds sometimes. They lay their eggs and it's the larvae we use to help us pinpoint the time of death. Since we know how long it takes for each species of larva to develop into a fly, and we know they sometimes colonize within minutes, we can count backwards and find the time of death by finding the time when the flies deposited their eggs."

"How can my protagonist know that the body's been moved?"

"There are different species of flies in different habitats. In this situation you would have larvae growing right from death in Quebec and larva growing from three days later when the body was moved to Ontario. Not only would you know the body had been moved, but you could pinpoint when it was moved. Forensic entomology is pretty straightforward."

It went on like this for some time. I was hoping maybe the questions were over when a chair scraped back and the tall slender woman who had whisked Peter away stood up. She looked me straight in the eye. "My book is set on a ship. That's why I'm on this trip. What would be the best way to murder one of my characters and get away with it?"

"That's not really about forensic biology, since there aren't too many flies out here at sea. And I'm sure you've thought of the best way: just upend them overboard."

"I had thought of that but there's so much pack ice."

"You could," I said gently, "write the pack ice out of the book."

She looked at me then and I thought I saw a look of sudden desperation, but I must have been mistaken because all she said was "How stupid of me," and sat back down.

Over the next few days the weather was too socked in for us to take any trips ashore and everyone was getting cabin fever. I spent my spare time in my berth, watching people strolling around the bow of the ship. All of them were wearing winter jackets and some were wearing balaclavas so that they looked like criminals. We were at anchor in some bay we could not see, hoping the fog would break so we could go ashore. But at least it was calm.

From where I stood I could see the entire bow with its myriad ropes and chains, and things that looked like horns. Someone had randomly painted lime green squares on the forest green deck, making it look as though some sort of tropical disease had taken hold and spread.

I was stir-crazy in that cabin. Thumbing my nose at my stomach I went on deck to explore. I needed air the way a sagging balloon does. The *Susanna Moodie* was a working ship, its provenance in days past as a research vessel made it utilitarian. As I strolled around the bow I looked up at the bridge, which was perched on the top deck of what looked like a big, white, square apartment building. It was supremely ugly.

I poked around the bow and checked out the anchor line, which was enormous and snaked its way down a hole about one and a half times my circumference. You could ride it up if it was calm — if there was no choice. As I stood there, looking down through the hole at the sea below and the waifs of fog that clung to it, the anchor line came to life and began reeling itself in. Each loop of the chain was bigger than my hand. As it rattled up onto the deck from its hidden visit beneath the sea it hugged one side of the tunnel. We were in a dead calm. I wondered what the chain would do in a rolling sea.

"Cordi!"

I turned and followed the voice; Duncan, out for a stroll in the fog, just like me.

"Dear girl," he said. Duncan was the only person I'd never corrected for calling me girl. It just seemed so innocuous and well meant coming from him. "How's the stomach?" He flung his arm around my shoulder and I staggered, not at the weight of him but because the sea was wreaking havoc with my balance.

I gave him what felt like a sick little grimace. "Not great."

"You just have to suck it up, as they say," he said, and I could tell he was proud of himself for getting the lingo right.

"When it's going the other way?" I asked.

He looked at me curiously and then grinned. "Well, I admit, that's a tad difficult."

He withdrew his arm, put his hands on my shoulders and stared into my face. "You don't look so well," he proclaimed.

Since I already knew that I didn't bother to answer. Instead I said, "What do you suppose that Peter guy meant when he asked Terry if the Zodiac ropes had been cut?"

"Dunno. Doesn't make any kind of sense. I mean, why would anyone want to cut the ropes?"

"I could have been killed."

Duncan looked at me. "I hope you're not suggesting someone was out to get you?"

I didn't answer.

"My dear girl, no one could have known you'd have to take over the boat. And there's the little question of why."

"So maybe someone was out to get Peter."

"Cordi, where do you get such a vivid imagination? Besides, I've heard from the captain that the ropes weren't cut — they were just badly frayed."

He stared at me until I looked away. I could see Owen and Terry huddled on the bow in deep conversation.

Duncan followed my gaze. "Have you met Owen and Terry yet?"

I nodded. "I sat beside them both on the plane."

"Lucky you."

"Terry's a bit of a handful, but Owen seems nice enough. A bit stiff but okay."

"You mean Terry's right-hand floor mat."

"He's a floor mat?" I asked.

"He does everything she tells him to do and gets no thanks whatsoever. He comes to every writing meeting just in case she wants him." Duncan flicked an imaginary piece of fluff over the railing and turned to look at me. "I think he must be in love with her because I can see no other reason why he would do that."

We stood at the railing, watching the ship being pushed about by the sea.

Duncan was twiddling his thumbs, looking like someone who wanted to say something but couldn't get it out.

"What?" I finally asked.

He looked at me. "Have you met Sally yet?"

I looked back at him with interest. "No. Who is she?"

"She's a member of the writing group. Good-looking with a hell of a head of red hair."

Sally. The one on the plane. I slowly nodded. "Yeah, I've seen her. Why?"

"She's not right," he said.

"Not right?"

"You know what I mean. You've been there." There was a long pause between us.

"She's depressed?" I finally asked.

Duncan nodded. "Looks like her boyfriend left her."

"Arthur?"

"How did you know that? You've spent most of your time in your room."

"I overheard the breakup on the plane," I said.

We stood in silence for a while. "She could use a friend."

"Surely she has friends on board."

Duncan hesitated. "Yes," he said. But he said it the way you say it when you're not really sure.

"Ah ha! An ulterior motive."

"I can't put my finger on it. She's been to every writing class and I still don't know why she bothers me. Something about her isn't right."

"You think it's the depression?"

"Could be," he said thoughtfully. "Could be ... She seemed sad even before Arthur dropped her." But he didn't sound as though he was convincing himself.

"I'll see what I can find out," I said, with a noted lack of enthusiasm.

We went back to watching the dull grey sea.

"What do you know about Terry's trial?"

"Don't tell me you don't know?" Duncan said. "Where were you when that happened? It was in all the papers."

"I can't remember. I must have been out of town," I said, somewhat defensively.

"She killed a friend of hers named Michael in her sleep."

I stared at him as I thought about all the implications that simple sentence embodied. "And was acquitted?"

"Yes. They determined that she didn't know what she was doing, and based the case on several others where sleepwalkers were acquitted of violent crimes."

We talked some more about the case and I wondered how easy it would be to fake walking in your sleep and killing someone. But I was beginning to feel unwell and didn't feel like pursuing my thoughts.

I left Duncan and sought refuge in my room. I must have fallen asleep because the next thing I knew Martha was prancing in, carrying a vermilion and bilious green bathing suit draped over her shoulder and partially hidden by a multicoloured towel covered in teddy bears. Where she ever got her sense of colour I didn't want to know.

"C'mon, Cordi! It's sauna time!"

Sauna time. I groaned.

"C'mon, it'll do you good. Where's your bathing suit?"

I waved in the direction of the dresser, or whatever it's called on a ship.

Martha began fishing out everything until there was nothing left. She looked at me questioningly.

"It's the navy blue thing right there." I moved towards her to get it when she pulled it out and waved it around.

"There's hardly anything here, for god's sake. Where do you put yourself?"

I grabbed the bathing suit from her and went into the head to find a towel. The sauna was right down at the end of my corridor — aft of my cabin in nautical terms. The change rooms were big enough for five people, but the sauna could have held ten because it lay midway between the men's and the woman's change room so that both could use it.

I changed into my bathing suit and opined that it had to be a coed sauna. Martha took an inordinate amount of time changing into her suit and while I was waiting for her I started counting the blue flowers on the wildly floral wallpaper. I got to three hundred when Martha emerged from her cubicle and I was very proud of myself for not leaping backwards in shock. She was wearing the most amazing bathing suit. She looked like a ballerina with a little skirt that refused to sit tight to her hips but stuck up, making her look even bigger. Colourful little fish were flitting to and fro, their eyes glittering with multicoloured sequins, and at discrete locations there were clear circular discs exposing the skin beneath. It was definitely not the type of suit someone of her ample size should attempt to wear.

I guess I didn't hide my reaction very well after all because Martha's face caved-in. "I bought it because I thought everybody would be so busy looking at it that they wouldn't notice how big I am."

I felt about two centimetres tall.

She turned from me and as she opened the sauna door a voice squeaked out, "You just have to bide your time, Sal. Be patient. But I still don't understand why you have to do it at all."

The voice stopped as our eyes met. She was a woman of curves, like a Reubens, with raven black hair and burnt umber eyes. She instinctively hunched forward as if to protect her body from a blow and then relaxed.

"Hello, I'm Sandy."

I nodded my head at her. She'd been in the writing class. I turned to look at the only other person in the sauna — the redhead.

Martha waded in and introduced me to Sally as we found our spots on the benches. She really was a big woman — not fat but big boned. Her luxurious, curly, red hair billowed around her face, making her watery blue eyes look like an afterthought.

"I was just telling Sally here," said Sandy, "that she's got to be patient. She's frustrated that she hasn't seen a polar bear yet."

I smiled and said, "Hard to see anything in this fog."

Sandy and Sally exchanged glances. Maybe I'd been too flippant?

"Did you know they are the largest land based carnivore in the world and their hair is actually translucent so the sun will go through it to the skin beneath?" I pushed on. "Their skin is black to absorb the sun and the fur is like a wetsuit when they swim."

No one said anything after that nice little piece of didactic information.

"Your lecture was fun," said Sandy suddenly. Fun was a strange word to use and I just nodded.

"Did you really solve a murder?"

I nodded again.

"It sounds fascinating, all the clues and sleuth work that you had to do."

I thought about the state the body had been in and involuntarily shivered.

"Lord love you, Cordi. How can you be shivering in a sauna?" Martha asked.

"Maybe someone stepped on her grave thinking it was mine." I swivelled my eyes over to look at Sally. That was a funny thing to say. These were a rum pair.

Martha jumped into the silence and changed the subject rather too abruptly. "Sally is part of our writing group and rumour has it she's a dynamite writer."

Sally, who looked as though she had been crying for twenty years, waved away the compliment.

"I just wish you'd read some of your novel to us in class so we could enjoy your talent."

"Sorry, it's just something I never do."

"Couldn't you hand out a copy, or even just an excerpt? Anything?"

Sally mournfully shook her head. "Sorry, I can't do that because …"

Sally was interrupted by Sandy, who said with the finality of a full stop period, "Sally doesn't like crowds," and again they exchanged glances.

"But that doesn't mean she can't …" Martha started, before thinking better of it when she caught sight of Sally, who had large tears pounding down her face. For a while I thought that maybe it was just a whole lot of sweat and we could ignore it, but then she started to gurgle a bit.

Martha and I looked at each other and then at Sally.

"You know, it's okay to cry," said Martha. "It helps the pain."

"How would you know what kind of pain I'm in?"

"Sweetie, we're on a boat. There are only a hundred and ten or so of us and the rumours have been flying. You haven't exactly kept your sorrow to yourself. You've been moping about the ship for all to see."

"What rumours?" she asked.

"Take your pick. For example: you just lost a child in childbirth and are suffering from postpartum depression."

Sally gave a weak smile and shook her head.

"How about: your business just went bankrupt and you are in debt over your earlobes?" Where did Martha find these metaphors?

Sally slowly shook her head.

"Okay then. You're a murderer, intent on revenge."

Sally suddenly covered her face and shook her head. Sandy squeezed her on the shoulder, in an attempt to comfort her, but Sally shook her off.

Martha caught my eye and knowing what she was about to do I began shaking my head, but she pretended not to see me. "Final scenario: Cordi here accidentally overheard your conversation with Arthur on the plane. He broke up with you."

Sally began sobbing then and Sandy gave us the hairy eyeball, but we stayed put.

Eventually Sally choked out, "He said he loved me." The words, though muffled and tear laden, were easy to hear — the universal story of love's cruel side.

"I don't know how I can survive without him," she said, then whimpered. "I don't think I can."

We were saved from all the normal useless platitudes that accompany such a statement by the sauna door opening and two more women coming in. They were as close to Mutt and Jeff in size as any friends I'd ever seen. One was the woman who had tried to muzzle Peter, and had asked the question about how to get away with murder on the boat. She was very thin and at least six feet tall. She had short, wavy black hair and a no-nonsense sort of face with an aristocratic air to it.

The other was the woman who Terry had skewered.

She was nudging five feet on her tippy toes. She had really frizzy, grey streaked hair and watery grey eyes that matched her complexion. She was a woman of angles — everything sharp and pointy from the top of her head to her nose and chin to the hipbones sticking out through her bathing suit.

I thought that Sally and Sandy might leave because they had been in longer than we had, but they stayed put. Martha introduced me to Elizabeth Goodal and Tracey Dunne, from the writing group. I was beginning to feel hemmed in, and where, I wondered, were all the men? This was a shared sauna after all, but it would be a hell of a lot nicer without bathing suits. Tracey had taken up a position beside me, making me feel like a giant.

Elizabeth broke the awkward silence by saying to no one in particular, "I just came from the dining room and Terry was lacing into some poor guy, telling him he was incompetent and the cause of the Zodiac fiasco." She looked at me with a deprecating smile and said, "Nice work by the way."

I opened and closed my return smile in a fraction of a second. "Is Terry always like this?"

There was a long silence and then Martha asked, "Like what?" As if she didn't know.

I took a deep breath and said, "Arrogant, rude, demanding."

"Pretty much, yes," said Elizabeth.

"Why do you all put up with her?"

I watched as the group looked at each other and literally closed ranks, even Martha, who said, "She's a really good teacher and she knows all the right people in the writing world."

"You mean she can get your book placed in the hands of the right agent?" I looked at them and they all nodded in unison like a bunch of synchronized swimmers. Is that really how it worked?

"I've never heard of her," I said, wondering how someone so abrasive could know all the right people.

"She was in all the newspapers." It was the first time that Tracey had spoken, even in greeting, and I was struck by the depth of negativity in her voice, like Eeyore in a bathing suit.

"You mean her trial?"

"Yes." Tracey glanced at Elizabeth and Sally as if seeking corroboration.

"She spent time in jail for a murder she didn't commit. Right?"

Tracey slowly nodded.

"What happened to her? How did she get involved?"

I looked around at the lot of them, but no one seemed to want to answer so I focused my gaze on Martha.

"Just read the book she wrote about it, Cordi. It's all in there."

"Yeah, but can't you give me some more detail?" Duncan's version had been sparse to say the least.

Martha made a big show of letting out her breath. "Okay, here goes, but it's really long and convoluted, and you should read the book to do it justice."

"In case you haven't noticed, we're on a boat, Martha. Where am I going to find her book?"

"Ship, Cordi. As in *umiajuaq.*" I stared at her and she laughed. "The Inuit distinguish between them too. *Umiaq* is a boat, *umiajuaq* is a giant boat." When I didn't say anything she shrugged. "It's a ship if it can carry a boat and it does have a library."

Yeah, right. As if it'll be in the ship's library, I thought.

"One of the guys in Terry's adult ed writing class, Michael," said Martha, as she settled into her storytelling role, "was an archaeologist doing research on the Queen Charlottes...."

The sauna seemed suddenly very quiet, except for a sudden muffled cough somewhere — probably Sally.

Martha continued, "Terry thought it would be a good idea to tag along and write a book and Michael agreed."

"Reluctantly," said Elizabeth.

"They were in the western part of the Queen Charlotte Islands on the west coast, with a group, camping out at the site. It was almost morn …"

The door to the sauna suddenly flew open and in walked Terry, as naked as the day she was born with a white towel coolly slung over her shoulder.

I don't know who met her eyes but the atmosphere must have blazoned out, "We are talking about you," because she went on the offensive right away.

"Look at you sissies. All in bathing suits for god's sake."

"I should point out to you," said Martha, "that this is a coed sauna and nudity is not a bright idea."

Terry smirked at Martha. "Scared?"

"You bet. In case you haven't noticed I'm not thirty-six, twenty-four, thirty-six."

"Oh, I've noticed alright. But in case you haven't noticed, it's women's night. Or hadn't you wondered why there weren't any men?"

I think we all felt like taking off our suits then and there, but Terry's smirk would have just got bigger and more carnivorous, so we didn't.

Terry snorted and moved over to take her place by Sally, who had to move over to make way. We were crammed like sardines and I was getting really hot. I couldn't figure out how on earth Sally and Sandy could stand the sauna for so long. I was only staying out of curiosity. Maybe they were too.

Terry sat on the top tier and scanned the room, looking at each of us in turn, as if we were insect specimens. As she got to Sally she suddenly recoiled. "Jesus, Sally. What the hell's the matter with you?" We all looked at Sally who had managed to dry up her tears and was looking pretty normal. Sally frowned and said nothing.

"Your necklace, girl. For god's sake, can't you feel it?"

Sally looked down at the cross around her neck as if she had never seen it before. She picked it up and quickly dropped it, looking at her fingers in surprise. Sandy moved closer to Sally and amid some ouches and ows got the necklace off and unceremoniously dropped it on the cedar bench. There was a red cross on her skin and no one said anything, but you could feel the question on every lip: "Why didn't you feel it?" Just showed how far gone she was over Arthur, I figured.

"Jesus. What kind of a person wears a bloody necklace into a sauna?" asked Terry. No one said anything. "Talk about dumb."

In response Sally looked up in despair and said, "But it's so hard to be Sally." She gulped, looking like she'd swallowed a big hunk of sorrow, or had quietly gone mad.

"What I mean is it's hard to be me, hard to be Sally when Arthur is gone. I don't feel anything." She looked around at the rest of us and made an effort to smile. "I just thought I'd found the right guy you know?"

Elizabeth and Tracey exchanged glances and Terry rolled her eyes. "Oh Lord, stop crying over spilt milk."

Sally jerked her head up and whispered. "At least with spilt milk you can lap it up, so nothing's wasted. This is not spilt milk."

"Okay, so it's spilt milk on sand. What's the difference? Your analogy stinks. If you think you're unique, think again. We've all been through it." Terry looked around at the rest of us but no one said anything, no one nodded either. It was as if we were isolating her by refusing to agree with what we all knew was the truth. I wondered why.

Suddenly Sally stood up and lurched for the door. Terry smiled and caught her by the arm. I didn't see what passed between them because Sandy suddenly stood up and blocked my vision.

Martha grabbed my arm. Terry looked at Martha. "Is it possible that you have no idea what you look like in that thing?"

Martha daintily opened the sauna door wider and gracefully walked out, calling over her shoulder, "Is it possible that you have no idea what you just said?"

As I left I looked back at Terry, who languidly raised her hand as if giving me permission to leave. "I cannot believe that you are going to jump in the pool in your bathing suits," she said. "Bunch of cowards."

"Now for the good part," Martha said as we trooped out the changing room door in our bathing suits, down the hall, past two cabins, and out the aft door onto a metal catwalk.

Somewhere along the way we lost Elizabeth and Tracey, but they must have gone into the showers rather than brave the Arctic wind. And the pool. It looked like something you'd see at a really old zoo. It was very small and completely square, enclosed by a serious looking iron railing that came right down to the edge of the water. You certainly couldn't swim lengths in this kid-sized pool, unless they were vertical. The water was very deep and very clear. I figured they must have used it to contain wild aquatic animals because it looked like a prison. And it sat half a deck below the top observation deck, which meant that anybody could come and watch us frolic in the icy cold waters, making fools of ourselves.

As we skittered down the fire escape type stairs the cold Arctic wind was threatening to beat the pool to the punch. By the time we got down there and draped our towels over the railing I was feeling decidedly less hot and hoped the pool wasn't as cold as it looked. Fat chance. The maniacal scream as Martha made the first leap was not reassuring. There are sauna-induced screams and then there are sauna-induced screams. The higher the pitch the greater the shock, and I think her scream would have broken a wineglass. If I had had any doubts they were all dispelled by Sandy's high-pitched squeal and Sally's awful, long, drawn out moan. I knew that I should have gone first. And then it was my turn but I had to fight my way to the jumping off spot as everyone raced to get out. Suddenly I stood alone, everyone chattering around me and draped in nice warm towels, feeling the rosy glow you get after you survive the breath stopping cold.

"Go for it, Cordi," called Martha. "It'll fix your stomach for sure."

"Yeah, by killing it outright," I replied.

They all yelled their encouragement until finally I leapt. The cold nearly knocked me out, sucking away my breath like a siphon. I came up clawing for the ladder and grabbed something soft and warm instead. I looked up anxiously, wanting to get the hell out of the pool and there was Terry looking down at me, grinning like the cat who ate the canary, still without a stitch of clothing on her body.

"This is how you're supposed to do it, ladies." She stood there for a while as if we were both enjoying a dip in the tropical south and then she suddenly let out an unholy bellow and jumped over my head into the water. I scampered out and Martha draped my towel over my shoulders as I began to shiver. We were all watching Terry as she dog-paddled to the ladder, got out, slipped on her slippers and wrapped her towel around herself.

Something made me look up at the open deck immediately above the pool. Arthur was standing there, the fog swirling around him, making him look indistinct and wraithlike. He was dressed in a down jacket and watch cap, resting his arms on the railing, completely still, staring down at Terry. His face was expressionless, like a man staring at something he couldn't see. His gaze flitted to me for a split second and then he slowly turned away and disappeared. He didn't seem to care that I had seen him, which was very disquieting. Peeping Toms are usually secretive.

Chapter Six

Back in my cabin I opened the porthole and looked out at a swirl of fog and ragged masses of pack ice. What if we got caught in the ice, I wondered. The pack ice was fragmented — huge hunks of it were drifting about — but the winds could blow the separate floes together to form an impenetrable prison of ice. This was the land of Franklin's ill-fated expedition in search of the Northwest Passage to the Orient. It wouldn't be quite like Franklin because we had cell phones and GPS and helicopters and lifeboats, but I shuddered at the thought of the power of the ice creeping around the hull and squeezing until the rivets shot out and the water rushed in.

I craned my neck down the length of the ship. I was really restless. It felt like about 8:00, but the clock by my bed said it was 1:30 in the morning. There's something about a ship at night — even in the land of the midnight sun — that is ghostlike. The ship lay at anchor near Baffin Island, where we were supposed to go ashore to see if we could find some polar bears to ogle, but we couldn't because of the pack ice. I wondered when the captain would weigh anchor and move us out. Surely it wasn't a good idea to stay here? I tried sleeping but it was so hard with the light streaming in the window. A couple of sleepless hours went by.

Finally I got up, thinking I'd heard a knock on my door, but when I opened it there was no one there. The hallway was empty in both directions. I refrained from looking up, blocking out thoughts of a spider-like man clinging to the ceiling. As I stood there in the hallway the door at the aft end banged shut and then eased open and gathered for another bang. I smiled at my own jumpy nerves and went back into my cabin.

I still couldn't sleep so I kicked into my sweats and runners and looked around for my winter jacket. I couldn't find it so I grabbed my rain jacket and toque and went up on deck, past the eerie and sombre orange hulls of the steel life rafts, and around to the port side where the gangway went down to the sea when an expedition was afoot.

As I reached the railing I was surprised to see that the gangway was lowered. I looked out to sea, the wind buffeting me. The fog was playing tricks with my mind but then I saw a shadow move out on the ice — a little white dog on white ice in a white fog. LuEllen's little white dog; it had to be, there wasn't any other little white dog on board. In fact, there were no other dogs on board.

I'm a real sucker for animals so I left the observation deck to get a better look. I went down the stairs to the gangway where I stopped and surveyed the situation. The dog was about twenty-five feet from the gangway and was eating away at an unappetizing lump of stuff on the ice, which had moved in on the ship. Why hadn't Jason moved away? It looked like the cook had just dumped a bunch of garbage there. Was that allowed? There was only a one foot gap between the platform and the pack ice and I realized I couldn't just leave the dog there. The ship could leave him behind.

I ran down the gangway, stepped onto the ice, and walked over to the dog, still gorging himself on the windfall. As I got closer he glanced up but went right back to eating. I approached slowly, so as not to frighten him, and wondered if he liked strangers. Martha had told me he was never out of LuEllen's arms. Well, he sure was now. I reached down and grabbed him around his stomach; he was so small my fingers met. That's not all they met. He wanted nothing to do with me and let me know by whipping his head around and sinking his teeth into my arm. Predictably, I threw him away from me. He landed in a puddle of ice-cold water and I watched as he struggled to regain his footing. I looked down at my arm and saw a row of indentations in my nice new rain jacket. Who'd have thought such a little dog could act like a pit bull. I looked back at the dog. He was standing now, looking uncertain and very stiff legged.

As I approached the dog again I heard some piece of machinery, or maybe it was several, come alive in a gentle hum. He'd begun to shiver and this time he let me pick him up without a protest. He was whimpering now, trembling and wet, and I put him inside my jacket where he took up hardly any room, but he felt like a little ice ball next to my heart.

I stood up and looked over the pack ice, wondering with a shiver what it must have been like to be Franklin, lost in this cruel white desert. That's when I heard the drums begin to reel in the anchor. I wheeled to look at the ship, my heart and the dog's wildly beating. I ran back toward the gangway and stared in horror at what I saw, or rather at what I did not see. The gangway was being raised. There was no way up and the pack ice and the ship had drifted away from each other.

I began to yell, my voice sounding lonely and useless in the eerie dawnish light, the sun sending shafts of golden light across the ship. It must have been about 3:00 a.m. When would they notice I was gone? Maybe not until 9:00 a.m. It could be twelve hours before they doubled back along their course and found me — assuming they did find me. My piece of pack ice wasn't standing still. It was drifting with the current. I weighed my options and eyed the watery distance between myself and the ship. Even if I could survive the cold of a five-foot swim, once I got to the ship there was nothing to hold onto.

I yelled and yelled until my voice was hoarse. At one point I thought I saw someone looking my way, standing partly in shadow near the controls for the gangway. I renewed my yelling, but I must have been mistaken because they seemed to melt away. I turned and watched the anchor line going up and thought, "Is this how I'm going to die?"

The dog whimpered in my arms, bringing me back to my senses. I had to do something. I couldn't just stand there. I walked along the pack ice towards the bow, yelling the whole way and scanning the ship for anything that might rescue me, but the noise of the engine drowned out my voice. I might as well have been yelling at a rock for all the help it would bring.

Again I became aware of the anchor line being reeled out of the water and panicked. The ship was leaving me here to freeze to death, just like Franklin. I looked at the chain for some moments before my mind got itself around it. My heart, already racing, had gone into overdrive. I wondered if I was crazy, but I couldn't see a better way out of the situation. I ran along the pack ice to the anchor chain. Just three feet away, in a calm sea, if I had no choice I could do it. Even with the dog, I could do it. I was small enough. I put the dog in the hood of my jacket and before I could think anymore I backed up and ran, planting my feet at the edge of the ice at the last moment and jumping out and up, my hands reaching high.

Both my hands grabbed a link in the chain and immediately began to slip. I heard the little dog yip and then start whimpering. Frantically I coiled my legs around the chain and forced one hand through to grab the other hand. I looked up and saw the gaping hole, the chain ahead of me sliding into it, the rusty stains from where the anchor had rested against the side of the ship at sea. Slowly the anchor chain raised me up. As I entered the hole the chain slid sideways, catching three fingers of my left hand that were clasped with my right, and I screamed. I nearly let go in pain — which made me almost cry out again.

There was no danger of me slipping into the sea unless I lost my three fingers, which I decided wasn't a good thing to dwell on. As my body entered the hole I had to let go of the chain with my legs and hung from my arms.

The dog was no longer whimpering, just shivering like aspen leaves in the wind, but I really had no mind for it or anything else except the light at the end of the tunnel. I had no idea how slowly an anchor comes back to its mooring, but by the time my head broke out into the light my arms were screaming with pain. And suddenly, as the anchor chain hauled my body out of the hole my hands were clear, the awful, grinding pressure gone. I had the strongest urge to let go then, but I hung on until the chain pulled me clear of the tunnel and I flopped down on the deck like a stranded fish.

I felt the dog escape from my hood as I tried to get to my feet. I looked at my hand to see the damage, expecting to see a mangled mess of flesh, but all that was there was an innocent looking scrape on the three fingers that had been dragged along the tunnel wall.

The dog stuck its nose into my face, not knowing how lucky it had just been. I looked up at the bridge but didn't see anyone. They must have been busy steering out of the pack ice because I could feel the ship bumping and grinding against the ice.

I got up and put the shivering dog inside my jacket, close to my chest, and made my way up to the bridge. In the twilight of 3:00 a.m. there were only two people up there: the captain and the third mate. I looked out the windows for the anchor hole, but it was hidden behind its giant roll of rope. So no one had seen me. I wasn't sure whether that was a good thing or not.

"Bit late to be up isn't it?" Jason had spotted me before I spotted him.

"Couldn't sleep," I said.

Jason looked at me curiously. "You look like you just crawled through a rusty pipe."

I looked at him in astonishment. Had he seen me come up the anchor hole? Then I followed his gaze and looked down at my jacket. There were huge, wet, rusty smears all down the front of it and my pants bore the marks of where I'd twined my legs around the chain.

"You're not far off. I've just come up the anchor hole."

He looked at me, momentarily taken off guard, and then began to laugh. "Good joke. And it's called a hawse-hole for future reference. But seriously, where HAVE you been? You're a rusty mess."

"Seriously, I have just come up the anchor hole — hawsehole — along with the chain."

"You're pulling my leg." He said it uncertainly. And that's when the dog suddenly started yapping under my coat. He must have warmed up a bit. The shivering wasn't as seismic as before.

"What are you doing with Scruffy?" said Jason, relieved to be changing the subject. He didn't believe me!

"Scruffy?" I asked.

"The dog."

"Oh. The dog. He was on the pack ice, eating tonight's leftovers."

"He was what?"

I told Jason the whole story — and then wished I hadn't.

"You must have been dreaming, Cordi. No one could come up the hawsehole. It's insane."

"But I did."

He didn't answer and he didn't return my gaze. Instead he said, "You said you thought you saw a person near the gangway who saw you on the ice. Why didn't they help you?"

I must admit I didn't know the answer to that question. It seemed fantastical even to me, and I'd lived it. No wonder he didn't believe me.

"I think you must have been imagining things."

I looked down at my jacket, at all the rust on it, and back up at him.

He chewed his lip. "I'll find out if the cook dumped food overboard, but I very much doubt it. We may be small but we're a class act. As for the walkway being down? I'll look into that too," but he said it in a patronizing way.

I nodded and extricated the dog from my jacket to give it to Jason.

"No, oh no," he said. "Dogs aren't allowed on the bridge." He had the grace to look sheepish about that last comment since I knew that Scruffy had been on the bridge before. "Can you keep it till morning? I'll let the owner know as soon as it's decent to knock."

"On second thought, maybe I'll slip a note under her door."

I stuffed the shivering little Scruffy back inside my jacket and had turned to go when Jason said, "We checked the ropes on the Zodiac. They were frayed." He looked at me strangely. I wondered why he was telling me this. "I asked Peter, since he was the first to bring it up, but he didn't know. Anyway, whoever started the rumour is going to get a piece of my mind once I find them. An angry piece. The last thing we need are a bunch of tourists who think the ship is sabotaged." Somehow he didn't sound very convincing and I wondered for a second if he was telling me the truth.

I smiled. "The only person on board who seems nasty enough to create a rumour and get everybody all upset" — including myself, I thought — "is Terry."

A dark look flitted across Jason's face. "Yes. It'd be just like Terry to pull a stunt like that."

"Has she pulled other stunts?"

Jason eyed me for a moment before answering. "We think so, but we've never been able to prove anything because there is always a believable reason for what she did. It's why she's still allowed on the ship."

"And what did she do?"

"There have only been two incidents but the polar bear was the hardest to take." He reached over to pat the dog's head as it peered out of my jacket and was rewarded with a high-pitched growl.

"We were making a stop in Croker Bay in Lancaster Sound. If the fog melts we'll be stopping there, probably tomorrow. Anyway, it's hilly and barren and there are a lot of polar bears around so we stationed three guards with guns and asked everybody to stay within the boundary formed by the guards."

"And Terry didn't."

"No. She wandered out of the perimeter and a female with two cubs came over the hill near where she was. The guard closest to her called to her to turn back but she didn't pay any attention to him."

"How close was he?"

"Close enough to hear easily. Anyway, she had her video camera out and was advancing toward the bears when the female charged. We had to shoot her." Jason smacked his fist into his hand in remembered anger. "I was livid, but when I confronted her and asked why she hadn't listened to the guard she smiled her pretty little smile, held up her headphones, and said, 'But Jason, I couldn't hear through these, now could I?' The guard was positive she hadn't been wearing them."

"But why would she do that?"

"Material for one of her books? Stories to tell her friends?"

"You're kidding."

He shrugged his shoulders.

I must have looked dubious because he added, "Look at all the embedded journalists — what do you think that's all about? They're not just doing it for their bosses, that's for sure. They can feel a book coming out of it. There are hundreds of examples. Next time you see a nature film of running giraffes my money's on a troop of trucks chasing them just off camera."

He laughed a dry hollow laugh. "But that wasn't the end of it for Terry. It never is with her type. That night she had the nerve to come up to me and say, 'Please have the pelt sent to my home address, but make sure it's tanned first.' I told her it was illegal and all she said was,

'You'll find a way, I'm sure.'"

I looked out the bridge windows. The fog was glowing like an illuminated globe and I thought I could see blue sky skittering through it — a real stranger to this land of ice and snow. It was 3:30 am. The dog had started to squirm and I felt a sudden wet warmth on my chest. I felt like yanking open my jacket and catapulting the dog at Jason, but a cooler head prevailed and I merely said goodbye and hightailed it back to my room.

The door at the end of the corridor to the outside was still ajar and I wondered what deck LuEllen's berth was on. I closed the door and went into my room. I got Scruffy out of my jacket and watched him standing there, looking at me with big doleful eyes and shivering at high speed. I washed him off with nice warm water and then got a big towel and rubbed him until he was dry, which didn't take long because he was so small. Then I cleaned myself up and went to bed. But Scruffy kept whimpering and whining and trying to get on the bed until I finally gave in and picked him up. He checked out the entire bed and walked across my chest to sniff the stuff on my night table. After three or four perambulations he settled in the crook of my knees, a warm little ball of fur.

Chapter Seven

I awoke suddenly to the sound of a rhythmic and desperate thumping. At first I thought the ship's engines must have malfunctioned and we were about to hit an iceberg. But as I slowly woke up I realized it was just someone knocking very loudly on my door. I started to swing my legs over the side of the bed and was suddenly aware of a flurry of movement. I couldn't figure out what was going on until Scruffy catapulted himself into my lap. If I'd had a bad heart I'd have died then and there.

The knocking was getting louder and more frantic and was now accompanied by "Cordi ... Cordi ... Wake up!" I looked at the clock on my bedside table: 5:00 a.m. One and a half hours sleep and I felt like a zombie — but at least I didn't feel sick. The relentless pounding continued and I cradled the little dog in my arm and went to answer the door in my PJs.

I should have known. Perhaps if I'd had more sleep I would have. When I opened the door there stood LuEllen, looking desperate enough to highjack a ship. The hall lighting wasn't kind to her face and I tried not to react to what the baseball cap and jacket had hidden. Who knows how much cosmetic surgery she'd had to try to fix the crooked, flattened nose, the caved-in cheekbone, and the numerous scars snaking across her face. In this light I could see the skin stretched so taut under one eye and along her forehead that it looked like it would spring apart at any time. But even her badly distorted face couldn't hide her joy and relief as she caught sight of Scruffy. As for Scruffy, his legs were moving like windmills as he tried to get a purchase on my arm to jump into hers. I took him in my hands and handed him over.

We stood there on the threshold of my door; me feeling uncomfortable, LuEllen ignoring everything but Scruffy. She was talking to him a mile a minute when she suddenly must have realized how rude she was being.

"Oh, I'm so sorry," she said. "It's just that Scruffy is everything to me. Since my accident he's been my only ..." she hesitated, "my friend."

I tried to see in her face the woman she once was, but it wasn't possible to imagine anything but what was in front of me. And I didn't really know who that was. She must have seen the indecision in my face, having seen it countless times before, but she made no effort to help me.

"What the hell happened to you?" was what I wanted to say. But I didn't. I mumbled something that I couldn't even hear and one side of her face went up in a smile but the other side didn't follow.

"Where did you find him?" she asked as Scruffy basked in her love. Some people never get loved that much.

I hesitated and then told her about the garbage on the pack ice. I didn't think I had to tell her everything so I didn't mention the hawsehole. I could still see the look of incredulity on Jason's face when I told him and I didn't much want to repeat it.

LuEllen looked down at Scruffy. "We went to bed together as usual, and when I woke up ten minutes ago he wasn't snuggling against me. I was frantic until I found the note from the captain. I'm so sorry I woke you so early."

I nodded away her apologies. "How did he get out? Did you leave your door open?"

She suddenly looked guilty and stammered, "Th-h-he b-b-berth was so hot. You know what it's like. I'm just down the hall from you, between Sally and Terry." She cooed in Scruffy's ear. "Sometimes he wanders, but I really thought we were okay and it was so stuffy. Scruffy could have died if you hadn't had insomnia."

And I wouldn't have had a brush with death either, I thought.

"So you think Scruffy walked around the ship trying to find a way back to me and smelled the food on the pack ice?" She looked dubious. "I don't know. Scruffy doesn't like water." Dear god, the poor dog, trapped on a ship and it doesn't like water. "But he does like food." I remembered the apple and smiled. Food triumphs over water!

After LuEllen was gone I went back to bed, thinking about the sequence of events and wondering if they were as they seemed. The image of someone at the controls of the gangway haunted me; why would they not sound the alarm? It didn't make sense — unless someone wanted me dead. An odd little shiver cascaded down my spine.

The morning, when I finally met it, was gloriously sunny. And when I looked out my bow window I could see land. Colourless, barren, lonely, desolate land; the sun glinting golden on the cliffs making it look deceptively benign, a landscape suffering from depression and no more. But, of course, Franklin had known better and perhaps the landscape looked so barren and lonely because of all the sorrow it had wrought.

I was about to turn away from the window when I noticed a familiar figure sitting on the deck. Sally was in profile and was staring intently at something, her face a tapestry of misery. Curious, I followed her gaze. On the starboard railing I saw Terry and that Arthur fellow standing side by side, with Arthur's arm flung lazily around Terry's shoulders. I looked back at Sally. What was going through her mind?

I put her out of my thoughts and got ready for our first trip ashore. We were going to Franklin's grave — not his real grave, but a memorial. The Zodiacs deposited us on a rocky beach. It was an eerie place, with the last tendrils of fog wisping their way up the cliff face that lowered over the gravesite. How anyone could have lived here I couldn't fathom, and we were there on a sunny summer day. Franklin and one hundred twenty-nine of his men had spent the winter of 1845–46 here. They built Northumberland

House with spars and masts from a wrecked rescue ship. Three of Franklin's men died that winter and many would-be rescuers would succumb over the years.

It was a place full of pathos — you could feel the pent up strength of nature in the shadows, waiting to pounce, biding its time. Revealing its softer side, like a polar bear satiated from an evening meal turning a benevolent eye on a wayward tourist, but when hunger strikes unleashing its full fury on any innocent wanderer. The terrifying gulf between the softness and the anger is what makes it so frighteningly lonely and touches even those who never knew the men who died in anger's eye.

Franklin's widow had spent a fortune paying people to search for him and on his gravestone had had engraved the inscription: "... and the anguish, subdued by faith, of her who lost, in the heroic leader of the expedition, the most devoted and affectionate of husbands." As I was reading this, with a little lump in my throat, I heard a strangled sob and turned to see Elizabeth looking over my shoulder. She sniffed and hastily wiped her eyes with her hands.

"Sorry, I can't help it. My husband died far from home too." She hesitated then added, "Lady Franklin was a brave woman searching for the truth about her husband." Her words were laced with such wistfulness that I turned to face her, but she had already turned away and was walking briskly toward the Zodiacs.

As I left the memorial I could see Martha down by the water's edge, Duncan at her side. I couldn't figure out what they were doing. Martha was taking up a weird sort of bent-at-the-knees, elbows-cranked-out pose. Then I saw the pebble. Duncan was teaching her how to skip stones. At least, he was trying. Martha's stone took a nosedive from her hand straight down into the water.

I told them what had happened to me and Scruffy, and they looked at each other and then back to me, their faces blank. I couldn't believe it. "You don't believe me either," I said incredulously.

"It's not that we don't believe you, Cordi. It's just that it all sounds a bit far fetched," said Martha. "The hawsehole?"

"My hand. Look at my hand" I said flapping it in front of their faces. It was scraped raw, and looked angry and very real.

Duncan took my hand and gazed at it for a while. "Cordi, if there really was someone there, as you say, why would they have not raised the alarm?" Echoes of Jason.

I stared at him and he stared back.

"No, Cordi. You can't be thinking what I think you're thinking," he said.

I looked down at my hands and said, "That someone was trying to kill me?"

"Whoa, Cordi. Put your head back on. Why would anybody want to do that? And in such a roundabout way?"

"I don't know and I've put a lot of thought into it. I admit that planning this whole thing out sounds crazy, but maybe whoever it is just took advantage of a situation. The dog was already on the ice. All whoever it was had to do was lower and then raise the gangway."

"Yes, but why?"

"Maybe I saw something or overheard something. Maybe I have something they want. I don't know."

"Look, Cordi. You've been popping Gravol like peanuts, you've been sick, you're stressed out. I think you're imagining demons where there simply aren't any." He hesitated, clearly wanting to say something more but deciding against it.

I looked at him suspiciously and then at Martha, who shrugged and said, "Sleep on it, Cordi. See how you feel tomorrow."

I didn't stay with them, but walked down the beach instead. I was actually feeling kind of, very, unsocial. I wasn't used to sharing my free time with so many people night after night and I felt irritable and sort of sad. I wondered if I WAS imagining things, but then I looked down at my hand and knew it had been real. Why did I sometimes let people talk me out of my feelings? Why do we all?

When we got back to the ship I headed out on deck to look for icebergs. It was late afternoon and the fog had rolled in. I prowled around all four sides but I found nothing except for the dampness of the sea, enshrouded by fog. As if on cue the foghorn sounded practically beside me and I jumped. I nosed about the deck where the pool is, poking my head here and there, not knowing what I was looking for or even if I would recognize it when I saw it. One of the huge orange metal lifeboats loomed out of the fog and I went over to take a look. It seemed to be made of multiple hatches all with numerous tie downs. I tried the handle of one of them and raised it slowly to an upright position. As I did so I heard a man and a woman arguing as they approached.

"We're playing with fire," said the man.

"It's worth every risk if it works. She can't just take my man away from me," said a woman, her voice rising.

"She's going to catch on, I know it." Their voices were getting closer. "There's a lot of risk."

"No one said it was going to be easy," the woman said.

I felt like an eavesdropper, which I guess I was, but I was struck by the intensity of their voices. I frantically looked around for a place to hide. I didn't want them to think I'd overheard them. Without hesitating I swung my body through the hatch and crouched just below the opening as their footsteps came close and stopped. They had reached the lifeboat and I heard one of them lean up against it.

"I know that." The man.

"Are you getting cold feet?"

There was no answer, just silence. I tried to peek out one of the portholes to see if one of them was nodding or shaking their head, but all I saw were shoulders and then the man's voice, "Who left the hatch open?"

There was a scuffling and a couple of grunts and then the hatch came down. I moved to the porthole and peered out. I could just make them out. The woman was facing me. Elizabeth. Suddenly the other one turned and I saw the bushy black beard: Peter. I heard their footsteps move away and I was left alone in the cold metal hull of that lifeboat with the hatch battened down.

Think like a mariner, I told myself, as I began to feel a tad uneasy. Lifeboats are for saving lives not locking people inside. Just because this hatch was locked down didn't mean they all were. Right? And there were more. I'd seen them sprouting their little levers like dozens of curling rocks. The portholes threw a gloomy light over everything so that I could just make out how awful it would be to have to be in one of these things for real. The seats were solid metal benches with room for maybe seventy people. Being stuck in one would mean bouncing around inside an unforgiving metal hull the shape of a walnut with people in various stages of seasickness. I was already feeling claustrophobic and I'd only been inside for five minutes.

It was cold. The metal of the boat was taking up the cold of the air like a sponge takes up water. I felt my way around until my hands found the outline of a hatch. I pushed, but nothing happened. In the twilight I could see eight levers, two on each side of the hatch, and I began turning them. When I tried to push up again and nothing happened I felt a little twinge of fear. What if I couldn't get out? What if they never found me? How often did they do lifeboat drills? I tried again and felt it budge. After several more attempts the hatch flew open and I was free to wonder about the conversation I had just overheard.

I went back to my berth and flopped down on the bed. Next thing I knew my stomach was in my mouth and my semi-circulars had lassoed my entire body, making me reel with nausea. I got up on my knees and opened the porthole. The sun was sinking toward the horizon that it would barely get to touch before being shot back up into the sky. The sea was roiling around in swells and the ship was doing a pretty good job of not roiling with them — something to do with stabilizers, we'd been told by the orientation crew. The PA system on the boat crackled to life and the captain's voice filled my little room. We were into some rough waters for a few hours before we could sneak around a headland and into calmer seas.

I spent those hours with my eyes glued to the barren mainland mountains. It helped keep the nausea at bay, but it was pretty tiring so at about 11:00 p.m. I got up and went to sit in the outer room, only once daring to take my eyes off the horizon to look at the time. Eventually we did hit calm water and I went back to bed and fell into a blanket-churning sleep. But before long I was awakened by a light tapping on my door and my name being whispered. I thought it was LuEllen, back for a repeat, but being mercifully quieter this time. I started to get up when the door opened — there were no locks on any of the berths on the ship — and in walked Martha, dressed in a floor-length, lime green velvet dressing gown and wearing enormous fuzzy Guinness slippers.

"You awake?" she whispered.

"I am now."

The room was lit by the stream of light coming through the open door and I felt no need to turn on the lamp.

"Cordi — you've got to see this. Look out your window!"

Looking out that window was the last thing I wanted to do after spending five hours at it, but I turned and looked. All I saw was a never ending expanse of sea and pack ice, a deep blue sky, and the mainland. I turned back and shrugged at her.

Martha came closer and looked. "Oh, you're on the wrong side. Come on!" and she grabbed me by the hand and pulled. I was a dead weight and she let go.

"Cordi, you'll regret it if you don't come and see."

"See what?"

"You'll see. Now where is your dressing gown?"

I was feeling groggy from the Gravol. "I don't have one."

"You don't? Why not?"

"Because most people don't travel with dressing gowns."

She stood there looking at me for a second and was about to say something when she thought better of it. Instead she flung me a pair of sweats, a top, and my runners. By the time I put my jacket on I was feeling a little better and thought that maybe Martha was right after all, until I caught sight of the time. It was 3:00 a.m. Was I doomed to always be awake at 3:00 a.m. on this ship?

As we moved out into the corridor, Martha leading the way, I said, "Martha, what are you doing up at this time of night?"

She stopped in the corridor and I crashed into her. "Some weird noises woke me up and I couldn't get back to sleep. I looked out the porthole and there it was. I knew you'd want to see it." Martha continued down the hall. She could be so infuriating.

We walked up a couple of decks and then outside, where we took the starboard stairs up to the observation deck. And there it was. Actually, there they were. Two vibrant rainbows, one snuggled inside the other and arching across the deep blue of the sky. The sun was balanced on the horizon, a red orange globe.

I could clearly see each colour of each rainbow — so clear and precise that there was no fading out at the edges or anywhere along the enormous arcs. They were perfect, stretching from Baffin Island across the ship and halfway to Greenland. We were the only ones up there and we stood and watched as the ship knifed its way through Baffin Bay to Lancaster Sound. In this uninhabited place of history and intrigue we could have been sent back three thousand years and it would have looked exactly the same.

I turned and looked toward the stern of the ship and gasped. In the golden light of the sun, which was trying — unsuccessfully — to set, lay a monster of an iceberg, taller than the ship and slowly receding from us. We moved to the far rail as if drawn by a magnet and watched it as it slowly glided away — or that's what it seemed like as we moved away from it.

I glanced down over the railing and saw the pool below. There was a white towel hanging over the rail. But that's not what caught my attention. There was a hunk of some sort of clothing floating near the surface, rising and falling with the movement of the ship. I was trying to make out what it was when my eyes shifted and I found myself looking down into the depths of the pool. At first it looked like some kind of weird white reflection through the wavy water, but then I recoiled when the reflection materialized into the unmistakable body of a naked woman.

Chapter Eight

I charged over to the stairs and, grabbing one railing in each hand, swung myself down the stairs, two at a time. I could hear Martha struggling down behind me, cursing her long flowing gown. Even before I got to the ladder I'd whipped off my sweatshirt and kicked off my shoes.

"Get help!" I yelled at Martha, and in a flash I had my sweats off and jumped into the pool. I felt nothing. No cold. No fear. Just the incredible focus of my goal. I swam down and took hold of the person under the chin, my finger momentarily getting caught on her necklace. I kicked hard and slowly rose to the surface. As I did so I could see the bundle of clothes, her clothes I guessed, floating languidly like a ballet dancer. And that's when I saw it: a face among the clothes was staring back at me, wide-eyed and lifeless. I nearly choked on a mouthful of water and almost let go of the first body. But I managed to kick up and broke the surface, raking in the air the way a croupier rakes in the chips.

Martha had disappeared to get help. I was all alone. I tried to hoist the body up the ladder but the superhuman strength that visits some people in moments like this wasn't calling on me. I wasn't sure what to do. I couldn't save them both, so I closed my eyes and did artificial respiration, trying not to think about anything at all, especially about who I was trying to save.

Suddenly an extra pair of hands reached down and grabbed the body under the arms, pulling it out of the pool. I watched as Duncan laid her down on the deck and began to take her pulse. The captain had arrived and went over to help Duncan. I heard him suck in his breath and looked over to see him stooping over the body, one hand holding his head, his expression, what? Dumfounded? Shocked? No, there was more. If I hadn't been so cold and shaking that I could barely see I would have sworn that Jason was crying. Someone threw a blanket over me as I looked up at Jason and said through chattering teeth, "There's another one."

"Save your strength," said Jason as he glanced back at me. And I realized he hadn't heard me.

"There's another one," I said loudly.

"Another what?" asked Jason, his voice strangely hoarse.

"Another body."

I pointed with my finger at the bundle of clothes, but I didn't take my eyes off the body Duncan was working on. It was Terry. Her face was grey and lifeless, but still as beautiful in death as it had been in life. I felt sick and cold and hopeless. How can life be so tenuous? I turned away, my stomach heaving, and saw the second mate jump in the water to rescue whoever was in the bundle of clothes. I think we all knew our actions were in vain. Their bodies looked as though they'd been deserted for a long time. The doctor had arrived, and she and Jason pulled the sodden mass out of the water and laid it down beside Duncan, who was resting on his haunches, a look of resignation on his face. He moved over to the body clad in the salt and pepper coat, and pushed the hair from her face.

Jason gasped and I heard him mutter "Oh, no," as we gazed down on Sally, who had finally realized her wish to be free of her torment.

It seemed surreal, standing there wrapped in a blanket that wouldn't keep Scruffy warm, in the land of the midnight sun, with the bodies of two women lying at our feet. I noticed someone had covered Terry. Beautiful, arrogant Terry. Timid, lovelorn Sally.

What had happened here that took two lives away? I shivered. Looking up, I saw a row of people gaping at the bodies, and then felt angry that the end of two lives could become a spectator sport. How had they found out at this crazy hour of the morning?

Martha tugged me on the arm, pulling me toward the stairs. I hadn't even known she was there. I stopped and looked toward where the rainbows had been but they had evaporated, just like the souls of those two women had. I started walking down the corridor when Martha grabbed my arm and steered me into the sauna.

"You get in the sauna. I'll get you some dry clothes," she said and was gone.

Like an automaton I stripped off my wet under-
clothes and went into the sauna. It was lonely in there, the
chattering voices of moments past assailing my ears as I
sought to make sense of what had just happened. Terry
must have been taking a late night sauna or it wouldn't
have still been warm in there. Thumbing her nose at the
world she jumped, alone and naked, into the pool. I was
remembering her the other night. She'd stayed close to
the ladder and used the dog-paddle. Perhaps she couldn't
really swim. Perhaps she'd inhaled some water or jumped
too far away from the ladder. Sally had happened upon
her, roaming the decks in sorrow, or insomnia, or both?
She'd jumped in to rescue her and they'd both drowned.

But other, less charitable, ideas were crowding my
mind. Something suddenly flitted through my brain so
fast that all I knew for sure was that it was important. I
idly wondered how something can be important if you
can't remember it.

Martha came back and collected me as if I was some
fragile vase, shepherding me down the hall to my room.
She wouldn't let me do anything except get into bed and
drink the hot chocolate she had somehow made materi-
alize. My body glowed with the warmth from the sauna,
and the heat of the hot chocolate was delicious.

I was exhausted, but just as I was snuggling down into
my covers, as Martha heaped yet another blanket on top of
me, there were three soft raps on my door. I started to get
up but Martha held up her hand and went to get the door.

"How is she?" Even in a whisper Duncan's voice is
loud, deep, and rumbly. "Dear girl. I thought I should
make a house call, make sure everything's okay."

Since Duncan's "house calls" usually involved dead bodies, that wasn't very reassuring. He came into my room and took up a position leaning against my porthole, which Martha had shut down tight, so that the air was already getting stale.

"The ship's doctor kicked me out. Took umbrage at my being at the scene before she was."

"She wouldn't do that," said Martha.

"No, but she did usher me out."

"What have they done with the, um, bodies?" I asked as I sat up in bed. I always felt at a disadvantage with Duncan because he's over six feet tall, but now I was a whole lot shorter and had to tilt my head back farther than usual just to see his face.

"The authorities have ordered the captain to put them on ice until they can be delivered to pathology back in Ottawa."

"Any guesses?" I asked innocently.

"Guesses?"

"About how they died?"

"Whoa, whoa, Cordi. Put the reins on your imagination. It looks like a straightforward situation. No guesses needed. No hanky-panky here." Duncan's mention of hanky-panky stopped me dead.

"I didn't say anything about hanky-panky," I said slowly. But maybe subconsciously I had. Or maybe I was just too damn tired to know my own mind.

"I wondered if you had a guess about the sequence of events."

"You mean who died first?"

I nodded.

"We may never know that, but one thing's pretty sure — one of them must have tried to save the other and they both died in the attempt. Of course, forensics could turn up something else, but if you're a betting woman put your money on the former."

I wasn't a betting woman, but I suddenly knew why Duncan's scenario didn't wash.

Chapter Nine

I lay sleepless in bed until early morning. I was thinking about giving in and getting up when I heard my door quietly opening. Who the hell could be visiting at this ungodly hour? I wasn't about to wait in bed to find out. In a flash I grabbed my blanket and flattened myself against the wall by my inner door. I could hear somebody padding around the outer room and time seemed to stand still, as it is wont to do when someone scares the shit out of you. Whoever it was started towards my door. I tensed myself, making sure I timed it just right. As they entered the door I raised the blanket over my head, flinging myself and it over the intruder, and we both crashed to the floor.

The blanket began flopping around like a giant jumping bean. I could hear the muffled cries of protest coming from under the blanket and suddenly realized they were saying something I could understand. "Cordi, you idiot, it's me!"

Who the hell was "me"? I thought.

"Martha!" yelled the big lump inside the blanket.

Shit. Hastily I got up and pulled the blanket off Martha, who looked as though she had just been bagged by a hunter, which she sort of had.

"Lord love a duck, Cordi. What are you doing?"

"Trying to defend myself. Why didn't you knock?"

"I did."

"You didn't."

Martha groaned and rolled onto all fours and pushed herself up with some difficulty.

She brushed her staticky hair off her face. "Who did you think I was for god's sake? Don't tell me you're still thinking there's some mad person on board out to get you? First the frayed ropes and then the mystery person and the hawsehole. I thought you'd got over that."

"I have." I lied.

Martha gave a sign of relief. "That's good."

"But I do think we now have a possible murderer on board."

Martha pinioned me with her astonished stare. "Listen to yourself, Cordi. You're going off half-cocked. Who ever wanted you dead anyway? As for Terry and Sally … accidental deaths — that's what they'll say. I know it's early yet, but so far there's nothing to say otherwise."

"Yes there is," I said.

Martha cocked her head at me. I waited, relishing the silence leading up to my revelation.

"Terry was wearing a necklace," I said triumphantly.

"So?"

I stared at her. This was not the reaction I'd had in mind. "Remember what happened in the sauna?" I asked.

And suddenly Martha's light bulb went on. "She chewed Sally out for being so stupid as to wear a necklace," she said slowly.

"Right. So what was she doing in that pool while wearing a necklace?"

Martha screwed up her face in thought. "She decided to take a late night dip."

"Without a sauna? That water is barely above freezing. No one in their right mind would do that.'

"Okay. She came out to see the midnight sun before turning in. Lost her balance and fell in. That's when Sally saved her."

"Stark naked?" I was going through the scene again in my mind's eye. The single towel over the railing.

She looked at me then and I saw the beginnings of a convert. "So how did she get into the pool?"

Just then the PA system crackled to life. "Would Cordi O'Callaghan and Martha Bathgate please report to the bridge at your earliest convenience?"

Martha and I exchanged glances. I started searching around for my clothes while she went into the head to calm down her electrified hair.

When we came up on deck the sun was washing the distant hills of Devon Island with golden tones. The pack ice prowled off the port side, making it impossible for us to go into Pond Inlet. People were very disappointed about that, but the ice was acting strangely this summer and the ship's crew couldn't do anything about it. No one wanted to be stranded in the pack ice.

Martha and I marched up to the bridge. Jason was talking to a few passengers and there were at least six other people lined up along the fore windows, binoculars glued to their eyes. I looked out the window and saw an iceberg the size of a three-storey apartment building slowly coming toward us, as graceful as a dancer. But that's not what everyone was looking at. We walked over to see what all the fuss was and saw two wrinkly walrus trying to sun themselves on the smallest little ice floe. Their massive bodies undulated with myriad folds of blubber and overlapped into the sea so that it looked as though they were sunbathing on water. Every time they moved their little ice floe bobbed them precariously up and down. All around them were dozens of much bigger ice floes, but for some reason they had chosen this tiny little one. I wondered which of the two would be left lying on the iceberg when it got too small for both of them. Of course, I knew, even though it made no sense in terms of the iceberg. The bigger one would win out. He was a monster, probably fourteen hundred kilograms.

By the time Jason noticed us standing by the helm, Martha was deep in conversation with some man who was telling her all about the life habits of walrus. I was glad I wasn't drawn into a conversation that would lead Martha to disclose that I was a zoology professor; although most of the ship probably already knew that.

Jason caught my eye and pointed back behind the bridge. I commandeered Martha and followed him into the privacy of the radio room, a room just behind the bridge with no windows. Seated at one of the radio consoles was Duncan, who was talking on the phone to someone who was having trouble hearing him. We were treated to his loud voice for several minutes.

"No, I am not the captain. He just passed the phone over to me. I am a pathologist. The captain asked me to … Yes that's right. We have two bodies on board. Preliminary exam points to accidental drowning of both. No, there were no obvious marks on the bodies, but that will have to wait for the autopsies. Yes, that's right. We have them on ice. What's that? Oh, right. Two females." He looked over at Jason. "But the captain says you have all that information. Yes. Alright. I'm losing you. Yes. Okay. Goodbye." I raised my eyebrows at Duncan, wondering where the ship's doctor was. He read my mind.

"Ship's doctor slipped and knocked herself out as we were getting the bodies to the cooler. She has quite a nice little concussion and Jason here has asked me to take over as best I can until she is able to resume her duties."

As if on cue we all looked at Jason.

"So, what happened?" he asked looking first at me and then at Martha.

Since our stories were almost identical it didn't take long to fill him in. He was about to get up to go back out onto the bridge when I hesitated. Martha started having facial fits trying to signal to me to think before I spoke. But I figured what the hell, if they thought I was crazy they'd ignore me, but if they thought what I said had some merit then it would be worth it.

"I don't think Terry died accidentally."

Jason looked up quickly with a "go on" expression on his face.

"I think someone murdered her, probably in the pool since Duncan says there were no marks on her,"

"And how in the name of god did you come up with that scenario?" asked Jason.

I told him about the necklace and Terry's derision of Sally, but he seemed completely unimpressed. Duncan, on the other hand, was having conniptions, shaking his head and chopping the air with his hand.

We all waited for Jason to respond.

"I don't know what to say, Cordi. You're a respected zoologist and you come to me with this weird story about the dog and the hawsehole and now this. Although the cook did admit to his assistant throwing leftovers on the ice, and the ramp was down to check on the hull. But the hawsehole? I hope you haven't blabbed this murder theory around ship and caused a panic that there's a murderer on board."

I sensed that maybe this was the time to say nothing and shake my head, so I said nothing. He fiddled with the hem of his sleeve.

"There was no murder. We have found a suicide note in Sally's room. Terry must have tried to rescue her and died in the attempt."

Did I feel dumb.

"What did the note say?" asked Martha.

Jason shook his head, rummaged around in his breast pocket, and pulled out a scrap of paper. When he saw the shocked expressions on our faces he said, "This isn't the real note. I just copied it down to look at it later."

We waited. He took his time. Then he began to read what Sally had written:

How hollow is time … Aching seconds I
cannot stand. The oozing emptiness that
is my mind. Sticky blackness. Nothing
there. I have to die. My friends, goodbye.

Haunting, melodramatic, and very, very sad.

Nobody said anything and through the door I could hear the second mate explaining to a passenger that port means left and starboard means right. I wondered if they had heard what we were saying.

Jason broke the silence. "So you see, it's not murder, but a good Samaritan dying in an attempt to save a suicide."

"But then why," I asked, "was she wearing noth …"

Duncan suddenly went into a paroxysm of coughing that bounced off all the walls and practically deafened us. He stood up and pointed to the door, and Martha and I went to help him. We got him out on the bridge and near the door where he gulped in fresh air.

Jason looked alarmed. "Is he all right?"

"He'll be okay," Martha said. "He's just allergic to plastics."

I looked at Martha in disbelief, but she refused to look at me. We took our leave of Jason, both of us supporting Duncan until we were well away from the bridge when Duncan shook us off and turned to me. "Cordi, are you nuts?"

I was getting used to that.

"You can't go blathering murder when there's no evidence. I have an idea what you were about to say back there, but it would not have been good."

We were standing on the port side of the ship near the Zodiacs. The view from the stern was spectacular: rolling, barren hills with glaciers creeping down them to the sea, leaving a splattered mass of ice. I reminded Duncan about the necklace and that Terry had been naked.

He peered at me the way doctors sometimes do when they're trying to make a diagnosis. "That's hardly evidence of murder."

"There's no evidence that it isn't, and there's no way Terry would have taken the time to strip naked to save someone in distress."

"She was coming from the sauna."

"Which brings us back to the necklace."

"She left the necklace on by mistake. All the evidence so far points to accidental drowning."

I wasn't about to give up. I had the bit in my teeth. "And I say there are way more scenarios than purely accidental or suicide."

Martha and Duncan looked at me expectantly.

"Terry murders Sally by drowning her and then accidentally drowns."

"Why?"

"I'm not sure. Or, Sally murders Terry and then drowns herself, or drowns accidentally."

"Why?"

"Do I hear an echo in here? Okay, maybe you like this better: Sally dies trying to rescue Terry, who is accidentally drowning, or vice versa. Nice and clean. No murder. No suicide."

"Enough already. We have a suicide note," Duncan said.

"Which can be faked."

"Cordi, you've made your point. There are lots of possibilities, including murder, but we'll just have to wait for the authorities to find out which scenario is the right one."

"There's another scenario."

"Why do I not want to hear this?"

"It was a suicide pact. They both committed suicide together."

Duncan looked slightly mollified by my retreat from murder, but Martha wasn't buying it at all. "Since when would Terry make a pact with Sally?" She had a point. They had not exactly been bosom buddies.

"Look on the bright side. If it's suicide we won't have to testify in court."

I wandered back up to the bridge to see what was happening and looked out the windows. That's when I noticed her. She was standing at the very bow of the ship, leaning into the railing as still as a figurehead. Sandy. I took the side stairs down from the bridge onto the deck. It was a beautiful day so there were lots of people around. I approached the bow slowly. She had her eyes closed and the wind was blowing her hair off her face. She looked peaceful and I felt like an intruder. I started to back away. Suddenly she opened her eyes and started. Clearly, she'd thought she was alone.

"Sorry," she said. "I'm hogging the bow." That was not what I had expected her to say considering her personal space had been invaded. She pulled herself upright so that we were now facing each other and I could see she had been crying.

"I'm sorry about Sally. You seemed like good friends."

"We were," she said. "More than you can know." She moved over to the railing and leaned against it. I followed suit.

"She was pretty upset about Arthur."

Sandy turned and looked at me, her face a mass of confusion, but I must have been mistaken because it suddenly turned to anger. "A lot of people used Sally. I had thought Arthur was different."

"There were others?"

She eyed me thoughtfully. "There are other ways to use people besides love affairs," she said, reading my mind.

"What do you think happened?"

"You want my version or the ship's version?"

"What's the ship's version?"

"They say she committed suicide, that there was a suicide note, and that Terry tried to save her and failed."

"And you don't think that's what happened?"

She rapped her fist against the railing and fixed her eye on the horizon. "No, I don't."

"But she was depressed and upset about Arthur."

"Was she? I mean was she upset enough to kill herself? No, she wasn't." She said it with such conviction that I wondered why she could be so sure. All I could see were images of a very miserable Sally in the sauna.

"What happened then?"

"I think she tried to save Terry and they both drowned. She wasn't a very good swimmer." Her voice caught on the last word and she turned to look at me. "Sally was not suicidal."

The words hung in the air like a dare and she stared at me, her eyes pleading for something I couldn't quite fathom. Finally she turned away and looked out across Lancaster Sound.

I left her standing by the rail and was headed back across the bow when I saw Peter and Elizabeth heading my way. I plastered a suitably sad look on my face and strode up to meet them.

"Terrible news about Sally and Terry," I said as we all came to a halt beside the hawsehole. I looked down it and shivered, but they didn't appear to notice.

Elizabeth looked awful, her face long and haggard, and so very pale, as if the lifeblood had been removed from it. You couldn't really tell what Peter looked like but he seemed slightly frantic, his eyes flitting about and alighting on nothing.

"It's so tragic," said Elizabeth, the words barely squeezing out of her mouth.

"It should never have happened," said Peter. I was surprised at his anger.

"But you hardly knew them," I said. "You aren't part of the writing group are you?" I remembered him coming late to that first lecture, but I hadn't seen him since.

He stared at me. Elizabeth jumped in. "He knew them through me."

Peter looked at Elizabeth and then slowly nodded. Elizabeth was fidgeting with one of her mitts. "Sally was a good woman," she said. "She's going to be missed."

The omission of Terry's name was glaring.

Peter took Elizabeth by the arm, signalling the end of the conversation, and I headed back to the haven of my berth.

It was midnight, one full day after Martha and I had found the bodies, and there we were again, on the prowl. I'd managed to convince her to come with me to check things out by telling her I was just trying to prove that Sally had not committed suicide. If I had mentioned murder again she might have given me that sideways look that meant she didn't quite believe me.

We were tiptoeing down my hallway, one behind the other, towards Sally's room. I could hear someone snoring as we passed one of the berths — whoever it was had left their door open. Sally's room had white masking tape criss-crossing it in a big X. I guess the captain didn't have any of the yellow stuff, which made it look sort of amateurish.

"We can't get through that without breaking it," said Martha. She was standing right by the door and I reached past her with my gloved hand, opened it, and turned on the light switch. I let it swing gently and the two of us stood and stared inside. Sally's room was just a two-bunk berth with a sink, a dresser, and a desk and chair. She probably shared facilities with LuEllen. I made a note of that. The bed sheets were all messed up as if she had been having a fitful sleep and her briefcase was open, some handwritten papers were scattered about.

I couldn't see clearly enough and leaned in over the tape, trying to get a better view. Martha tapped me on the shoulder and said, "Allow me." She nudged me aside, whipped out a pair of binoculars and began eyeballing the room. It was all I could do to keep from asking for the binocs, she was taking so long. I kept looking anxiously up and down the hall. Finally, I couldn't stand it anymore and grabbed Martha by the shoulder. She turned round and gave me the binoculars.

"All the papers are handwritten and the suicide note is just to the left of the sink."

I scanned the sink and zoomed in on the note. It was handwritten on a ripped sheet of paper with scalloped edges, which seemed somehow pathetic for a last communication. I scanned the other sheets, just a handful that could have been blown about by the porthole being open. There was a biography of Audrey Hepburn and Terry's book, which looked old and tattered. There were some clothes draped over a chair and a little teddy bear propped up on the desk.

Suddenly Martha hauled down on my coat hissing, "Someone's coming."

I could hear footsteps coming up the stairs to the outer door at the end of the hallway. I quickly reached in to close the door and found that my arm wasn't long enough. I looked at the binocs in my hand and against all odds lassoed the handle with the strap and pulled it closed just as the door at the end of the hall opened.

Martha and I had started walking down toward the door when Elizabeth appeared, still looking haggard and demolished. I could see the surprise in her eyes when she saw us but she covered it well, saying in a monotone, "Good evening ladies. What are you doing up so late?"

There was a moment's silence and then Martha replied, "Just bird watching."

She kicked me in the foot. It took me a second to figure out what she meant by that and I quickly raised the binoculars in a salute.

Elizabeth didn't give any indication that this might be a bit unusual at 12:30 a.m. We'd have looked like fools had we not been in the land of the midnight sun. She didn't even look at the binocs. Instead she said, "I wish you luck," and we flattened up against the wall so that she could get by.

We continued down the hall, past the tape on Terry's door to the outside door. When we reached it I glanced back quickly, but Elizabeth was gone. To be on the safe side we made a show of trying to find some birds to ogle, but we didn't last long. It was cold and we weren't really dressed for it. Besides, our minds were somewhere else.

When we opened the door and peered down the hall it was deserted, but then it was 12:30 a.m. For the first time I wondered what Elizabeth had been doing up. Why hadn't we asked her? When we reached Terry's cabin Martha was fidgeting like a hummingbird on speed. I opened the door in the same way as I had opened Sally's and let it swing open. I turned on the light switch.

Terry's room was palatial compared to all the other ones I'd seen. She had a big living room with six portholes so that the light streamed in. There was a bright red corduroy sofa that had such an upright back that it must have felt like sitting against a wall. The two matching chairs were no better. There was a writing desk that ran the length of four portholes. It was covered in papers, typewritten and handwritten. There was a laptop computer and a printer.

Right by the door was a small desk with a dull bronze elephant, about the size of a cherry, on it. It had a broken right tusk that looked as though the artist had fashioned it on purpose. I dimly remembered seeing something similar fall out of Terry's briefcase on the plane. I marvelled at what people took with them on trips to make them feel at home.

There was an open door into the bedroom and beyond that another open door into the bathroom. Part of the rug by the bathroom door was wet and from the reflection in the bathroom mirror I could see a bathtub and the sink, which was full of makeup bottles and lipsticks; nothing there. Martha nudged me. "Let's get out of here, Cordi."

I quickly turned off the light and tried to lasso the door with the binocular strap, but missed three times before I got it. Martha was beating a tattoo on the floor with her feet. As soon as the door closed we scampered back to my room.

"Cordi, that was close."

"Martha, she was just a woman in the hall," I said, but my voice croaked. I cleared my throat and tried again. Martha was looking at me the way my mother used to when I'd get a cold — kind of predatory.

"What's wrong with your throat?" she asked.

"Must be laryngitis." The words came out all scratchy and Martha was on me in a flash. She wouldn't leave until I was in bed with several different cold remedies sloshing around in my stomach.

As she turned to go she poked her head back around the door and said, "I wish to god these doors had locks."

So do I, I thought in alarm. I retrieved my only chair and wedged it up under the doorknob before I went to bed.

Next morning I felt awful. Not my stomach this time, but my head, and when I went to clear my throat I found I had no voice. I had to cancel my lectures and after breakfast I pretty much stuck to my room all day, until bedtime when I sheepishly did the doorknob and chair routine again. Just in case.

Chapter Ten

*T*he sun floated down on me like a soft warm blanket.
I was lying on my belly on an ice floe no bigger than
I was, and wearing a blue and white polka dot bikini.
There was some sunscreen and a book about frogs at my
left hand and a short, squat little Margarita on my right.
I looked around, wondering how I had got here. There
were dozens of other little ice floes, but they were all
black and seemed to be moving. When I looked closer
I could see the rolls of fat cascading from the backs of
hundreds of walrus. Some of them had human faces. I
could make out Sally's and Terry's and Arthur's, but the
others were turned from me. Was I a walrus? But then I
remembered the bikini — it hadn't been on a walrus.

There was no ship in sight, just me and the wal-
ruses, until a three-storey iceberg sailed into our midst.
It was shaped just like a polar bear climbing an iceberg.
I took a sip of my margarita, adjusted the sunglasses

that suddenly appeared on my nose, and idly watched
as it came nearer. Or perhaps I was moving and it was
still. The midnight sun left rose-coloured streaks on
its snowy sides, making it look warm and soft when
really it was neither. I watched it glide by my ice floe,
which suddenly reared and dipped violently, catapult-
ing me off. As I struggled to breathe I saw a huge black,
water slicked walrus hauling itself up onto my ice floe,
water streaming off its sides like little rivers. While it
usurped my tiny island I was plunged into the violently
cold waters of Lancaster Sound. As I went under I saw
the magnificent statue of the iceberg give way to what
lay, sombre, quiet, and deadly, beneath — an enor-
mous mountain of luminous blue and aquamarine ice,
a good twenty times larger than my polar bear. The tip
of the iceberg....

I sat up in bed. The dream was as real as my breathing. I sat there for a long time, thinking about the iceberg
and the revolting shock of just how big its hidden sec-
tions were, like cancer run amok inside while the outside looks benign. It's true what they say — that eighty
percent of an iceberg is hidden beneath the sea. Amazing
considering that some are huge, calved from a Greenland
or Ellesmere glacier.

The thought was chased out of my mind by a dull
thud in my outer room — the door shutting. I heard
someone quietly moving around and found myself staring at my doorknob with dreaded fascination. I consid-
ered pounding on the walls, but two of them were outside walls, the third was occupied by my intruder, and
the fourth — the one in the head — was a common wall

with the library, and who would be up reading at this hour? But then, maybe it was Martha?

I watched as the doorknob began to shake and the chair began to shift at the first suggestion that the intruder was pushing against the door. Not Martha. I flung the sheets off me, grabbed my down vest, and turned to the only escape hatch I had — my porthole. The doorknob was rattling now as I frantically looked out. I was three decks above the main deck and there were no convenient trellises or other handholds. I looked up and my hopes went up too. Above me, just within reach, was the barred metal catwalk that ran alongside the bridge so that the officers could see sternwards. I looked back at my door, hoping the thudding was a dream, but the door was shaking the chair free and it looked ready to give at any moment.

I threaded my body out through the porthole. I sat on the edge and reached up, my fingers gripping one of the metal bars. I took a deep breath and glanced back at the door, which suddenly swung open. A person in a balaclava moved quickly towards me. I pushed myself off the porthole, swinging rather violently and wrenching my arms. I made the mistake of looking down and nearly swallowed my teeth. I quieted my body but found, as I walked my hands along the bar toward the edge of the underside of the deck, that I had to kick out with my legs. That's when it happened. Balaclava grabbed one of my legs and started to pull. I could see him or her squeezing through the porthole, trying to reel me in. I could feel the strain on my arms get worse as I tried to shake off their hands. I gave one almighty shout but nothing came out. I could see whoever it was now, their eyes glinting through the holes of the balaclava.

I figured I had one shot at this. I braced my mind and on the next violent tug I went with it, at the same time kicking viciously with my other foot. There was a muffled gasp and the pressure on my foot lightened. I immediately kicked out and was free! I brought my legs up to my chin and walked my hands along the bar as fast as I could. I could see that Balaclava was trying to get through the porthole. My arms were screaming and my fingers were so cold I was beginning to lose feeling in them. I had very little time left.

When I reached the end of the catwalk I tilted my head way back and could see that the railing was a latticework of squares made from bars. I painfully reached up and grabbed one, then began to haul myself up. I nearly cried when I reached the top of the railing and fell like a clod of earth onto the metal deck without feeling a thing. My arms felt like jelly and my hands didn't feel anything at all. I rolled over onto all fours, got to my feet, and ran toward the bridge and help. But the bridge was empty. Where the hell was everybody? I remembered that the ship was at anchor, but even so there should have been a watch.

I ran into the map room and tried to remember what exits there were from the bridge — through the radio room. I ran into the radio room, all the dials and blinking lights mocking me, and ran for the door. I burst out into a corridor and couldn't remember which way led down. There was no time; I could hear Balaclava behind me. I turned left and fled down the corridor, braced my arm on the wall and skidded around the next right turn. There was the door at the end of the hall. I pelted towards it and burst through, the slapping of Balaclava's footsteps close behind. I turned to see if I could lock the door, but it only lost me precious time. I looked ahead of me and my heart sank. I was on a catwalk that led to a set of stairs that went up, not down, to an observation deck. I couldn't remember if there was another way down or not.

I scrambled up the stairs as the door behind me crashed open. When I reached the top I knew I was in trouble. There was no way out — just a big deck surrounded by a metal railing and a small padlocked room with loud rumblings coming from it. I ran to one of the side rails and looked down three decks. I raced to the other side, but there was nothing. Suddenly Balaclava was there, standing on the top of the stairs. I backed up towards the stern railing as Balaclava began walking toward me. I judged the height and the weight of the person — large woman or medium sized man, but I couldn't tell which because they were wearing a bulky down coat. When I felt the railing hit the small of my back I quickly turned my head and glanced down, then immediately back. Balaclava was closing in on me. It was now or never. I turned, gripped the railing with both hands, hoisted myself up, and swung my body over.

As I fell I heard Balaclava's running footsteps, but I was too busy looking at what I was falling into to care: a bevy of naked men taking a dip in the pool, or hovering around the ladder waiting their turn. As I plunged into the water I almost laughed at the expressions on their faces. It seemed to take a long time to reach bottom and I'd tucked up my legs so they'd be bent on impact. I was just glad they'd refilled the pool after draining it to clean it. It was still a jolt and as I unbent my legs and pushed off to the surface I could feel my PJs and down vest holding me back.

When I came to the surface there was a flurry of male bottoms frantically disappearing up the ladder to the safety of their towels. They stood aside to let me through and as I passed them I smiled and said, "Excuse me, gentlemen. I seem to have lost my way."

"Cordi, you realize that these things that have been happening to you — nobody can corroborate them."

'The men in the pool can," I croaked.

"They only saw *you*. They didn't see anybody chasing you. And the anchor thing; same deal. Besides, why would anyone want to kill you and do such a bad job?"

Duncan, Martha, and I were sitting in the library the next morning. Duncan was looking at me with such concern that I was getting uneasy. "Cordi, you know you have problems with depression."

I narrowed my eyes and looked at Martha, who unnerved me by staring right back at me. "I'm definitely not depressed." It was summer and summers are good. "Don't tell me: you think I'm delusional, that I've been hallucinating or something?"

Duncan had the good grace to look sheepish.

"Duncan, I'm your friend. How can you not believe me?"

"Because I'm a physician too. And I didn't say I don't believe you. I'm worried about you. I think maybe you've had some sort of psychotic episode triggered by the twenty-four hour light cycle."

"Which made me imagine these things?"

"Possibly." At least he wasn't saying definitely.

"And what about my murder theory? Delusion?"

"I don't know. We have to wait for the autopsy results."

"Since I believe these so-called delusions are real, I figure I must have seen something to do with the deaths. Except the hawsehole happened before the murder, so it can't have anything to do with it."

"We don't know that it's murder, Cordi," said Duncan.

Suddenly Martha jumped in. "Hold on. Maybe Cordi overheard someone or saw something that could have twigged her to the murder *before* it happened." Duncan glared at Martha, but she ignored him.

"Oh great. So I could have saved their lives?"

"Cordi, why do you always look on the dark side of things?"

"Because the things I'm looking at are dark!"

"Look — if it had to do with the deaths then maybe whoever it is has lost interest in you. Realizes you aren't a threat."

Yeah right, I thought, and wished I knew what they thought I knew that I didn't know I knew.

"It was just an accident, Cordi," said Duncan quietly.

"But if it wasn't?"

"Would you at least promise to see someone when we get back to Ottawa? I can set you up with an excellent specialist I know." He looked so serious and so concerned that I agreed. The way one does when they don't really mean it. After all, I was not delusional.

By the time we'd figured out the state of my depressive nature and the fate of the bodies it was 9:00 a.m. Since it was a foggy day there were no shore excursions' and I wasn't slated to give a lecture until the afternoon. I took off for the bridge, deciding to retrace my route of the night before, in case Balaclava had dropped anything. When I got there I thought there was no one on it, just like last night. But I was wrong: Jason was leaning against the starboard side of the ship, staring out to sea, his face completely still except for the tear dribbling its way down it.

I cleared my throat and he hastily looked away, bringing up his sleeve to his cheek, and then turning to face me. Who did he keep crying for? Sally? Terry? Surely not Terry. Or was it something else altogether? His eyes were red and I wanted to say something, but since I didn't know why he'd been crying I was limited to saying "Hello."

"What's wrong with your voice?"

"Laryngitis on the mend."

He gave me a weak smile and flung out his arm at his fog-enshrouded ship. "Zero visibility. I've never seen such bad weather. Storm moving in too. You people have hardly been ashore at all and we're due in Nanisivik in forty-eight hours." He stopped abruptly, moved over and twiddled with something next to the helm, while I digested the fact that the trip was almost over. We were due to fly out of Nanisivik. I'd lost count of the days, but I couldn't honestly say that I wasn't happy to be going home. The ship was beginning to feel like a prison, or maybe Tweety Bird's cage with a human sized Sylvester on the loose.

We talked a bit about the awful weather and the pack ice, then I asked him who was on watch last night at about 1:00.

"That'd be the second mate," he said. "Why?"

I didn't tell him everything but I did tell him I'd been on the bridge at 1:00 and nobody had been there.

"Probably in the washroom. Did you call out?"

I pointed at my throat and shook my head. Why hadn't I thought of the washroom? Not that I knew where it was. Even so, it couldn't be far, so there'd been someone right there to help me all along. If nothing else, Balaclava lived with a lot of luck. But then, if there had been someone on the bridge, Balaclava would have gone down the outside stairs, which I had completely failed to notice, and left me in peace. I sighed. I wondered what else I had failed to notice.

Chapter Eleven

I left the bridge and followed my route from the night before, all the way up to the sixth observation deck. I was alone.

I could feel the motion of the ship swaying gently in the quickening breeze. I looked out over Lancaster Sound and thought again about the men who came looking for the Northwest Passage — Frobisher, Davis, Hudson, Bylot, Parry, Ross, Amundsen, Franklin. It didn't exist at the time, but now, with global warming, it did. I wondered what they would have thought of our world. Ship after ship had come to sail the ice-infested waters, their men to chart the unknown land, and, for far too many, to die in this vast and barren place, so cold and far from home.

I was in my own little world up here on the grass green deck with the white railings hemming me in, keeping me from the sea, which seemed to come alive and begin throwing itself at the ship. I felt it in my legs too and not long after, in my stomach. I walked over to the stern rail and looked down. Overnight someone had drained the pool. It looked like a giant cement tube capped on the bottom, lifeless the way only empty pools can be. The rails stood guard around three sides, like sentinels who don't know their quarry has flown. The inside of the pool was painted a pale ocean blue that was flaking off like spindrift, reminding me of the wind that was whipping all around me. I felt the hundred and seventeen metre ship groan and quiver up through my legs. I headed back to my berth.

The following day I awoke to a dead calm and brilliant sunshine. When I looked out the porthole I could see Dundas Harbour, cradled by stark, eroded cliffs that looked like one of those cakes with scalloped sides. The cliffs swept down to the sea and turned into gravel spits left behind by the glaciers. As I watched, a single Zodiac headed out, presumably to check things out before we all descended.

I took the last boat out, spending the intervening time standing at the railing watching the Zodiacs being swung over and lowered to the water below. There was a biting wind, but on the lee side of the ship, with the sun shining down, it was almost warm. But I was still glad I had my orange jacket on.

I noticed the group below were being handed some hot chocolate and I scurried down to get some. I could see Martha and Duncan heading toward the gangway.

"Are you coming? You're going to miss the last boat!" yelled Martha.

I waved and started moving for the gangway.

It was a relief to be in a Zodiac that didn't bounce and grind. As we motored in, some harp seals came swimming alongside us, their sleek, shiny backs glinting in the sun as they porpoised along. Every now and then they would dive and when they surfaced their curious whiskered little faces bobbed up and down out of the water as they tried to place us. Thousands of seabirds skimmed the waters and soared overhead. A small herd of walrus was lazing about on the ice floes, their huge slug-like bodies and delicate whiskers in soft contrast to their long, white, dagger-like tusks. I remembered learning that those selfsame tusks were used to break through a breathing hole that had frozen over and it gave me shivers imagining swimming up to a hole and finding it blocked. They looked so out of shape with their rolls of fat, but it was all a mirage. The blubber in those rolls of skin provides heavy-duty insulation to see them through a long, hard Arctic winter. As I thought about being a big fat, almost hairless human, just like the walrus, except with no chance in hell of surviving even a second of minus fifty, we landed on a gravel spit that led gently up a whaleback and into a secluded cove.

Martha and Duncan strolled over. Martha said, "This is unreal. Nothing grows here, Cordi. It's dead, sterile, barren, stark, cold, hard, rocky."

"What's this then?" I asked as I pointed at something at my feet.

"What? I can't see anything. You mean that little red thing?"

"Yeah. That's a prickly saxifrage."

"How do you know that? You're not a botanist."

"I read the brochure. And this one," I crouched down and touched a golden yellow plant, "is an Arctic willow. They've already changed colours. The Arctic summer is ending."

"What summer? I don't see a summer," said Martha. "Ooooo, look! There's a big ball of fluff galloping up the hill." And she pointed up the whaleback beneath a cliff. We all whipped out our binoculars, but I already knew what it was, I'd just never seen one before: a muskox, its hair so long as to hide its legs even in flight. But take away the insulating hair and like a grape to a raisin the animal shrinks. We watched it run by two unsuspecting tourists who visibly jumped as it careened over the whaleback and disappeared.

Duncan and Martha moved off and I continued climbing until the cove came into view. Backed by a cliff were four or five deserted wooden buildings, abandoned by the RCMP many, many years ago. The biggest one was built in the shape of an L and had a rusted old stovepipe poking up through the roof. I went and looked inside. It was little more than a one-storey shack and all the windows had long since ceased to function as windows, merrily letting the weather in instead of keeping it out. There was a jumble of old stuff on the floor, books, a coffee pot, some plates, all left behind long ago. As I snooped about I heard a footfall and looked up to see LuEllen enter the building. I looked behind her expecting to see Scruffy, but there was no little dog in sight.

"Where's Scruffy?" I asked. She started and then stared in my direction, her eyes getting accustomed to the dark.

"Is that you, Cordi? They won't let Scruffy ashore in case he harasses the polar bears." I wasn't sure if she was joking or not, but the image of tiny little Scruffy harassing a polar bear was comical. It suddenly occurred to me that maybe Scruffy had wakened LuEllen the night of the deaths — he was quite the little yapper. I asked her.

"We slept right through it all. Poor sweet Sally."

I took note of her not mentioning Terry and didn't want to let it slide by this time. "I'm sure you're going to miss Terry too?"

"Why would I miss Terry?" Her voice was cold and lifeless.

"Because she was your teacher?"

"That doesn't mean I had to like her."

"I gather you didn't."

"Would you like someone who ..." she stopped abruptly, turned on her heel, and left, leaving me with my mouth wide open, wondering how that sentence was meant to finish.

I went back outside to see if she had maybe changed her mind and saw her standing by an old handmade wooden ladder that was leaning against the outside of the building. But she had her back to me so I went and looked at the little graveyard. It had a little white picket fence around it that looked so brave and so forlorn guarding its graves. There were three graves. I walked over to the farthest one: Constable William Robert Stephens, RCMP 1902–1927. He was only twenty-five years old when he died. I shivered. It seemed so benign here, the sun warm on my back. But it hadn't been for William. I wondered if he had died alone with no one to hear his final words. Such a lonely, lonely place. As I was leaving the little graveyard, feeling forlorn, I bumped into Tracey and her husband, George.

"Sad thing about Sally and Terry," I said.

George scowled at me. "Sad about Sally, yes, but that bitch Terry deserved everything she got." I was taken aback by his vehemence and Tracey plucked him on the sleeve, trying to stop him. He ignored her.

"You were there," he said. "You saw what she did to Tracey. Totally humiliated her, trampling every vestige of her self-respect. I wasn't there, but if I had been I'd have killed her."

I looked at Tracey, who refused to meet my eyes, and then back at George. Was he the right size to be Balaclava? Possibly. We turned to a safer topic and after five minutes of discussing the weather I escaped and walked down near the shore.

I was feeling very sleepy from the bucket loads of Gravol that I'd been taking, so when I saw a nice piece of grass in front of a fairly smooth rock I sat down and leaned back, face to the warmth of the sun, and in an instant I was asleep.

When I woke up the sun had moved. I stood up and looked around. There were no people milling about any of the buildings, no people around the gravesite, and no one on the beach. I was alone. Uneasily I checked my watch. It was 4:30, half an hour after I was supposed to meet the last Zodiac. I felt a moment of panic as I picked up my binoculars and headed up toward the shack and the path over the whaleback to the beach.

I don't know what it was that made me turn and look back, but what I saw froze me: a polar bear standing some distance behind me, sniffing the wind. Everything I knew about polar bears told me it had seen me and was interested. And then I saw movement off to my right. Two small cubs came gambolling over to the female and I knew I had to do something. I felt caught in a dream, on some gigantic treadmill of time where I could not get away, no matter what. I'd been here before, facing a black bear in the wilds of West Quebec and I couldn't believe it was happening again. I knew one thing for sure: I'd pick the black bear over a polar bear any day. I glanced quickly over my shoulder to look at the building where LuEllen had become tongue-tied. I'd have very little time — polar bears can outrun a man so it could certainly outrun me. She made up my mind for me by starting to amble towards me.

I bolted, dodging old oil barrels and rocky outcrops, forcing myself not to waste time by looking back. I took the ladder on the run and began to climb it. One of the rungs broke and I found myself hanging from my hands, wildly searching for another rung. I could hear the bear now. Frantically I reached for the next rung and pulled my body up until I found my footing. I clambered up and onto the roof; only then did I turn around. The bear was ten feet away and coming fast. A large white slash against the drab grey browns and greens of the rocks and grass. White. The colour of purity. How can purity be so fierce?

I pushed out the ladder and the bear ran into it, slowing its pace, as I scrambled backwards up towards the middle of the gently sloping roof, all the while watching the bear. It came up to the shed and disappeared from view. I held my breath and suddenly there she was, all nine feet of her, her head and shoulders rearing above the shack as if it was a doll's house. Her front paws and forearms made contact with the roof and she slowly pulled herself up until she was on all fours and gaining purchase to make the final lunge. I scrambled back over the ridge, avoiding the holes and trying to think up some fantastic getaway plan. But my mind was not co-operating and the bear was barrelling down on me. And then, just as suddenly, she wasn't there anymore. A huge rending of splintering wood and she was gone. I peered down through one of the holes, but I couldn't see her. Worse, I couldn't hear her. Maybe she'd knocked herself out.

It was so fast that I had no warning: an enormous white paw at least ten inches long and ten inches wide came flailing up through the hole beside me and caught my leg a glancing blow before I could move away. As I scrambled back the bear's head came through the hole, her paws gripping the roof, and we just stared at each other. It went on like that for what seemed like a long time, until suddenly she dropped from view and I could hear her muddling around inside the shack.

I sat and waited — for her to get me, or for the expedition guys to realize I was gone and come rescue me. I wondered what had happened to the young constable and shuddered. I wouldn't want to die here, I thought, hugging my knees in fear. And then I saw her, fifteen feet from the shack, looking back at me. I could see the cubs some distance away and thought about the power of every female's dedication to her offspring. It's scary how violent and vicious it can be.

Suddenly a gunshot reverberated off the cliffs and the polar bear began loping towards her cubs. I looked behind me and saw three men up on the whaleback — all wearing crew uniforms. I felt devoid of emotion. Almost as if it were an anticlimax to still be alive. It was a weird and ugly feeling. I wondered if this was what Terry and Sally had felt.

I waited on the roof until they came, afraid the bear would double back. As they approached I could see that they were handling their guns casually as if there was no longer any threat. I slowly crawled down the roof as Peter came around the corner, the shock on his face visible even through the beard. He seemed to be struggling with finding the right thing to say to me.

Finally, he said, "You were lucky you weren't killed." He was wrestling with the ladder, finally leaning it up against the roof. I climbed down just as the other two men arrived. "How did you manage to miss the rendezvous time?" His voice wasn't giving anything away.

"I fell asleep."

He looked out to sea. "Where?"

I pointed to the group of boulders. He followed my arm and then looked at the two men at his side.

One of them shifted his gun and said, "I checked the boulders."

"Yourself?" asked Peter.

The man took the cap off his head and ruffled his dark brown hair. "Well, not exactly" he said.

"What, exactly?"

"There was someone in a grey parka over in the area so I yelled at them to check for anyone in among the boulders." He put his cap back on. "I didn't see any harm in it. I guess they missed this lady though."

"Evidently they did," said Peter. I looked down at my bright orange jacket and shivered.

My last night on board turned into a repeat of my first night as the sea whipped itself into a frenzy and the ship struggled toward Nanisivik. Even Martha didn't come calling and I wondered if maybe she had finally succumbed. I spent a fitful night and was wakened by Jason, who came on over the PA system to announce that we had docked at Nanisivik and disembarkation would commence in an hour. I looked out the porthole and the sea had calmed down quite a bit, but my stomach wouldn't follow its lead. I spent a miserable half hour packing my things. Just as I was finishing there was a knock on the door and in flew Martha.

"All set to go?" She stood in my door with little bits of luggage hanging from every conceivable spot. Definitely had not succumbed. Duncan was right behind her, carrying more than his own luggage, judging by the pink flight bag in his massive paw.

"Looking forward to dry land?" he asked. It was a question unworthy of an answer judging by the green tinge I saw in my face when I caught a glimpse of myself in the mirror. Half an hour later we disembarked down the gangway into Nanisivik, a desolate mining town on the shores of the Hall Peninsula, Baffin Island. When I first touched land with my feet, as barren and cold as it was, I felt like I'd won the lottery by regaining ownership of my stomach. Or so I thought. The flight back was long and bumpy — their definition — mine would have touched on words like major turbulence and jaw-dropping altitude changes. I spent the time dreaming about my polar bear and wondering how someone could have missed my bright orange jacket.

Ottawa International Airport was a tangled mess of people trying to get where they were not allowed to go because some diplomat had arrived in town and security took priority over the rest of us. I scanned the crowd, hoping to see Patrick, but why would he be there? I'd driven myself to the airport and tonight was the night he usually taught a course at the university. All the same, it was disappointing. We hadn't seen each other in nearly three weeks. I guess I'd have to wait until tomorrow.

We'd arrived during rush hour. It took me more than half an hour to get to the Champlain Bridge and cross over into Quebec. I live under the eye of the Eardley Escarpment, in a lovely corner of rural West Quebec. It's a bit of a commute into work every day, but worth it. I came over the rise in Highway 148 and the Ottawa River lay below me, the setting sun spreading a red orange sheen down its length. Eventually I turned right, onto the dirt road that leads to my log cabin.

August. Glorious August, with the fields full of ripening hay and the dairy cows out to pasture in the back forty. My brother Ryan and his wife, Rose, live in the old farmhouse. My cabin is further down the lane, beyond the barns. I pulled my car up by the barn, behind Ryan's car, and got out. As I was about to go inside to look for him, a voice floated out at me from underneath the car. "Welcome back, Sis."

I turned and watched as Ryan came gliding out from underneath the car on a little trolley, all six feet of him. I didn't even bother to ask how he knew it was me — he could identify the sound of any car he'd ever worked on and even ones he hadn't. His red-blond hair was all askelter, as usual, and there were a few dabs of oil trying to obscure the thousand freckles on his face.

"How'd it go?" he asked before he'd even looked at me. He eyed me critically. "You look like you've been through hell."

I laughed and began to fill him in when he stopped me. "Go get settled. Come for dinner, 7:30."

I wondered why he was trying to get rid of me. I looked at my watch. Only 5:30 and I did feel like having a shower. "Sounds good," I said and took my leave.

My little log cabin, hidden in the woods on three sides, with a view from the front over the endless fields of hay, looked friendly and cozy. The curtains were open and I figured Ryan or Rose had come in and opened things up for me. I took my bag out of the car and went up the stairs to the wraparound porch — my prize possession. I'd spent all of one summer building it and now, in the summer months, it was the space I used most often. I'd even screened in a section of it so that I could enjoy the nighttime without the bugs enjoying me.

I dumped my bag in order to unlock the natural oak front door. I walked in, breathing in the wood smell of the logs and scent of fresh flowers. Without warning something suddenly whipped around my chest and held me tight. Visions of Balaclava darted through my mind. I squirmed around to face the intruder and brought up my knee with a vicious jerk as I looked up at my attacker, and felt the blood drain from my face. Patrick. I couldn't stop the momentum of my leg in time. The roar of pain that came out of his mouth felt like a physical blow. He was doubled over and twirling in little circles, then he suddenly slumped to the floor and writhed on the ground. I didn't quite know what to do. Fortunately, after about five agonizing minutes the writhing slowly abated and he gasped. "Jesus Christ, Cordi!"

That wasn't very informative. Or maybe it was. But what else should I have done under the circumstances? I couldn't think of any other route that my reflexes could have taken.

I made little mumbly noises and tried to put a pillow under his head, but he pushed it away and got up on all fours, his head down so I couldn't see his face. What a homecoming, I thought. He just stayed that way for a long time. He wouldn't let me help him get up, but when he did he stood there, bent over, hands on his knees. I said nothing, just listened to the crickets and the robin that used one of my trees to blast out its song. When Patrick finally straightened up, sort of, his face was pale and wincing.

"Remind me never to surprise you again." His voice was stiff and guttural. I put my arm around his shoulders and he put both arms around mine and kissed me. But when I moved against him he quickly pulled away. "Sorry, Cordi. I think I have to lie down."

I helped him to the sofa and went and got an icepack. That's when I knew it was really bad because he wouldn't let me help him with it. I got him a painkiller and covered him with a blanket and then began to unpack. This was not quite how I'd envisioned my first night back with Patrick. I felt like an idiot and I kind of wanted to cry at having messed up his plans. In racing around to find him a painkiller and blanket I saw that he had set the dining room table and there was a single red rose in a vase as the centrepiece. In the kitchen there were some half unpacked bags of groceries and when I looked in the fridge I saw two T-bone steaks. Patrick was asleep when I went back to check on him and I puttered around, glad to be home, but angry at myself for letting my imagination knee Patrick in the groin. I mean, what was that? I was home. I was safe.

Chapter Twelve

The next morning I woke to the song of a cardinal, intermingled with the sweet gurgle of a bobolink. I tried to imagine what the notes would look like on a sonogram — a magical musical sheet of paper where the musical notes of birds are translated. Some of my current research was working with bird song and how it developed. My thoughts came back to Patrick. The sun was flooding through my bedroom window and flinging itself across my bed, across Patrick's face. His thick blond hair had flopped over his left eye and he was breathing deeply. All the pain lines from the night before were gone. I snuggled up against him and he shuffled the covers and suddenly opened his eyes and smiled at me.

"How are you?" I asked as I draped my arm across his chest.

He grimaced. "I'm not about to hit any homeruns any time soon."

I giggled, tightened my grip, and plunked my head on his shoulder. We lay there for a while, listening to the birds and the distant mooing of the cows, until he gently shifted me off him and gingerly swung his legs over the edge of the bed.

I lay there, listening to the shower pinging against the plastic of my awful molded shower stall. I had always meant to tear it out and put something nice in, tiled, but I never seemed to get around to it. The shower went on forever and ever until I figured he'd drained my well. Finally I got up, and staggered. My legs were still at sea, my mind convincing them that the land was a swirling mass of waves. It calmed down, coming in spurts, and I got dressed and padded down to the kitchen to scare something up for breakfast. I was glad the trip had ended on a Saturday so that I had a full day to recover.

Somebody had bought eggs, bread, bacon, and milk, and dumped them in the fridge, still in the bag. Couldn't have been Rose, I thought, so it was Ryan or Patrick. I dragged the bag out of the fridge and began making breakfast. By the time I had the bacon sizzling, Patrick had appeared in the door and leaned up against the doorjamb to watch me. It was silly but I felt like a little kid having to give a presentation in class, and when he came over and took me in his arms my knees went another kind of wobbly.

The bacon got burned, but that was okay because Patrick was back! I cracked the first and second egg and watched their little sunny eyes looking up at me, wrapped in a little cocoon of happiness, until Patrick raised the topic that neither of us wanted to talk about. "I'm going to London on Wednesday for the job interview."

All I really remember immediately after hearing that statement was how quiet it was and how loud my heartbeat sounded crashing against my chest. The third egg, which I had cracked as he told me, now lay on the floor between us like an accusatory finger. Wasn't love supposed to be all-powerful? How can people truly be in love if one can choose to leave for the lifespan of a job? Love endures even that?

Patrick went over to the kitchen sink, picked up the dishrag and came back. I didn't meet his eyes. I just stared at the stupid egg as he began to mop it up.

"I have to go, Cordi. It's a big chance for me. Two years working with a great parasitologist."

I rallied then, mumbling some inane idiocies about our being able to survive two years. That's all it would be. I mean what were two years in a lifetime? A lot, I thought. By my calculations two years might mean, if we were lucky, six visits a year — three each. Very lucky. I wasn't even sure our budgets would stretch that high. Would we survive? My thoughts started travelling down a lane where I didn't want to go.

"Tell me about your trip. How did it go?" Patrick was way too eager to change the topic too.

"Well, apart from the two dead bodies I found, the three attempts on my life, the twenty-four/seven seasickness, the rampaging polar bear, and a dysfunctional writing class, it was great."

Patrick laughed. "Oh, Cordi, that's why I love you so much. You have such a fantastic sense of humour."

Ooops. I stared at him with an expression that must

have said "I hear you and are you ever wrong" because his laughter dissolved. "You're kidding, right?"

I slowly shook my head.

"Two dead bodies?"

I slowly nodded my head.

"Two seagulls? Two polar bears?"

I slowly shook my head. "Although, there was that one polar bear, but it was very much alive."

Patrick suddenly reached out his hand, grabbed the spatula, and expertly whipped the two solid white eggs off the burner onto our plates. Then he pointed the spatula at me, gun fashion. "Okay, O'Callaghan, spill it."

I laughed despite myself and began telling him about the bodies because that's what he would want to hear first. That's what anyone would want to hear first.

When I had finished he said, "Okay. Let me get this straight. You and Martha find two bodies in the pool. One is a woman who was acquitted of murder and the other is a member of her writing course. Right?"

I nodded as we moved over to the kitchen table and sat down.

"What happened?"

"We won't know for sure until the autopsy results come back, and even then we might never know."

When I didn't say anything more he raised his eyebrows at me.

"The current theory is that the writer, Sally, decided to commit suicide and Terry attempted to rescue her and drowned too."

"How big is this pool?" I could see where he was going with this.

"About ten feet by ten feet, and twenty feet deep, but Terry couldn't swim. At least, I don't think she could."

"Go on."

"That's it."

"Oh c'mon, Cordi. I know you have a theory."

"I think Terry was murdered."

Patrick didn't say anything for the longest time and then he put his fork carefully down on the table, as if he was afraid to dent it. "What makes you think that?"

I told him about the necklace. He was noncommittal, but I could see his face wrestling with his thoughts.

"Maybe she didn't go to the sauna, just wanted a dip?"

"It's possible, but unlikely. The pool isn't heated."

Patrick scraped back his chair and whisked my plate and his back to the kitchen.

"There's more," I said to his back. He turned around and looked at me, then nodded for me to go on.

I told him about Scruffy and the hawsehole without any interruption from him. He just stood there leaning against the kitchen sink, watching me.

When I was finally done he said, "You're lucky to be alive." But he didn't get up and hug me or anything, and when I didn't say anything he continued, "Now let me get this part straight. You're on board two or three days and you go and rescue a white dog from the pack ice, who's gorging himself on garbage the cook's assistant dumped overboard?"

"Well, yeah. Presumably the assistant cook meant to hit water, but he hit the pack ice instead. The captain was furious when he found out."

"So the dog walks down a conveniently lowered gang-way to get at the food."

I was starting to get defensive. "The captain said it was accidentally left down."

"So you get insomnia, take a hike around the ship, and see the dog. You go down to rescue it and then the ship up and leaves?"

"The pack ice was closing in. The captain said they had to leave or we'd have become stuck in the ice."

"So you see someone raising the gangway and call out, but the engine noise drowns out your voice. Jesus, Cordi, you could have been killed."

"I think I was meant to be," I said quietly.

Patrick was in mid bite when I dropped that bombshell.

"Holy shit! Where did you get that idea?"

"Because the person pulling up the ramp saw me."

"How do you know that?"

"Because they were looking my way."

"Maybe they didn't see you. You could have blended in with the snow."

"In an orange jacket?"

"Cordi, your eyesight isn't the greatest. Maybe you thought they were looking at you but they were actually looking somewhere else, or maybe their eyesight was bad and they didn't see you."

But he was wrong. I knew what I'd seen and I'd been wearing my contacts. The person had been staring down at me while the ramp was still moving and then had inexplicably disappeared as if they were a ghost — but they weren't. Of that I was sure. Or pretty sure.

"They were too far away for you to know for sure and besides, why would anyone want to kill you? This happened before the murders right?"

I nodded. "And twice afterwards."

Patrick looked at me incredulously. "You rescued the dog two more times?"

"No," I said, exasperated. "Someone tried to kill me two more times. I think."

He just looked at me and shook his head. I couldn't tell whether the headshake meant he didn't believe me or that he was still taking it all in. I decided it was the latter and began telling him about Balaclava.

When I was done he said, "Did you actually see Balaclava climbing on the gangway out of your porthole? Were they even small enough to fit through it?"

I knew where he was headed and I didn't like it one bit. "No."

"So the Balaclava on the bridge could have been someone else altogether?"

"Yes, but ..."

"Could have been someone out for a stroll who happened to follow you?"

"That's a hell of a coincidence. Two Balaclavas near the bridge so early in the morning."

"You said yourself that lots of people wore balaclavas. And you have a broken trail where you didn't see Balaclava the whole time. It could have been someone else innocently following you and you jumped into the pool because you jumped to conclusions."

"Even if that's the case, Balaclava still broke into

my room. I saw him." And I had felt their hand on my leg. Definitely alive.

I rubbed my face with my hands and wondered how I could explain to the man I loved that he was wrong and I was right, when a lot of the evidence was against me. After all, Martha and Duncan hadn't exactly supported me.

"Are you okay, Cordi?" he asked, his voice soft and warm. "Is there something you aren't telling me?"

I looked at him between my fingers and sighed. "Duncan and Martha think I'm crazy."

"Well, they are quite amazing stories."

I let my hands fall into my lap. "That's what they say. They think I had a delusional episode on the ship that made me believe these things were real. Nobody else saw them."

"You mean they don't believe any of these things actually happened to you?"

"Well, not exactly. They're reserving judgment. They believe I believe it."

"But why would they ever think you were delusional in the first place? Anybody else but Duncan, Martha, and I would have laughed. Tell me why I shouldn't."

I hesitated. "I get periodic depressions, usually in the winter, and I'm sure Duncan thinks I've got some psychological problem like manic depression. I don't, of course. I may have SAD but I'm not bipolar."

"Shit." We sat there and let his word of wisdom sink in. "That's why you were so down this past winter? Sometimes it seemed I could hardly reach you."

"Yeah," I said, remembering how much I'd pushed him away.

"How long has this been going on?" he asked.

"Long enough."

"But surely your doctor has you on something?"

I shifted uneasily in my seat as the silence lengthened and then blurted, "I don't have a doctor."

He cocked his head at me. "Don't you think you should?"

"I don't want to talk about this anymore."

He looked at me, the concern written all over his face, but he didn't pursue it. I could have hugged him when he said nothing at all.

I felt trapped by my need to be in control, so it was disconcerting having people telling me I needed help. Patrick stared at me and I stared back. When things got bad, in the winter, I was sometimes too depressed to help myself. When things were good I convinced myself that I was perfectly normal, which I was most of the time. I was okay. I could handle it.

"Tell me about the rampaging polar bear," he said. And I did.

Chapter Thirteen

Monday morning on the drive into Ottawa, I mulled over the conversation Patrick and I had had. But the only thing that stuck was that he was going to the job interview tomorrow. I distracted myself by looking at the view of the Ottawa River and the Eardley Escarpment, as I skirted it on my way in to Aylmer, Quebec.

The drive got nasty over the Champlain Bridge. Bumper to bumper and everybody a singleton so the only traffic using the carpool lane were the infrequent buses. It always felt wrong to get angry over that — environmentally wrong — but at least I had an excuse for being solo. I lived in the country where there was no mass transit. I wondered how many of the other drivers had the same excuse. Boy, was I in a bad mood.

By the time I got to the zoology building at Sussex University I felt like I needed a vacation. I avoided the elevator and walked up the five flights to my office, ever grateful that the profession I had chosen did not include dress suits and high heels. How can anybody walk up five flights of stairs in high heels? Which got me to thinking of all those movies with women in high heels being chased down laneways, up fire escapes, and just about everywhere else. I felt pretty sure that stunt-women were underpaid.

We are an anomaly in the animal kingdom. I know of no other species whose males invent things for the females to wear. In fact, in the animal kingdom the male is usually the one "dressing up" to entice the female, who eschews the spotlight so that it doesn't fall on her young.

Amazing how the mind free flows, I thought, as I hauled open the stairwell door and headed down the corridor. I could see an oblong of light staining the floor outside my door and knew that it was open and Martha was there. I share her with two other assistant professors, and uncharitable as it is, I am always happy when she's in my office and not theirs.

I poked my head through my door and stopped in amazement. Martha was sitting just inside the door perched on the little milking stool our hired hand had given her and giggling her head off. Ten feet away, sitting on top of the table next to the computer, was a television tuned to *The Simpsons*. Since we normally didn't have a TV, and Martha had once told me she hated *The Simpsons*, I was at a loss as to what was going on. Martha glanced at me and stood up, her little milking stool waggling behind her.

"Sorry, Cordi. I have to watch this. I'll tell you why when it's over."

I squeezed by her and made my way into my inner office where a stack of work obscured my desk. I sat down, fished around for the phone, and listened to my messages. Lots of stuff about courses, students needing help, grants people wanting more information, and then one I hadn't expected:

"Hello, Cordi. This is the Dean. I need to talk to you about Martha. Please call me when you get back from your holiday." The cold click sounded like a gun without a bullet. Why did he want to talk to me about Martha?

I hung up and then dialed the Dean, getting his secretary, Cindy. "Oh hi, Cordi. Yeah, the Dean wanted to talk to you but he had to go on unexpected business to Vancouver. Won't be back for awhile."

I tried to pump her for information, but she clammed up so I hung up. I'd have to wait for an explanation. Plenty of time to come up with a hundred bad reasons why he wanted to talk to me about Martha. I marvelled at how we all routinely put other people through the wringer without even knowing it.

I dialed up the rest of my messages.

"Cordi. This is Sandy from the ship." She sounded harried and hurried. I could still picture her tear-streaked face in the bow of the ship after Sally died. "I need your help. Please call as soon as you can." And she left a number.

Out of curiosity I dialed, but there was no answer and no machine so I put it out of my mind and tackled my desk. I hadn't got very far when the phone rang again. I picked it up and the past came tumbling down around me.

"Cordi, this is Shannon Johnson."

The name brought dozens of images flashing through my mind, none of them particularly nice. Shannon had been Jake Diamond's girlfriend, the man whose body I had stumbled across in the wilderness the previous summer, and whose secret had damn near killed me.

"Hello, Shannon. It's been a long time. What can I do for you?"

"Do you remember Paulie?" No small talk here.

Paulie. Diamond's three-legged cat. It had hung around the body for four days and then disappeared and was never found.

"She's been found."

"That's terrific, Shannon. I know how heartbroken you were."

"Not so terrific. My new partner hates cats and they hate him so I can't take Paulie."

The ensuing silence was filled with her obvious intentions and I was trying to find some way to deflect her next question, but she was too quick off the mark.

"I thought maybe you could take her. You live on a farm and she'd be happy there."

I groaned. As I said, I'm a real pushover when it comes to animals but I wasn't sure I wanted a cat. Still, I backpedalled my way into saying yes.

She gave me the name and number of a family in Dumoine who were looking after her, thanked me again, and hung up. I stared at the phone for a while, happy the cat was alive but not so sure I wanted a pet. Reluctantly, I picked up the phone and dialed the Andersons.

"Mrs. Anderson. My name is Cordi...."

"Thank god. I thought you'd never call. When can you come and pick up Paulie?"

"Not until the weekend. I live a couple of hours away from you."

"We can't wait that long. You have to come and get her." The desperation in her voice was deafening and I felt a queer sense of unease as I asked her what was wrong.

"The cats is a hellion. It's terrorized all of us, including our pit bull."

Oh Jesus. "What's wrong with her?"

"Too wild, that's all. She's no cat for us. I have a four-year-old and a two-year-old, both covered in scratches. Come and get her today or we're taking her to the pound."

I told her I'd get back to her in an hour and hung up. Part of me thought the pound would be okay until I realized no family would ever adopt her. I could bring her home, make her an outdoor cat, and just make sure she got fed. I could do that. I picked up the phone and called Duncan.

"Hey, Duncan. How are you doing?"

"I should ask that of you, Cordi. You were the one who got seasick, among other things. Got your legs back?"

"Finally. It took a few days though. My semi-circulars kept thinking I was still on the ship." I paused. "You live in Dumoine ..."

"Last time I checked, yes," he said. "What's up?"

"Paulie has been found up in your area."

"The little cat?"

"Yeah, but no one seems to want her except me."

"And what has this to do with me?"

"I need you to go and pick her up and look after her until I can come and get her."

I could hear Duncan thinking it over.

"Why not?" he finally said and I thanked him a little too much because he got suspicious and asked, "What am I getting myself into?"

"Nothing much. She's just a tad frisky, that's all."

I hung up quickly, before he could change his mind, and went upstairs to check on my birds and insects. Leah had left a detailed report on their health and had meticulously recorded all the relevant data for two separate experiments, one on bird song and the other on cricket song. When I got back ten minutes later the cartoon voices were gone and Martha was hard at work.

She looked up when I came in. "Sorry. I promised my niece I'd help her write a critique of the show."

I tilted my head to one side and she interrupted what I was about to say.

"I know, I know. I should have taped it, but my VCR is on the fritz."

"And your niece is too?"

"What?" asked Martha.

"It's a school day and she's ..."

"Home sick," finished Martha. "Look, if you need me I'll be in the labs upstairs. I need to clean the cages." She turned to leave. "Leah says there were no problems."

I nodded as she left and thought about all the things that can go wrong when you have a research experiment with live animals. I was trying some new stuff on how young birds develop song. I allowed some young birds to interact vocally with an adult male and another group where the young birds only overheard a male bird singing. Part of the reasoning was to find out how different the songs were when both groups of birds grew up.

I heard Martha rustling around in the outer office. She reappeared, brandishing a book that she dropped in front of me, and then left me to the mess in my office. Curious, I picked up the book and saw that it was Terry's. I turned it over to the back cover and read the description. It was about the murder, and her trial and subsequent release. Better late than never, I thought, as the phone rang and drew me away for the rest of the day. I stayed late, partly to catch up and partly to miss the traffic on the Champlain Bridge. It made it an easy ride across the bridge, through Aylmer, and northwest up Highway 148 toward Luskville. I stopped in at the barn to see if Rose or Ryan were there, but the cows had already been milked and they were probably soon for bed so I didn't go in. I threw dinner together, fished out Terry's book, and began to read.

She'd started with the night terror and then the murder itself, or rather the accidental killing — presumably taking artistic license at the parts she couldn't remember. How much was that? I wondered. Do sleepwalkers remember anything? Whatever. This is what she had written:

> *The wind crashed into her face and eddied by on either side, her hair streaming back. She was standing above the windshield, head flung back at the night. They were going so fast, skimming across the inky black waters, stirring*

up the stars with their wake. They were
running without lights, running wild,
running free, running full speed ahead,
right into the sickening sound of rending metal and the ripping of fiberglass.
It drowned the noise of the engines, and
the grisly sound of people screaming
drowned out everything else.

The boat jackknifed as they were
hit by a much bigger powerboat. They
exploded out of the water like a breach-
ing whale and she was caught as the
boat folded in on her. She could hear
people moaning, even see them in the
water, crying, but it was all so surreal,
like watching paper cutouts of people
rehearsing the motions of disaster. She
felt invincible. She had survived!

As she struggled to free herself from
the splintered boat she became aware
that her right foot was caught, trapped
by some unseen piece of the disintegrat-
ing hull. She tried to jerk her leg free.
Nothing happened. The water sloshed
all around her as she reached beneath
the surface, grabbed her leg with both
hands and pulled, but there was no give
at all, just a deep throbbing pain. There
was more water now, gallons of it, pour-
ing in all around her. Suddenly everything lost its surreal quality, like a mask

*quickly withdrawn from a hideous face;
she threw back her head and screamed.*

*In the darkness she felt someone grip
her under the shoulders and pull. He
was strong; it would work. Three times
he braced himself against some unseen
part of the boat and pulled, and three
times he failed to release her. What the
hell was the matter with him? Suddenly
he let go and the void of fear that rushed
in made her scream out in terror. But he
hadn't left her. She could feel his hands
now, moving down her leg, gripping it in
his hands. The water was rising. It was
almost up to her face now. Why was he
taking so long? She heard the man take
a deep breath, felt him go under, pulling on her leg again and again until
she thought it would break. He pulled
harder and harder and the pain scorched
her brain as she realized how desperate
his movements had become.*

*And then, suddenly, he stopped. Just
like that. It was an odd sensation until
she realized with mind numbing horror
that he had given up. Dear god, he had
given up. The water was up to her chin
now. She struggled to breathe. He surfaced beside her and the water poured
over her face. She felt his hand gripping
hers and saw his face floating in front*

of her, full of concern, full of fear. She lashed out then in panic, in uncontrollable anger, with her arms, with her free leg, with her whole body, until the man gripping her hand suddenly let it go.

"How could the bastard let go?" she thought, before the water slowly stole her last breath away.

She reared up in bed, her face sweaty, her legs tangled up in her sheets, her eyes glazed, her face expressionless. Her heart was beating too fast. Slowly she untangled her legs and swung them over the edge of the cot. The moon pushed its way through the wide doorway of the large canvas tent, lighting up three other blanketed figures — all asleep. She slowly put on her belted jeans, a jacket, and her runners and — without looking at anything in the tent — walked out into the moonlight. Her tent was pitched between two tall pine trees; many more lay just beyond, swaying in the wind and flinging shadows that danced on the ground like maniacs. But she didn't notice them. She had only one thing on her mind.

She weaved her way through the trees to a clearing. The moonlight touched the tops of three large tents, making them seem only half there, their bottom halves blending in with the darkness of *the forest floor. Without hesitating she headed toward the tent that was farthest away, picking her way through the bleak remains of the campfire and the paraphernalia of a camping expedition. She looked neither to the right nor to the left. When she reached the tent she slowly unzipped the door and walked inside. Only one of the two cots was occupied, and she stood over it and stared for a very long time. Suddenly she reached for her belt, grabbing a hunting knife in her right hand and withdrawing it from its sheath.*

Carefully, she raised the knife with both hands, and then stopped as if paralyzed, the light from the moon spraying the grotesqueness of her shadow across the canvas. Then a force seemed to grip her hands and the blade came down hard. It juddered as it plunged into the man's chest and she let go. He sat up violently, wordlessly, his face childlike in its surprise, before falling back lifeless onto his cot.

An hour later I put down the book and whistled. No wonder Martha hadn't told me all the details. I probably wouldn't have gone on the cruise if she had.

∞∞∞∞∞∞∞∞∞∞∞

Tuesday night came before I knew it. Patrick and I spent our last evening together getting caught in a giant traffic jam en route to a nice restaurant. We got there too late and had to settle for fish and chips at a greasy spoon. Then the car broke down and it was 2:00 a.m. before we got to Patrick's and he hadn't even started to pack. His flight out was a charter that left at dawn, so we didn't have much time to discuss anything or do anything either — which was probably just as well. One wrenching kiss and he was gone. I moped around his apartment after he'd left, but it just depressed me, so I locked up and went home for a couple of hours.

At the university I immersed myself in work, even doing some of the statistics I hate doing with the sonograms of my song sparrows. Several days after Patrick left Martha waltzed into my office and plopped herself down in my guest chair.

"Have you read the book?"

"What book?" I asked absently.

"Cordi! Terry's book!"

"Oh yeah. What a weird scenario. She has a night terror where she believes a boat is drowning her. She 'wakes' from that dream and in a glazed, dazed torpor leaves her tent, crosses a clearing, enters another tent, and murders this guy Michael with a knife." I straightened out some papers in a huge pile teetering on my desk.

"Pretty hard to believe she got acquitted."

"Cordi, where do you hide yourself? There was another case in Ottawa. This guy sleep walked his way out of his house, into his car, drove I don't know how far, got out of the car, entered the house of his in-laws, killed her with a tire iron and almost choked him to death."

"Yeah, I vaguely remember that one."

"Then he called 911 — still asleep."

"Terry didn't do that, did she?"

"Cordi! Didn't you read it all? She was in the bush!"

"I skimmed through it."

Martha rolled her eyes at me. "Well, Terry apparently left the tent and went and woke up somebody else and said 'I've just killed Michael.' After which she woke up and freaked out about the blood all over her. She couldn't remember a thing. Apparently that's normal for sleepwalkers."

"I didn't know you could use sleepwalking as a defence," I said.

"Neither did I. She had two experts testify that she had a long history of sleepwalking since her childhood."

"Yes, but killing somebody so ruthlessly? In her sleep? Does that mean we are all capable of doing something like that? I mean, where does that come from? Decent when you're awake, deadly when you're asleep. It's like Dr. Jekyll and Mr. Hyde."

Martha was looking at me dubiously. "Are you saying she is guilty?"

"Well, obviously not. Not when a jury found her innocent and the judge freed her on the proviso that she take some kind of drug to help stop her sleepwalking. That was about eight years ago, right?" I fiddled with the papers on my desk.

"I wonder what that experience did to her though," I continued. "I mean, think about it: You're a good person.

You savagely kill someone and can't remember it, then you're charged with murder."

"Now you're saying she's innocent."

"It's a tough one. It's really hard to believe that someone technically asleep could kill somebody and not be found responsible."

"Guilty, you mean," Martha said.

"Well — it's the perfect murder isn't it? If you're a good actor why wouldn't it work?" Why indeed. But thinking about this was really just academic. Nobody had tried to kill me since I got home and Terry wasn't my problem anymore. Martha got up to leave and I cleared my throat. "Why didn't you tell me about all this before the trip?"

Martha shook her head. "If I'd told you, you would have jumped to conclusions. You would have said she was guilty. And you wouldn't have come on the trip."

I had my feet up on my desk, and was leaning back in my chair eating a very sloppy tomato sandwich, when I heard footsteps in my outer office. Too long a stride for Martha. I nearly choked on my sandwich when I heard a man's voice call out and in strode the Dean; earlier than expected, I noted.

He doesn't look like a Dean, either in profession or name. By some quirk of fate whereby Dr. Fish becomes an ichthyologist and Dr. Hart a cardiologist, Dean Anderson had followed his name into his profession and become Dean Dean Anderson, or Dean Squared for short. He's long, lean, ageless, and totally bald, having come in to work one day with his little circlet of hair gone. He was obviously bashed around at birth because his head is sort of misshapen, though he doesn't seem to notice. I wondered how often he had to shave his head to keep it so smooth.

With as much dignity as I could muster I got my feet down onto hard ground, deposited my sandwich on my desk, and wiped my mouth with a scrap of napkin. As I started to get up he waved me down, unloaded some files onto the desk from my sole chair, and sat.

I smiled at him uncertainly. I had visited Dean many times and he had been in my labs just as often, but he had never visited me in my office before. I felt a premonition that I did not like. What did he want with Martha?

"Good trip?"

"Yeah," I said, lying through my teeth, figuring he didn't know how bad it had been. Besides, I didn't really want to talk about it.

"I heard two people died. That doesn't sound so good."

"Yeah, well, if you must know, the whole trip was a disaster."

"So, I've heard." I looked at him in surprise, wondering if I had missed coverage in the papers.

"Martha told me. She's been helping me out on and off for the last four weeks because my tech has been ill."

Martha, I thought, with a sinking feeling. Why hadn't she told me that? No wonder I hadn't seen as much of her. Why didn't he just get to the point, whatever it was?

"Speaking of Martha, I wanted to talk to you about her."

My mind was racing thinking of all the reasons he might want to talk to me about her: I'd asked her to do something she wasn't supposed to do; they were going to fire her; she was being let go because her other two bosses had complained; she was retiring and was afraid to tell me; she was ill and was afraid to tell me; three bosses were too many and she wanted out. I could have gone on but he was looking at me, waiting for me to acknowledge what he had said. I nodded and he continued.

"I'm going to offer Martha a job with me. It'll mean a promotion for her. She is the most efficient tech we have in this department. I wanted to give you the courtesy of hearing it from me first."

I tried to neutralize my face so that he wouldn't know what I was thinking. "What about your own tech?" I asked.

"She's on sick leave and has told me she is not coming back. I've already talked to your colleagues and they are okay with it."

I was speechless. And terribly conflicted. On the one hand I wanted the best for Martha. On the other hand what would I do without her?

"I thought it courteous to let you know. I'm speaking to Martha this afternoon."

After he'd gone I looked at the soggy mess of my sandwich and suddenly didn't feel hungry anymore. But I didn't have much time to think about losing Martha because the phone rang. Why couldn't they design a bell tone that started softly and grew in volume as your ears adjusted? That would be a good feature on alarm clocks too. I wondered how many people had died of a heart attack after their alarm clocks woke them up. Wake 'em up to make 'em die. God, how macabre.

I picked up the phone. "Cordi, it's Duncan. Please come and get your cat." There was a lot of meaning pent up in those last six words.

"It's that bad?"

"No, not if you find constant whining, meowing, fidgeting, scratching, and hissing acceptable."

"She's just disoriented. She'll come around."

"I don't want her to come around, I want you to come around and get her."

"I can come up tomorrow, if you can wait that long?"

He grumbled some response I couldn't hear — probably wasn't meant to — and then changed the subject. "I've got the autopsy results back."

"You have?"

"Yup."

"But you're not officially on the case. The autopsy was done in Ottawa."

"Right. And the guy who did it is an old student of mine." Trust Duncan.

I laughed. "Anything of interest?" I asked, expecting nothing.

"Well, actually, yes there is."

I waited.

"With apologies to you, Terry didn't die in the swimming pool."

I pulled the phone away from my ear and looked at it, as if it could make everything comprehensible. "She what?"

"The autopsy says that she drowned."

"We know that."

"But she drowned in fresh water."

I wasn't getting this.

"Cordi, the swimming pool. It's salt water.

The possibilities of what this meant swarmed my mind like a hive of angry bees. I was speechless. I remembered the prickly feeling on my skin after going in the pool and having to take a shower to get the salt off. And I remembered the necklace. I'd been right.

"You there?"

"So where did she drown?" But I knew already. I could see her bathroom clear as day, with the only bathtub on the ship aside from the captain's. I could see the wet carpet.

"The police theory is she was somehow drowned in her own bathtub and then carried outside with the intention of throwing her overboard. They must have been interrupted and instead had to throw her in the pool."

"And Sally?"

"The police think Sally drowned Terry and then committed suicide. Sally drowned in salt water." He paused. "Sally was a big woman, strong enough to carry Terry to the pool."

That was certainly convenient for the police; no murderer to find and no one to try. Sally writes a suicide note, stalks Terry, kills her, and then kills herself. I thought back to Sally, who was indeed a big woman, physically capable of such a deed, but emotionally? I doubted it. I doubted it very much. She'd been pretty much a basket case.

"Do you think Sally could have done that?" I asked.

"No, I don't think so," said Duncan. "I would like to think Sally came along, saw Terry in the pool, and reacted instinctively. She jumped in fully clothed to try and save her, and her heavy clothes took her under. But the suicide note clearly kyboshes that."

"Could be fake."

"Not according to the police. It's definitely her handwriting scrawled on a little, ripped piece of paper."

I thought about that for awhile and was caught off guard when Duncan said, "I have a name for you, Cordi." His voice came softly down the line, interrupting my chain of thought. "Dr. Geraldine McKinnon."

What the hell was he talking about, I wondered, and then froze. Duncan was nothing, if not persistent.

"Just because you were right about the necklace, and about one of them being murdered, doesn't mean you don't need help." He proceeded to rattle off the woman's phone number, admonishing, "Just call her, Cordi. It can't hurt you."

Then the line went dead and I stared at the mouthpiece for a long time. A very long time indeed. I hung the phone up and stared at it some more, willing the conversation I had just had to crawl back into the receiver and die. I didn't want anything more to do with Sally and Terry. It wasn't my problem. And I didn't want anything to do with Dr. Geraldine McKinnon.

Chapter Fourteen

I spent the next bunch of days catching up on work, planning the courses I'd have to teach in the fall, and marking some lab assignments from my comparative anatomy course. I called Duncan to beg off the five hour round trip drive to get Paulie. He wasn't too happy about it, but both of us were swamped and couldn't take the time. I hadn't seen Martha for a while and I wondered if the Dean had already snatched her, but then I realized that all her things were still here, and besides, Martha would never leave without saying goodbye. I was actually grateful when there was a heavy footfall outside my door.

It was a policeman, wanting to take my statement about Terry's death. I answered all of his questions, basically outlining everything I remembered, but when I began to ask him questions about the fresh water in her lungs he politely begged off. It was, after all, an official investigation. Frustrated, I saw him to the door. Then the phone rang and I ran back to get it.

"Cordi?" The voice was strong, almost angry, or was it something else?

"Yes," I said, warily.

"It's Sandy. From the ship."

Shit. I'd forgotten to ring her back, or at least there was no answer when I did. How many days now? Four? It couldn't have been much of an emergency. There was a lot of commotion in the background — children's voices. Must be a birthday party.

"Sandy. How are you?"

Instead of answering my question she said, "I'm sorry I wasn't around if you tried to call." She hesitated, letting the implication sink in and then quickly added, "I had a sick kid," by way of her explanation.

"That's too bad. Everything okay now?" I asked.

She bulldozed over my questions and got to the point. "I need to talk to you very badly." When I didn't respond she said, "It's about Sally."

"What about her?"

"Please, I need to talk to you in person. Can we meet today?"

I sighed and rummaged around on my desk for my laptop and calendar, buried under a stack of research papers. "Why don't you come here around 5:00?" I said, cursing myself for not just saying no. I'd just finished telling myself I wanted nothing more to do with Terry and Sally and the lot. Tell that to the niggling little thought in the back of my head.

There was a long pause at the end of the phone. I

waited, listening to children's voices laughing and giggling. I was wondering what it would be like to have children when Sally broke up my dog's breakfast of thoughts. "I know this is asking a lot, but could you come here? I have the kids and no car...."

I blew air into my cheeks so they popped out like a puffer fish and then let the air slowly stream out of my mouth. "Where's here?" I heard myself asking the question that had just committed me.

"Manotick" she said slowly, as if I might react badly.

I did, but not to her. I hauled the receiver away from my ear and made nasty faces at it before bringing it back and politely saying, "Where in Manotick?"

Manotick is in the countryside, fifteen kilometres south of Ottawa, but is officially part of the City of Ottawa — the rural part. It was going to take me about twenty-five minutes to get there if there wasn't much traffic. When I'd realized I was going to have to go to her I changed the time to 6:30, dinner time, so I could get my work in. She hadn't protested.

Just as I was grabbing my keys and stuffing a notebook into my pocket, Martha walked into the outer office. At the same time the phone rang. I picked it up and got some guy at the grant office telling me I hadn't sent in all the required information. As I sorted it out with him I watched Martha in the mirror in my office. She was just wandering around aimlessly, picking up specimens, holding up her milking stool and then putting it down, and even touching the pictures she'd taken of one of my indigo buntings as if she'd never seen them before.

I caught my breath. She'd talked to the Dean. It was written all over her face — indecision, nervousness, excitement, nostalgia, and regret. I felt my heart sink. Had she said yes? If she had I'd have to let her tell me. I didn't want her thinking I had talked about her behind her back, even if the Dean had initiated it.

"Hi," I said as I stepped out of my office. Martha was holding the little rubber ducky I'd given her as a joke at least four years ago. I hadn't even known she still had it. Guiltily she dumped it in her drawer and shut it.

"Hi, Cordi."

We were two solitudes, each with our own knowledge, but no bridge to communicate it. Why do friends do that to each other? I felt powerless to even begin to build a bridge. Of course, I could have swum across, but I didn't.

I gave her lots of time to say something, but she didn't. Maybe that meant she hadn't yet made up her mind. I couldn't believe she'd stay with me and the other two guys she didn't care about one way or the other. Put that way, I knew what her answer would be. It was a promotion after all — to work for a full professor with his added research funding, equipment, and experiments.

"Gotta go," I said and she smiled.

"See ya."

I should not have turned around in the doorway. She was blowing her nose and looking out the window, the indecision usurping every line in her face.

I practically ran to my car, shoving thoughts of Martha out of my head as fast as they came in — and they were breaking the speed limit.

The ride out to Manotick was actually nice, once the four lane highway of Riverside gave way to the two lane River Road, and the houses gave way to fields with placidly grazing cows. Developers were having a field day out here, giving their developments such names as "Honey Gables" and, across the river, "Heart's Desire." I never understood developers' need to be so precious.

As I drove over the bridge spanning one branch of the Rideau River I could see Watson's Mill, now in shadow. It's a huge stone monolith that rises out of the water, and has been part of the river for almost one hundred fifty years. Every time I look at a mill I marvel at the strength of the stone — that the river could not carry it away — and I secretly wonder if they ever leak.

I drove down the town's main street and followed the river out the other end, until I came to a dirt road where I stopped to peer at my scribbled page of directions. When I finally found her house it was not what I had expected. The first indication was two monstrous brick gateposts with ornate wrought iron gates fastened to them. I had stopped the car and started getting out to open them, when they slowly opened on their own accord. A camera? I drove down a windy road and broke out onto lawns that would have held ten tennis courts. The house was huge and immensely ugly. It looked as though it had been built of Styrofoam blocks by a couple of children having fun. There wasn't a single straight wall. They angled or turned corners and slanted themselves in all directions. The door, however, was normal. I walked up to it and raised the leaden knocker that had been fashioned into a bolt of lightning.

It was a long time before the heavy oak door slowly opened.

"Hi," said a little voice some three and a half feet off the floor. A little boy, about six years old, stood dressed in a Robin Hood outfit complete with plastic bow and arrows.

"Are you Dr. O'Callaghan?" He stumbled over my name but smiled up at me as if he hadn't noticed, which he probably hadn't.

"Yes, I am," I said and smiled back.

"Mummy says to bring you to the living room. She's busy. Becky did a boo boo."

I followed the little boy into the house. The hallway was very dark, lined in grey slate, and the floor was dark grey slate too. I could see the light at the end of the short hall and when we broke out into the open I stood on the wide slate-grey stairs that led down into the house and gaped in astonishment.

The room I had just entered was enormous — about the size of half a football field, its ceiling three stories high. It was all one post and beam room. I could see the kitchen, the dining room, the rec room, and the living rooms, all formed into little pods by the strategic placement of the furniture. Enormous picture windows brought light streaming in, and focused your eyes on the view of the Rideau River as it wound its way through tree-clad banks. Incongruously, hanging from the wall between two of the picture windows, was the enormous head of a moose. Someone had festooned its antlers with silver bangles. I idly wondered about the history of this quite magnificent beast, until my eyes lighted on the centrepiece of the living room: a large green bronze birdbath with a little bronze bluebird flicking water over its wings, and a huge eagle, life size, wings fully outstretched, talons forever open and reaching, ready to make the kill. Artistic license allowed lots of odd things to happen, I thought wryly.

When I'd finally finished surveying the room I noticed my little friend had disappeared, or rather had gone to join a group of noisy children in the rec room. It suddenly occurred to me that Sandy must run a daycare here. I counted the kids, seven plus Becky. She must be right on the limit of what's allowed.

She must love kids, I thought. She certainly didn't need the money.

I stood there for a long while, wondering if I should just go and sit in the living room, but afraid Sandy wouldn't notice me in this enormous place.

"Daniel!" I turned in the direction of the adult voice and saw Sandy with a baby riding her hip, entering the kitchen. "I asked you to take Dr. O'Callaghan to the living room."

Daniel ignored his mother — he was too busy fitting an arrow to his bow.

Sandy came up, made some apologies, and led me to a sofa in the living room where a tray full of goodies and ice-cold lemonade were already ensconced. Becky kept trying to snafu some of the goodies, so Sandy put her down on the floor and pretty much ignored her. I watched Becky crawl her way through the living room toward the kitchen.

"She'll be okay," said Sandy. "This place is kid proof."

I smiled. She turned and looked at me. Her eyes were red and swollen and her cheeks were puffy. Sally must have been quite a friend. I wondered how she ever found the privacy to cry — unless she cried in front of the kids, which seemed unlikely. That would just cause more problems.

"Thank you for coming."

I nodded and waited.

"The police have been questioning me" she said, her voice tightly under control.

"That's a normal thing. Everybody involved in the deaths in any way has been questioned since we got back from the cruise."

"Yes, but they say Sally committed suicide, which I told you is absolutely impossible." She paused. "Sally was the most optimistic person I know."

I let my mind wander back to Sally and her tear streaked face and her needy, clingy personality. "Are you saying she wasn't upset about splitting up with Arthur?"

"Of course she was upset, but Sally was biologically incapable of being depressed for long."

Not the Sally I knew.

"Now the police are insinuating that she killed Terry. That she drowned her in her bathtub, carried the body out, dumped it into the pool, and then killed herself. Sally! As if she could do such a thing!" She fidgeted with her lemonade. "Sally could no more have murdered Terry than a baby could."

I reached over and picked up a cookie from the tray, trying to find the right words. "Sandy, look. Your friend was very quiet and very secretive. It's possible she didn't tell you everything."

"Sally was an outgoing extrovert who loved people and liked to tell everybody her stories; and she had some great ones."

I choked on my cookie and stared at her. "Are we talking about the same Sally here?" I asked.

Sandy put her lemonade carefully on the tray. "Sally was an actor."

I could hear a clock ticking somewhere in the enormous room. Two of the kids were fighting over a piece of Lego. I digested this piece of information. "Meaning what exactly?" I asked.

"She was acting a part on board the ship," Sandy said.

I could feel my jaw dropping and made a conscious effort to catch it before it fell too far. I thought back to the sauna — "It's hard to be Sally," she'd said. "Hard to be the mouse."

"She told me it could make her career. She told me she had a recall audition for a part in a play. She was to be a mousy, shy, and timid woman with low self-esteem — the exact opposite of Sally. She wanted to try and be this woman, live and breathe her while among strangers, and had settled for an Arctic cruise. She asked me to come along with her. It was a lot of juggling, what with the kids and all, but I said yes. She wanted me to come so much that she offered to pay for my ticket."

"Why didn't she just go alone? There'd be no distractions."

"Aw, you don't know Sally, not the real Sally. She cannot — could not — keep things to herself and she needed me to talk to at night so that she could play the mouse by day. She craved an audience, otherwise she would have blasted her secret to the rooftops. She was never very good at keeping secrets, but this meant so much to her."

Sandy put her lemonade glass down on the table and turned to look at me. "There was something more than just the acting happening."

I waited but she didn't go on. "You mean something with Sally?"

Sandy nodded. "She was a great actor, but every time she returned to our cabin where she could be herself she was on edge, almost fearful. When I asked her why, she was abrupt and clammed up."

"I'm sure it was just a case of actor fatigue. Imagine having to act a part eighteen hours a day? It would be enough to put anybody on edge."

When Sandy didn't say anything I said, "Why have you called me?"

"Because you were there, you found the bodies, and you've solved a murder before. Sally did not murder Terry. The police think she did. I want you to clear her name."

"Friends hide lots of things from each other," I said gently. "How can you be so sure she isn't a murderer?"

Sandy smiled then and said, "Do you have any siblings?"

What did that have to do with anything?

I nodded.

"How often have you been able to hide things from them?"

"Not often," I admitted. Especially if it was as important as a murder, I thought.

"Now maybe you understand."
I looked at her curiously.
"Sally was my sister."

Chapter Fifteen

I spent part of the drive home wondering why I was surprised that they were sisters. After all, why would they have thought it necessary to volunteer that information? Then I moved on to wonder about Sally's acting role and finally about how I had failed to say no to Sandy's request. I had told her that I was pretty busy with my job at the university, but she had refused to let me say no right then and there, which is what I wanted to do. I'm such a wimp. She had asked me to give it some thought before I made a decision. I had hesitated in the face of such determination, agreeing to think it over and get back to her. I had just delayed the inevitable and perhaps given her some false hope.

It was way too late to go back to work, and rush hour was over, so the ride home was easy. I rolled into the barn to see if Ryan was around. It was quiet — not yet milking time. I strolled over to our Olympic milk producer, Ethel, and gave her a pat on the schnozz. I checked the pens where the cows are kept, in case Ryan was in there, but he wasn't. I reached over one of the pens and let one of the little guys suck on my fingers. Being a steer is such a bummer. If your genes don't single you out for stud service your life is short. But at least you're well-fed.

I left the barn and walked around to the entrance to Ryan's studio. The red light outside the door was off — he wasn't in the darkroom. I wondered when he would change over to digital. It was a lot easier and surely the quality was good enough now? But I knew Ryan liked the peace and the quiet of the darkroom and the eerie red glow of the safe light. Life seems so far away when you're in there.

I opened the door and walked in. Ryan was over by the big bay window, looking at a fistful of prints.

"Hi, Cordi. What's up?"

I dawdled down his long table looking at the photos strewn all over it. He's a good photographer, my brother, and more and more magazines were after his services. One day he wouldn't have to be a farmer anymore, although I knew he would never give that up. It's in his blood, same as me. I looked at him and smiled. The summer sun had created so many freckles on his face that they had practically merged. His thick blond hair always makes me wonder how we ever came from the same parents. My hair is as black as it comes and not one single freckle can be found on my face. There are other differences too, of course, and no stranger had ever cottoned on to the fact that we were brother and sister.

"Spill it."

"I think I just agreed to investigate another murder."

"Whose murder?"

"The woman on the ship who I told you about."

Ryan dropped his photos on a chair and waited.

I told him about the police deciding that Sally had murdered Terry — because of the salt water/fresh water evidence that pointed to Terry being murdered. I told him that they couldn't prove it and then I told him that Sandy wanted her sister's name cleared, that she believed Sally couldn't have done it.

"You've got to be kidding," Ryan said, and I knew he was thinking of the bear ravaged body of my first murder case. He's as bad as I am with corpses. We want to be as far away from them as possible. You'd think a couple of farm kids who'd shot their share of groundhogs would be inured to dead bodies, but we weren't, at least, not dead human bodies.

"Why would you want to get mixed up in that stuff again?" asked Ryan.

"I'm not sure I do, but you have to admit it sounds intriguing." I told him about Sandy's and Duncan's version of Sally attempting to rescue Terry.

"But I thought you said Terry drowned in fresh water?"

"Yeah, that's right, but Sandy believes Sally saw Terry's body in the salt water pool and jumped in to rescue her without knowing she was already dead."

"But by your description it was a tiny pool."

"Sally was wearing winter clothing when she jumped in. A big ankle length wool coat that would have dragged her down."

"Why on earth wouldn't she have taken it off?"

"I don't know."

"And the suicide note?"

"That's a little tricky. Police say it's Sally's handwriting."

"So whether you should help or not depends on how much you believe this Sandy."

We bandied around some ideas for a while, and I told him what Sandy had said about Sally acting a part.

"That's one dedicated actress," he said and I let his words sink in. It was always restful being around Ryan. He's seldom judgmental and solid as a rock.

When I finally turned to leave he said, "I was in your cabin delivering a parcel when the phone rang. I answered it thinking it might be Rose."

"And?"

"It was somebody asking for you. Wanted to know if you would be in tonight so they could call you back. I told them yes. Hope that's okay."

"Telemarketer?"

"No." Why is it that telemarketers are so easy to spot?

Ryan could be exasperating sometimes, the way I had to crowbar information out of him. "Male? Female?"

"Couldn't tell. Whoever it was had laryngitis or something."

I thanked him for bringing in the parcel.

"Watch your back. It's heavy," he said, as I headed out the door.

I got in my car, drove past the farmhouse and waved to Rose, who was out playing baseball with the kids.

Ryan had dumped the box right in the middle of the hallway and I pushed it with my foot to move it. It was

immovable. I bent over and looked at the label. No clue.
It looked as though someone had used about five miles
of tape to seal it, and by the time I was through cutting it open I needed a shower. There was a covering of
brown paper hiding the contents, which I pulled aside,
and started to laugh. Inside was an enormous card with
an elephant riding on the back of a mouse, blaring his
love for me, and hiding twelve bottles of a good white
wine. Each bottle had a little stickum on the neck with a
corny little message meant only for me. No wonder he'd
used so much tape. It felt good to be loved like this, and I
resolutely refused to think about London and spoil it all,
so I didn't try to phone him.

I took the shower I needed, spent a leisurely hour
in the kitchen making dinner, popped the cork on one
of the bottles of wine, and took my dinner outside to
eat on the porch. Somewhere the moon was coming up
because its light was glinting off the oak trees on my
front lawn. The wine was light, fruity, and chased away
all my nerves. After I'd finished dinner I sat for a while,
contemplating life. Suddenly I remembered Ryan's mysterious phone call. They hadn't called back. I got up and
checked my messages. There weren't any. I scrolled back
through the people who had called me today. I knew
them all except one. It was a blocked number and I felt a
twinge of annoyance, easily chased away by another sip
of wine and the fact that I had once thought about blocking my own number.

The wine made me sleepy and I headed for bed where
romping dreams, surrealistic and disquieting, awaited me.
I'm not sure what woke me, but it woke me with such

suddenness that for a moment I was disoriented. Something wasn't right. I looked out the window and against the light of the moon saw swirls of smoke sending their tendrils across my room. I was out of bed in a flash, the smoke already beginning to sting my nostrils. I ran out through my open door into the hall where the smoke was thicker. I looked down the stairs and saw the blurred lights of flames dancing like maniacs on my living room wall.

The kitchen. It was in the kitchen. I raced downstairs, but the smoke got thicker as I ran. I stood on the landing and watched as a plume of black smoke whooshed out of the kitchen. That's when I ran. I stumbled up the stairs, holding my pajama top against my nose. Some of the killer black smoke had already reached the hallway.

I looked up at the smoke detector, wondering why it hadn't gone off. The batteries were brand new — I'd struggled on the stepladder on my tippy toes to put the damn things in so I knew it was working. Not anymore — the plastic protector was dangling from the ceiling and I felt my mind shudder. The battery was gone, which could mean only one thing: He was back. Or was it a she?

I ran back into my bedroom and shut the door. My cell phone was somewhere and I flung clothes and bags everywhere until I found it. I dialed Ryan because I knew 911 would need help finding me on a rural route. I was on a cell phone and I'd have no time to talk.

His sleepy voice came over the phone as the black smoke entered my bedroom.

"Ryan! My house is on fire. Call 911."

I didn't wait for an answer, couldn't wait. I ran to my window and hauled up on it but it wouldn't budge.

I checked the latches to make sure it was unlocked and tried again. Nothing. I looked around the room for something to break the window with and spied my favourite oak chair — I really loved that chair. I looked for something else but there was nothing, so I picked it up, held it over my head, and advanced on the window, coughing like crazy. I heaved the chair at the window and nothing happened. They made it look so easy in the movies. It took two tries to break the heavy glass and then another couple to make a hole big enough for me to get out. I was coughing hard now as I crawled out the window onto the roof of the porch. I skidded to the edge of the roof and looked down. A twenty-foot jump onto the steeply sloping part of my front lawn. Ankle breaking country.

"Cordi!" I heard Ryan screaming my name and looked over and saw him racing around from the kitchen door to the front door.

"Ryan, NO! I'm up here," I screamed, but he didn't hear me and he disappeared under the porch roof.

Two fire trucks finally arrived and I jumped up and down and waved my arms. At any other time I would have thought it pretty impressive for the trucks to arrive so fast, since we live in the country, but all I could think of was why didn't you get here sooner? One of the firemen saw me and I watched as he ran around, released a ladder, and hurried over to me.

I looked back. Behind me the smoke was billowing out the window, but all I could think of was Ryan. I stood helpless on that roof waiting for the firemen to come. When they did I yelled, "My brother! He's inside!"

I could see two firemen hauling out the hose and aiming it through the kitchen window, while another two firemen went in through the front door with their oxygen masks and tanks. A fifth fireman rescued me on the ladder.

I sat on my front lawn, a blanket over my shoulders, watching the front door until I heard a woman's voice. "Cordi? Where's Cordi?" It was Rose. I could see a fireman pointing me out to her and she came running over.

"Oh my god, Cordi. Are you all right? Ryan came to help."

"Rose, look, Ryan is ..."

Before I could finish my sentence two blackened firemen burst out the front door carrying my unrecognizable soot soaked brother between them. I felt like I was going to be sick. He was limp. No movement. No movement at all.

Confused, Rose had turned to look at the doorway as I stood up. "Dear god, Cordi. Who is it?" she cried.

I looked at her in total terror. "Ryan," I said. "It's Ryan."

Chapter Sixteen

I watched as they loaded Ryan into the ambulance and Rose got in beside him, calling out last minute instructions for their children. All I wanted to do was get in that ambulance too. But of course I didn't.

The firemen and the police questioned me briefly. A burner on the stove had been left on and there was a charred pot on it. Had I left a burner on? Something simmering? Like a pot of oil perhaps? Why had I taken the battery out of the smoke detector? I was too traumatized to answer.

When they were done I started back down the farm road to my brother's house, dragging my eyes away from my own tattered home, the white doors and windows now soot grey. I could just see the blackened frame of the kitchen door and the firemen making double sure the fire was out.

I should have felt glad that I still had my home,

damaged but still standing. Instead I was angry and frightened; for Ryan, for myself. The dangling plastic cover and the empty space where I had put a battery haunted me. And the strange phone call. Suddenly it made sense. Someone had wanted to be sure I would be home tonight. Were they just trying to scare me or did they want me dead? Was it the same person as on the ship? If they did want me dead they were really bad at it. Except that each incident easily could have ended in my death. So what was it? Why were they trying to scare me? I'd only just started doing some snooping. Did they know I might be helping Sandy?

I trudged down the darkness of the pockmarked road to the farmhouse. There was a light on in every room of the house, but that's not what I saw. Sitting on the porch, all by herself, grasping her knees and looking vulnerable and forlorn, was four-year-old Annie. As soon as she saw me she got uncertainly to her feet and hesitated on the stoop as if about to run away, then she started backing up. Suddenly I realized what she must be seeing — a soot-covered figure, wrapped in a dark blanket, looking like some evil creature come for her from out of the darkness of the night.

I called out gently, "Annie, it's me — Cordi."

She stopped then, still not sure. "Cordi?" she asked, hesitantly.

"Yes."

She ran down the porch and threw her arms around me. A string of rushed words came out of her mouth. "The phone rang and I woke up, and Daddy said it was you and your house was on fire and he had to go and help, and then there were all kinds of siren sounds and an ambulance, and then Mac came to look after us and Mummy went to help Daddy, and I'm scared."

I waved at Mac, our ageless farmhand, who had come out onto the porch. Annie was latched onto me like a limpet. I tried to soothe her as best I could as I braced myself for the inevitable questions.

"Where're Daddy and Mummy?" she asked, gazing up at me.

I bent down and lifted her into my arms and started up the porch stairs. "Daddy had to go to the hospital for a while," I said, looking at Mac.

"Did Daddy get hurt?" She looked as though she was going to cry.

"Yes. But Mummy has gone with him to look after him."

She seemed to rally at that. "You're really dirty, Cordi."

I smiled. "Yeah, I need a bath," I said, wishing that was all I needed.

I got Annie back into bed and then went and checked on Davy. I was grateful that he'd slept through the whole thing. Mac was pretty upset when I told him Ryan had been hurt, but there was nothing either of us could do, so he gave me a hug and left.

I had a shower and scrubbed the soot from my body, borrowed some of Rose's clothes, and then phoned her. There was no word yet and she promised to phone as soon as there was. God, how I wanted to be there with her.

∞∞∞∞∞∞∞∞

The phone call came while it was still dark, while imaginations were at their peak. I was afraid to answer the phone, afraid of the news at the other end. But then I remembered Annie being awakened by the phone. I snatched it up and gripped it so hard my nails dug into my palms.

"Cordi, he's going to be okay."

Every muscle in my body suddenly went slack, like an elastic band that had been stretched and suddenly let go.

"He inhaled a lot of that black gunk and they had to put a tube down his throat to keep his airway from closing in case there was swelling.

We didn't talk long. She told me her mother was coming at 8:00 to look after the kids and I thanked her for thinking of that. Then I rang off and stared into the night until it softened into dawn. I called Rose again at about 7:30, but she said there was no change.

I told her I'd be down as soon as her mother came but she said, "No point. He's not allowed visitors."

"Have you seen him?"

"Not even me, Cordi," she said. Was I that transparent?

When Rose's mother came I didn't stick around. I practically ran along the road to my house, phoning Patrick as I hustled along. But I don't think his cell phone was working and I didn't leave a message because what would I say? I hung up as I came around the corner — then stopped and stared.

The logs were darker now, parts of the white porch were streaked with soot and so were one or two windows. Except for the change in colour scheme, the house looked pretty much the same. All the hoses that had snaked across the lawn and all the trucks were gone now. A house is such a material thing. Just logs and plaster and glass, just a container for people who make it more than what it really is.

I walked around the whole house looking for structural damage. I didn't see any, except for the kitchen, which was a charred mess. And the little attached shed out back. It was gone and so were all the wonderful things in it. My two canoes, my kayak, my woodworking tools, my lawnmower — all gone.

When I finally picked my way inside the house it reeked of smoke and there was soot everywhere. I wondered how much of this damage would be covered by my insurance policy. I covered my nose with Rose's T-shirt, walked in the front door, and was initially surprised by all the damage in areas where the fire hadn't reached. Everything was soaked and covered in soot. Some of my glass animal figurines were smashed on the floor, furniture was shifted around. I tried to imagine what it would have been like in here last night after I left. Black, dark, with firemen carrying hoses in a house they did not know trying to find a man. My brother. And that's when the anger really surged through me. That's when Sandy got an ally.

I phoned her on my hands-free cell phone as I was driving in to work two hours later. Sandy answered on the eighth ring and I could hear all the kids yelling and laughing in the background. I didn't know how she did it, but at least the ones who weren't her own went home every day and she had a chance to recuperate.

I told her I'd help her, but not why. We arranged to meet at her house at 7:30, a bit late, but maybe that's when the last kid got picked up. Then I called my insurance company and they told me to put in a claim for damages and have a copy of the police report.

"I hope you didn't lose anything that is excluded from your policy," the agent said, just as I was about to disconnect. "Like an ATV for instance. You may have a rider on ATVs, boats, stuff like that. I'll check."

I disconnected and gripped the steering wheel like a lifeline. The insurance company wasn't going to recognize ANY of my claim, I just knew it. The police report would indicate my smoke detectors were not working, or some other little loophole written in miniscule print on the backside of my policy would void it because I'd done something wrong. If I told the police why the fire had happened to me they would think I was nuts. Plus everyone thought it was my pot of oil on the stove. I had no proof, just like all the other times. I worried about what to do about my insurance and the police the rest of the way into work, where I arrived frazzled, worried, and scared. In the parking lot I raised Rose, but she said nothing had changed and she'd call.

I almost took the elevator because I was feeling so lousy. The five flights didn't help much. As I was walking down the hall I suddenly realized I had forgotten to phone Martha and let her know about the fire. Had I missed any appointments? I turned into my office and

Martha was seated at her desk, doodling on her pad and staring into space, the phone cradled by one ear.

She glanced up when she heard my footfall and said, "I've been on hold for ten minutes." Then she looked at me again. "Lord, Cordi. What train ran over you?"

"Ryan's in hospital. They say he's going to be okay."

Martha hung up. "What happened?"

"My house burned down."

Martha brought her hand to her mouth. "All of it?"

"Well, no, just the kitchen. But the house is unlivable."

"And Ryan?"

"He tried to save me. Thought I was still inside."

Martha got up and gave me a big hug. "Do they know how it happened?"

"They suspect I left a pot of oil on the stove."

"A pot of oil?" Martha looked confused.

"There was a charred pot on the stove, which was on. They figure the fire started there and then spread, although they won't be sure until they do a proper investigation."

"A pot of oil? Why would you have a pot of oil on the stove?"

"To make deep-fried stuff."

"But you don't make deep-fried stuff."

"I know."

"What am I missing here, Cordi?"

I told her then about the phone call and the empty smoke detector. When I was done she was quiet.

"I think he's back, Martha."

"Wait a minute. You don't know for sure it was a pot of oil on the stove. In the heat of the moment the firemen just suggested it. You must have left the stove on by mistake. Maybe left a wooden spoon on the burner."

I felt discouraged. Once again my word against the evidence. I walked past Martha into my office.

"But just suppose you are right," said Martha and I popped my head back out. "I'm not saying you are, mind you, but if you are you're in danger. Where were you going to stay tonight?"

"At Ryan's."

"That's the first place they'll look. Anywhere else?" she asked.

I thought a bit and then said, "Well, I could stay at Patrick's. He's in London, but I have a key."

"Uh uh," she said. "You can't be alone."

"I can't sleep on the streets either," I quipped and popped my head back into my office.

"Come stay with me."

I walked back out and looked at her.

"My place isn't big, but there is room — just."

My knee jerk reaction was to say no, but then I reconsidered. I couldn't endanger Rose and the kids by staying there and I didn't relish the thought of living alone in Patrick's apartment with all the memories, perhaps with no more to come.

I said yes.

I was gazing out my office window when I suddenly remembered Paulie. I put a phone call through to Duncan and was relieved to get his answering machine. Then I felt guilty about being relieved. I told him what had happened and that I wouldn't be able to pick Paulie up for a few more days.

I spent the afternoon working on the logistics of a possible new experiment with cricket song; how the males stake out their little territories waiting for the females to answer their call. When I couldn't get my head around it I changed tacks and scanned the phone book looking for a private investigator. The one with the little eye looking out of a keyhole hooked me. I dialed and was put through to Derek. He seemed professional enough so I asked him if he could dig up all the information on the Terry Spencer case. I wanted to know more about it besides what I'd read in her book. There might be some clue in her past that could shed light on the deaths of these two women. I was encouraged that Derek had heard about the case and I hung up feeling satisfied that I was doing something to fit the pieces of the puzzle together.

Martha's incredibly sensitive hearing had her standing in my doorway as soon as I hung up. "What was that all about?"

"I've read Terry's book, but it's all from her angle and she uses pseudonyms. I realized I needed an unbiased view of things."

"You think that trial has something to do with her murder?"

"Could be."

I liked that Martha was talking murder. It made it seem that she was coming around to my viewpoint. Of course, the police thought it was murder too.

At 6:00 Martha poked her head around the corner. "I'm about to leave. If you want you can follow me."

I told her about Sandy so she scribbled her address down on a sheet of paper and left.

Half an hour later she was back. "My car won't start. Can I get a drive back with you and deal with it tomorrow?"

"If you don't mind going to Manotick first."

Half an hour later we were wending our way to Manotick, and I filled Martha in on everything Sandy had told me at our first meeting. We arrived at the front door just as it opened and four little kids came running out, the last one toddling. They stopped in surprise when they saw us and the biggest little boy ran back inside followed by all the rest. We could hear him yelling, "Mummy, it's not Daddy."

Shortly after, as we politely waited by the open door, Sandy appeared.

After Martha and Sandy got reacquainted, Sandy led us to the living room and sat down. Before the kids could interrupt I asked gently, "Did anybody else know that Sally was playing a part?"

"Nobody else knew except ..." she paused as one of the kids yelped.

"Except?"

"Arthur."

"Arthur?" I asked, wondering why I hadn't thought of that.

"Yeah, they really were going out together until he dumped her on the plane. I can't believe he did that. Poor Sally. Such a cruel place to say goodbye. And he had the nerve to come to her funeral all teary eyed."

"I don't understand. They were going out together but they didn't share a cabin?"

"Sure they did, but Sally moved in with me when they broke up, so it was lucky she'd invited me along or she'd have had to stay with him."

"How long had they been together?"

"A year maybe."

"Was there anything you noticed that was different about Sally on that trip?"

"You mean, besides her acting like a shy recluse?"

I nodded.

Sandy sighed. "Yes. But you have to understand that nobody but a sister would have picked up on it."

I nodded my encouragement.

"I told you she was holding something back from me. I could sense it." She looked from me to Martha and asked, "Do you have sisters?"

When we both shook our heads she sighed again. "Sally was guarded, as if she was keeping a big secret. She used to act that way whenever she was hiding something, even as an adult. She was lousy at keeping things to herself — usually spilled everything within a day — but when she didn't, when the secret was so important it had to be kept, she was guarded. That's what I saw. That, and something else that puzzled me."

"What was that?"

"Fear."

Just then the front door banged open and the children, in unison, charged the front door, all of them yelling, "Daddy!" or at least all of them who could talk and walk. I stared, mesmerized, at the tangle of twenty-eight little arms and legs all reaching up to a tall dark haired man who was smiling at his children. No daycare.

Martha pulled me out of my trance by saying, "Did Sally live near you?"

Sandy was smiling at her family but turned and nodded. "Yes."

"Could we see her place?"

Why hadn't I thought of that?

"I suppose that would be okay. The police are finished with it. I'll just get my purse and we can go now. You might as well follow me."

We followed Sally back through downtown Manotick, and turned off on a side road near the centre of town. Sally pulled her car up in a weed infested, crumbling asphalt parking lot that had seen better days. It seemed to be attached to a utilitarian two-storey building, the first floor of which was a tool depot. I could see two rust-red fire escapes climbing up the side of the wall running along beside the parking lot. Sandy led us to the one closest to the street. When she got to the top she fumbled for the keys and then we were in. It was hot and stuffy, and very messy. Sandy went over and pulled the curtains and opened a window, then turned to look at the room.

"Sally would have hated this. She was so neat. Why did the police have to be so boisterous about their search?"

She ran a hand along a sofa and then pushed it several inches westward to fit into the marks its feet had left from standing so long in one place. She sat down in an old corduroy chair with most of the corduroy gone.

The shabbiness of the place stood in sharp contrast to Sandy's. I could see Martha poking about, trying not to look like a snoop and failing miserably.

I went over to the phone and flipped through the pages of an address book, but nothing stood out. It was difficult for anything to stand out since I didn't know what I was looking for.

On impulse I turned to Sandy and asked her if she had the addresses of the writing group. She shook her head, but Martha piped up, "Cordi, don't you ever read anything? The expedition group sent us each a ship's log last week and everybody's particulars are in it. Besides, I'm in the writing group, remember?"

Jesus. How could I have forgotten? Something dawned on me. "Was Sally acting her part at all the writing lectures?"

"Yeah, she was. Pretty good actor too. I never cottoned on," said Martha. So the acting had preceded the ship and she'd stayed in role. I asked Sandy if she had the name of Sally's agent.

"Oh sure. She's great. I've got it right here on my PalmPilot. She's actually a friend of mine."

She tapped away at her Palm and came up with the number. I pulled out my cell phone and dialed. "What's her name?" I asked quickly, as someone picked up.

"Carol Stimpson."

When I got through to Carol I introduced myself and told her I wanted to talk to her about Sally. She didn't sound too enthusiastic until I told her I had Sandy in the room with me. I handed the phone over and the two talked for a while about who I was and then Sandy handed the phone back to me. "Sandy tells me Sally was working on a role as a shy reclusive woman."

Carol said nothing.

"She said she had a recall audition for the part when she got back from the ship."

"Impossible," said Carol. "There was no recall audition."

"How do you know?"

"Because I know all the auditions she takes. I'm her sole agent."

"So what you're saying is …"

"There was no audition. There was no shy, reclusive woman. Sally was having a hard time getting any role at all."

"Could she have been operating on her own?"

"Not without breaking her contract with me."

We rang off and I told Sandy and Martha what she had said.

"I knew she was hiding something," said Sandy. "Stupid lovable fool. What was she hiding?"

What indeed.

Chapter Seventeen

I could not believe that I had forgotten that Martha was part of the writing group. I turned to look at her sitting beside me in the car.

"Was Sally putting on a front the whole time?" I asked again.

"You mean acting shy and timid? Yeah, I never saw her as anything but. I can't imagine how hard that would be to play your exact opposite three hours a week and then on the ship for eighteen hours a day. It would be so easy to forget, especially if you were outgoing."

"So why the hell would she do that? There was no audition. What was she up to?"

Martha grunted and shook her head. "Maybe she was just keeping her hand in."

"How did the writing group work?" I asked, changing course.

She swivelled in her seat to look at me. "We met every Thursday night from seven to ten."

"How many were you?"

"Twenty-four, I think. Only eight of us went on the trip Terry had advertised. I guess the others had business or couldn't afford it."

"Was the trip part of the course?"

"Yes and no. It was advertised months in advance, probably as an enticement for the course, but of course the trip was very expensive."

"And Sally, who doesn't appear to be very wealthy, pays for herself, offers to pay for her sister, and then plays at being someone else. It doesn't make sense."

My cell phone went off then. Rose. If I hurried I could see Ryan for a few minutes before visiting hours were over. I dropped Martha at the bus stop and headed to Gatineau. My stomach was in knots because I didn't know what to expect.

He was lying in bed with his hands spread out on the sheets and Rose sitting beside him. When he saw me he rallied up a little smile and I smiled back. He had no bandages, so he hadn't been burned. It had been the smoke. We sat and talked for about five minutes, or at least I talked and he listened. His voice was pretty much shot. But when the nurse came in to tell us we had to leave he pulled me down to ear level and whispered, "I saw a pot on the stove, all in flames."

I stood back and searched his face. Was he blaming me?

He pulled me down again. "I heard the firemen say it was full of oil. You never deep-fry."

I stood up.

He mouthed, "What have you got yourself into this time?"

We know each other so well, my brother and I. I knew he was worried about me, but he was worried about Rose too.

"I'll be staying at Martha's for awhile," I said, and thought I saw the relief in his face. I gave him a hug, waved to Rose, and left them alone.

I'd never been to Martha's apartment before, but it turned out to be a twenty-four-storey affair, complete with gym and pool, and a doorman who directed me to apartment 1202. I knocked on the door and Martha opened it almost instantly. She was all sweaty and looked like she'd just run the marathon. I'd never seen her sweaty.

"Don't ask. You don't want to know," she said. But then immediately added, "I needed groceries so I walked to the store. How's Ryan?"

We had walked down a miniature hallway and entered a room that doubled as a living and dining room. If you blinked you'd miss the kitchen. Nervously I looked around for where I might be staying, but all I saw was one small bedroom with a single bed and the bathroom.

Martha must have been watching my face because she said, "Don't worry, Cordi. I've got it all worked out."

And indeed she had. Sort of. I watched in amazement as she unrolled some gaily coloured material, took hold of the ring at one end and hooked it over a ring in the doorway that held one of those spider plants that was spilling little spiders all over the place. She went over and retrieved the second ring, and hung it from another hook just outside the bathroom. She stood back with a pleased expression on her face and waved at the hammock. "Welcome to my guestroom."

I looked at the hammock, which just cleared one of her two comfy chairs and then soared over the tiny dining table and a standing plant beyond it.

"Just use the chair to get in and you won't get any broken bones," said Martha as she headed into the bathroom.

I stood there, gazing at my accommodation and marvelling that Martha didn't seem to feel as though it was an intrusion of any kind. Had the roles been reversed I would have been in quiet conniptions.

The next morning I was standing at the sink washing the little bowl I'd used for some Rice Krispies when Martha emerged from her bedroom, all set for a jog, and mumbled good morning. I was suddenly reminded of what stood between us and wondered when she would talk to me.

There was no room for both of us in the kitchen so I sidled out and let her in to check out the contents of the fridge. One night and my back was killing me from my tumultuous sleep in the hammock. I knew I'd have to find other accommodations or make a back specialist a very happy woman. I also couldn't understand why Martha hadn't told me about the job. Maybe because she hadn't decided yet, but still — I was a good friend.

"Cordi?"

Here it comes, I thought. She's taken the job. Why did I always seem to be waiting for people I cared about to take jobs that would take them away from me? Well, okay, Martha would just be down two flights, but Patrick would be across an ocean.

"This is a royal mess up," she said.

I waited.

"I mean, why would Sally pretend to be someone else?"

I let out a big breath.

"She didn't have anything on the horizon that would require practising for such a part. I mean, maybe it's why she's dead?"

"You mean the part called for her to jump in and rescue Terry?" I asked.

Martha shot me a venomous look. "No, of course not, but now we know it wasn't suicide," — she paused — "although I guess it still could be." She scratched her chin. "Could be a murder-suicide. But why would she kill Terry?"

"Arthur and Terry were together a lot. Maybe they were an item and Sally couldn't take it. She killed the woman who had stolen her lover and then killed herself."

"According to Sandy the police like that version of it."

"Yeah, nice and neat. Case closed." I picked up a magazine that had fallen on the floor and put it on the dining room table. "But suppose someone else murdered Terry? In that case it would make more sense to just throw her overboard. Why use the bathtub?"

"It must have been a spur of the moment thing. The murderer had to get rid of the body," said Martha.

"And then had the bad luck to be interrupted by Sally before they could dump the body into the sea. They were forced to dump the body in the pool. But Sally must have seen them and they drowned her."

"But what about the suicide note?"

"Right. Okay. To make us believe Sally killed herself and Terry tried to save her and drowned."

"Yeah, but that doesn't work with the autopsy results and the fresh water."

"Exactly, which means whoever killed Terry and Sally couldn't have known that the pool was salt water. Why would you, unless you'd actually been in it?" I remembered again how itchy it was.

"But the suicide note was genuine."

"That's trickier. I don't know how someone could force Sally to write a suicide note."

"Okay, if we set the suicide note aside for the time being that means we're dealing with a double murder." We looked at each other. "By the same person?"

We looked at each other some more and then I said, "Okay. Suppose someone else murdered Terry, or murdered both of them, and somehow managed to get Sally to write a suicide note. I figure it makes sense that it was someone from the creative writing group since they all knew her and I can't believe this was some random act."

"Or Jason."

"Right. Or Jason. Or Peter. Or even Arthur for that matter." I remembered how Jason and Terry had fought on the bridge and then the tears — what had they been all about? Sally? Couldn't be. He didn't even know Sally. And Peter and his outburst. Where had that come from?

"Or anybody else she knew who we didn't know she knew, and that maybe she didn't know she knew."

"Oh for heaven's sake, Martha. We have to start somewhere, so we pick the answer with the highest percentage of possibilities. That leaves the writing group."

"And Jason."

"And Peter."

"And Arthur."

And the entire rest of the ship, if I wanted to depress myself, which I didn't.

After getting into work I spent an hour up with my animals, checking on the tape recording equipment I was using to record their song. I went back to my office and was sitting at my desk trying to do statistical analysis on some of my data. I heard footsteps in my outer office. I glanced up and there was Duncan, holding a large plastic pet cage and looking around with interest. He'd never been to my office before. I came out to greet him and got a big bear hug.

"Cordi, Cordi. Rescue me from this damn cat."

The cage was bouncing around, but when I looked through the slats Paulie stopped moving and eyed me calmly. "Well that's a good omen, Cordi! She usually hisses at anybody new."

"Maybe it's because Cordi and Paulie already know each other," said Martha as she waltzed in the door and gave Duncan a big hug. "Paulie and Cordi spent a bit of time in the woods together before they found Jake Diamond's body last summer, remember?"

Martha picked up the cage. "I'm going to take her up to the lab where she'll be more comfortable until you can take her home."

I nodded. Duncan waited until Martha's footsteps were a distant thump. "You've got a real hellion on your hands. I had to stop off in Shawville and get something from the vet to calm her down. She goes wild in the car."

Shawville is a little town northwest of Ottawa, on the Quebec side. It has the best little café in the area, where you can get delicious and imaginative meals. I sort of suspected that that was the real reason Duncan had stopped in Shawville.

"I've come to take you out for lunch!"

I looked at the clock: 11:30. Guess I was wrong about Shawville.

"Oh, I know it's early but I simply could not spend any more time with that cat. I know the perfect restaurant."

I was flattered and suggested we invite Martha along as well, but he shook his head and said, "No, I think I want you all to myself."

I tidied up a few loose ends and we left the building. I wondered what restaurant he had in mind so I was a little surprised when he walked me three blocks to an outdoor vending cart and said magnanimously, "Have anything you want; it's on me. This guy makes the best damned sausages in the world." Which meant I was duty bound to order a sausage.

Once we had our drinks, sausages, fries, and napkins I looked around for a place to sit. There wasn't anywhere. We were going to have to eat standing up, which would be a real juggling act. I must say I was surprised at Duncan's choice. He paid for the food, then took my arm and steered me half a block down the street to a three-storey building where he opened the door for me. I was very curious by the time we took the elevator up and walked out into a very nicely appointed sports club, with tables of four and two lined up behind six glass-backed squash courts.

"You'll have to excuse me, my dear, but I'm a real fan of squash and there's a match today that I just can't miss. He led me to a table near the first court and we sat down facing the empty court. We spread out our food and began to eat the incredibly messy but remarkably tasty sausages. I waited for Duncan to make the first conversational salvo, wondering about what he might have to tell me. I should have known.

"Have you thought anymore about doing some forensic entomology for me?"

After Jake Diamond was discovered, Duncan had asked me to be a consultant forensic entomologist on any cases where he might need help from someone with a background in entomology. Someone like me. I'd never really answered him because I was torn.

"I wasn't too thrilled with how I reacted to finding Jake Diamond's body," I said. I'd thrown up and felt like the mass of maggots on his body had somehow jumped to mine. It was a feeling I didn't ever want to have again.

"You get used to it."

"I don't think so. And I'm not sure I want to." I remembered the lifeless forms of Sally and Terry. But at least there had been no maggots. That was what really grossed me out — a dead body writhing with maggots. I shivered.

"What's the difference between setting out dead pigs and porcupines and raccoons for your students, and eyeballing human remains?"

"Imagination."

"I don't understand."

"I can't imagine myself as a raccoon, but I can imagine myself being infested with maggots if they're on a human body."

"I'm not going to take this as a no."

I marvelled at his optimism, but then, stranger things have happened. You never knew what my life might bring.

Duncan wiped his mouth with his napkin, then scrunched up his sausage wrapper and threw it at the garbage can. To both our surprise it went in.

"Have you phoned Dr. McKinnon yet?" he asked out of the blue.

I watched as two men entered the squash court and Duncan's head swivelled to watch them too. But then he turned back and stared at me.

I was squirming in my chair and said nothing.

"I'll take that as a no," he said, and we sat in silence watching the two men bash the ball around the court. He tried another tact. "Martha told me about your house fire. I'm really sorry."

I grunted.

"She says a pot of oil was left on the burner."

I said nothing.

"She also said you never deep-fry anything."

I sighed, waiting for him to say I was delusional.

Instead he said, "That's one too many coincidences for me."

"What happened to my being delusional?"

He sighed. "Martha thinks your attacker could be real and I believe that while you have a problem with depression, I may have jumped the gun on thinking you were delusional. It's just that they are such fantastical stories — likely a series of unfortunate accidents — and knowing your history I thought it was possible you were in the manic phase of bipolar."

"I'm not bipolar."

"But you are something, Cordi. Maybe SAD."

Such an apt acronym for a real mouthful — Seasonal Affective Disorder. The winter blues with a bite.

"I'm managing just fine with my life." A defensive tone had snuck into my voice.

"But are you managing it? Martha says you're pretty bad in the winter. There are medications that can help you, Cordi, turn the dark to light. Just call the doctor. See what she has to say. For your own sake. It can't hurt."

One of the men in the squash court smashed into the back wall and made me jump. I felt trapped sitting there, trapped by Duncan, trapped by myself. I just wanted to get out. Duncan must have seen the panic slowly closing over me because he leaned forward and abruptly changed the subject. "I hear you're losing Martha."

From the frying pan into the fire. He must have seen the confusion on my face because he covered his mouth with his hand. "Oh no. You don't know."

"I know she's thinking of leaving, but so far she's said nothing to me." But she had confided in Duncan. Were they that close? I thought about the ship and all the times I'd come across them together. I thought about how she never invited me back to her cabin. And the penny dropped.

"I'm so sorry, Cordi. I thought you knew."

I ignored what he said and confronted him. "You and Martha are seeing each other."

He broke into a broad grin. "We wondered when you'd cotton on."

"And that's why she confided in you about her job."

He nodded. "But now I've mucked it up." He looked at me questioningly.

"Don't worry, Duncan. I'll keep it to myself until she tells me." I felt drained and wanted to get back to my office and drown myself in work. It was a good remedy for too many stray thoughts.

Back at the office I compiled a list of all the people who could have murdered Terry. I closed my eyes and plonked my finger down on one of them: Elizabeth. No. I didn't want to call her first for some reason. Instead I picked up the phone and asked for directory assistance for Tracey Dunne. As I figured out what my story would be I listened to the phone ringing, either in an empty house or someone was taking their own sweet time answering.

"Hello?" The voice was breathless, low, male.

"Could I speak to Tracey, please?" I heard the phone clattering on something that sounded like a marble surface.

"Hello?" The voice this time was high, tentative.

I reintroduced myself and was relieved that she remembered who I was. I let her talk about my lecture until it got too embarrassing. I interrupted her and asked if we could meet somewhere, I needed to talk to her about something.

She was immediately wary. When I told her it was about Sally she started making backing away noises and I thought I'd lost her.

"I'm just trying to piece things together for her sister, Sandy." Silence. "She deserves that much."

"Sandy's her sister?" She didn't wait for an answer. Instead she lowered her voice and said, "You can't come here. I'll meet you at Canal Ritz. Do you know that restaurant?"

I said yes. The cute little restaurant right on the Rideau Canal.

"5:00?"

"Yes," I said, and she hung up.

My comparative anatomy course ended early, so I got to the restaurant at ten to five so that I could get a table outside by the water. The inside is really nice, but it's dark. Tracey arrived at 5:00 exactly, but she went directly inside and I debated about getting up to get her. From where I sat I could see into the restaurant proper and I saw her talking to a waiter who pointed in my direction. We greeted each other and as she sat down a bullet-shaped speedboat came whizzing down the canal. She looked up at it, her face rippling with emotion, and suddenly got up and took the other seat with her back to the canal.

"Don't like speed boats?" I asked lightly.

"My sister died when she was hit by one," she said, her face white and drawn.

Oops. "I'm sorry. I shouldn't have said it like that."

She didn't respond so I asked her what had happened, but she wasn't going there.

I waited until our orders had been taken before bringing up what was on my mind. "I was there when Terry was so ruthless about your writing."

She turned away and I watched a swan paddling down the canal amongst a bunch of ducks.

"You must have been pretty angry."

She looked up quickly. "I wouldn't use the word angry. She humiliated me in a mean-spirited way, that's all."

"The police think Sally killed her, drowned her in the tub, threw her in the pool when someone chanced upon her, and then committed suicide." I was watching a hot air balloon lazily drifting over the canal.

"And you don't think that's what happened?"

"I don't think Sally killed her. I think someone else did."

"You think because I was humiliated that I might have done it?" Tracey asked, without a trace of emotion.

I hazarded a guess. "I think someone in the creative writing group knows something and is hiding it."

She brought her napkin up to her mouth and said, "I wouldn't know anything about that," but she wouldn't meet my eye.

I didn't get anything more out of her and I let her leave while I paid the bill. As the waiter came back with my credit card he was followed by a man who looked vaguely familiar.

He strode up to my table, planted his hands on the table cloth, and said, "What have you been telling my wife?"

George. The man with the temper. The man trying to control that temper and not doing a very good job.

I asked him to sit down but he preferred the advantage of looking down on me.

"I'm looking into Terry's death."

"The police have been all through it."

I just stared at him and waited.

"Look," he said, "Tracey had no involvement in those deaths."

"But someone in the creative writing group may have."

His right eye twitched and his hands pressed harder onto the table before he straightened up.

"Why did she keep going to class when Terry was so mean about the quality of her writing?"

"Her writing means everything to her."

"And Terry had the right contacts?"

"Yes. My wife kept hoping. But the bitch undermined her, took away her self-confidence, and finally, on board the ship, refused to help her find an agent. Said her writing stank."

"She ridiculed your wife's writing in front of all those people."

"My wife's a good writer." George's voice had become loud and defensive. "She'd do anything for her writing."

"Including murder?"

George made a sudden move toward me, but just then the waiter appeared to take my credit card slip and George stayed his hand. He glared at me before striding through the restaurant and out the door.

When I got back to my office the next day there was no sign of Martha, but there were four boxes blocking my way with a note stuck to one of them.

I yanked it off and read it.

> This is just for starters — do you want
> me to keep going?
>   Call me,
>   Derek.

I opened the boxes and discovered court transcripts and newspaper articles, lots of them. I pulled one out: "Sleepwalker Acquitted of Murder."

"Accused Pleads Sleepwalking as Defence." Terry's face loomed out at me.

"Michael Grady Murdered in his Sleep." Michael had been a very good-looking man.

I flicked through some more until I read "Juror #9 Injured." There was a picture of a pretty young woman, presumably juror number nine, but it wasn't the picture that caught my attention — not at first anyway. It was the name: LuEllen. I looked back at the picture and saw what she had lost.

I picked up the phone and got through to LuEllen, but she wasn't very enthusiastic about speaking to me after I told her why. In fact, she had been as guarded as Tracey until I asked her if she really believed that Sally could kill Terry. That seemed to change her mind. We arranged to meet at her house in Chelsea, just outside of Ottawa on the Quebec side of the Ottawa River, later that evening.

I put in four hours of work — I was wrestling with some of the sonograms that seemed to indicate that the birds allowed to interact vocally with a male learned twice as many songs as the isolated birds, corroborating other research. At one point Martha came in and interrupted me with my mail. I took it from her but she still said nothing, just looked around the office like a lost waif.

I couldn't stand it any longer. Into the silence that felt like a ten ton weight I asked, "Are you going to take the job?"

She reacted as if I had bitten her and I realized with chagrin that she still didn't know I knew. I had assumed Duncan had filled her in. Shit.

At that incredibly crucial moment the phone rang and we both stared at it. I had to get it. It was Rose. I watched as Martha left in what looked like a huff and I felt like a heel. But I was more angry at Dean, who should have told her he'd spoken to me instead of making it look like we were talking behind her back.

"Cordi, he's coming home today. He said you're to come and stay with us, and if you'd prefer to be on your own you can use his studio."

I started to protest. I was still worried about endangering my brother and his family, but she said, "We need you, Cordi. Ryan won't be able to milk the ladies for awhile and Mac can't do it alone. I can do some of it, but with the kids it's difficult."

I thought about our farmhand Mac and couldn't believe I had not thought about my brother's predicament sooner.

"Has Mac been doing it all?"

"Pretty much."

I told her I'd be back that evening.

"For supper?"

"No."

I hung up and went in search of Martha, but she was nowhere to be found. I called the police about my wreck of a house and they confirmed that it was a pot of oil on the stove. When I mentioned that I had not left a pot of oil on the stove the officer said, "Look, everybody can be forgetful sometimes. Or maybe a member of your family left it on the burner. That's what the evidence tells us."

"So that's what you've sent to the insurance company?"

"Unless you can prove otherwise, yes."

I then spoke to the insurance company but nobody seemed to be able to tell me anything. They were still waiting for the police report.

I pulled myself together and headed across the Ottawa River, through Hull, now Gatineau — one of those name changes that have stationary stores and letterhead designers rubbing their hands in glee — and headed up the highway to Chelsea. It was a twenty minute drive, half the distance I drive to and from work, and it landed me right in the heart of the country with the Gatineau Hills rolling all over the place and the Gatineau River rushing down to meet the Ottawa. The tree studded hills afford remarkable privacy for the myriad houses that have been built in their valleys and dales. They come in all sizes, shapes, and expense accounts.

I zipped off Highway 5 and made my way along the old highway that skirts the Gatineau River to find

Rosemount Place, a grandiose name for an unpaved, pot-holed road that climbed up into one of the Gatineau Hills. I drove past mansions and modest two bedroom homes, although the smaller houses were definitively older than the bigger, more ostentatious homes.

LuEllen's home was right at the top at the end of the road. It was tiny; from the outside it looked like little more than a wooden shingled shed with three enormous freezers lining one side. She'd painted her wooden shutters a coral colour to match the door, but there were no flowers, mostly because the house stood on bedrock and was surrounded by trees, except on the far side, which I could not see.

I walked up the flagstone walkway and took the little brass knocker, shaped like a dolphin swimming around a circle, in my hand and let it go. It didn't make much noise, but then it didn't have a big job to do. The door had two glass windows in it and I could see LuEllen sitting on a sofa facing an enormous picture window. Scruffy came flying around the corner of the sofa, yapping so hard it made it impossible for him to stay still, each yap jerking him sideways.

She turned as I knocked and got up and grabbed a baseball cap, but not before I'd seen her head. I thought I was prepared, but without her ball cap and her heavy winter jacket her disfigurement was frightening in its completeness. I tried to keep my features steady as I gripped her one good hand. She led me inside. It was a simple room, maybe fifteen by twenty feet, dominated by an enormous loom and a piano, with a bedroom off to one side and presumably a bathroom. There was a modest granite fireplace festooned with pictures.

What made the room was the view from the picture window. In front of the house the bedrock dropped away into a forest of trees and cliffs that landed far below on the shores of the Gatineau River. Her view encompassed the cliffs, the river, and the far side where the land was flat before it rose into another Gatineau Hill. She was very isolated and I wondered if she had lived here before the accident, or if the accident had caused her to seek solitude.

We took a seat at either end of the little sofa.

"You have a beautiful home here. Very isolated."

"I like it that way. I don't usually invite anyone here," she said, staring at me.

I found it very disconcerting and wondered why she had made an exception with me.

"You see? Look at your face. Pity, that's what's there. People find it uncomfortable to be with me, and because of that I find it uncomfortable to be with them. So I avoid people most of the time." She smiled a rictus smile and I tried to hide my discomfiture. "I'm self-contained here. I buy all my food once a year, I have satellite, and I have my weaving and my writing. No one needs to pity me." Her words echoed around my head. I thought of the three freezers and the loneliness that suddenly enveloped me was cold and hard, like a lump of ice.

"Sally was a good woman. I'm sorry she's dead," she said changing the subject so fast that it took me awhile to react.

"I don't believe that she killed Terry," I said, coming straight to my point.

"Is that what the police are saying?"

"Yes. They think she killed Terry and then committed suicide by drowning."

I was at a disadvantage. I couldn't read her face, it was so scarred and stretched. She reached over and picked up Scruffy, who began slathering kisses onto her face. "I think that's best left to the police," she said.

I changed tack. "Why did you take Terry's course?"

"I'd heard that she was a good teacher and I thought writing would be a good thing for someone like me. It's an isolating profession and that's the way I live."

"I don't understand. You go to great troubles to avoid people, but then you not only take a creative writing course, you go on a cruise."

She was still and Scruffy began to whine. LuEllen got up and put him on the floor, asking if I wanted some tea.

"I know you're juror number nine," I said.

She whirled to look at me. "How did you find that out?" she whispered.

I told her about the newspaper coverage of Terry's trial.

"But that was years ago."

"What happened?"

"You read the papers. You know."

"They said you were going to convict when the rest of the jury wasn't."

She didn't say anything.

"But you had an accident and Terry was acquitted."

She held the bridge of her nose between her thumb and forefinger and said nothing.

"Was she guilty?"

"What do you think? She sleepwalks and murders a man, then walks? What kind of justice is that?"

"Justice by jury."

"Yeah, but I was missing." She had raised her voice. "It would have ended in a hung jury and then gone on to another trial. She would have lost."

"Except that you accidentally tripped and fell down a twenty-five step flight of cement stairs."

"It was no goddamned accident," she yelled. "Someone pushed me."

She stopped then and stared at me, her eyes wide. "Please get out. I've said too much already."

Chapter Eighteen

I stopped at a St-Hubert restaurant for some chicken and fries, then headed back to Martha's apartment after wrestling with the option of going straight to Rose's and calling Martha from there. Cluck, cluck, I thought. By the time I got there it was already dark. She opened the door to me all sweaty and dressed in a black leotard.

Even before I saw it I could hear the TV intoning, "Stretch your arms. Good. Hold them for ten, nine, eight, seven, good, keep it up, four, three."

Martha switched off the TV. "Just watch, Cordi. I'll be as thin as you." She smiled. We both knew it was an empty threat since she had tried dozens of exercise regimens and hadn't been able to stomach them.

I plopped down on the sofa and closed my eyes. I was more tired than I knew and one more night in the hammock would have been a death sentence.

I had to stick to my resolve to tell her I had to leave tonight and tell her why.

"How did you know?" asked Martha, hands on hips.

I opened my eyes and found her staring at me.

"Know what?" I asked

"My job offer."

"Dean," I said.

"He told you?" she asked incredulously.

I nodded.

"But why?"

"He knew how much I valued you and I guess he was being considerate and giving me advance notice."

"And what about me? Don't I have any say in all this?"

I chose my words carefully. "Your word is the only word that matters here."

"Cordi, did you know that I didn't know he'd told you?"

"No, I didn't know. Not until I saw the look on your face when I asked you about the job offer. He shouldn't have done it without asking you first."

The defiance in her eyes died down and she whispered, "I thought I'd lost you, Cordi. Friends don't hide stuff like that from each other."

I wondered about that, since she hadn't bothered to tell me about the job offer either. She read my mind. "I didn't tell you because I don't know what I want to do. And if I decide to stay with you I didn't want you to always worry you were going to lose me." Martha sat down on a little stool.

"It's a good offer, Martha — a promotion and he's a nice guy. Not to mention he can pay you more because he is a full professor with full tenure. You'd have job

security. With my position I could be gone next month."
I could not believe that I was practically pushing her
toward the job. It sounded a little callous so I softened it
with, "On the downside, you'd be irreplaceable both as
a lab tech and as a friend."

"Lord love you, Cordi. Don't get so melodramatic.
Even if I take the job you'll still be my friend."

I smiled and closed my eyes.

"Hammock's getting to you isn't it?"

I opened my eyes. It was the opening I was looking
for. I nodded, "It's a bitch on the back."

She regarded me. "Why don't you go back and stay
with Ryan? I've been thinking, no one's going to go after
you with Ryan and Rose and a bunch of kids."

I sat forward on the edge of the sofa and rubbed
my eyes.

"I know you're afraid someone will try to kill you
again, but really Cordi, it's time you accepted that maybe
you've been the victim of a series of unfortunate accidents. I mean, if someone is trying to murder you they
aren't very good at it."

Odd that she'd used the same words as Duncan: "A
series of unfortunate accidents."

"Unless they're just trying to scare me."

"Cordi, let it go and go home. They're going to need
help with the milking until Ryan's better, aren't they?"

I nodded and began to protest — I didn't even feel
guilty about my charade, I was so tired.

I stood up and began collecting my things, but Martha wasn't finished. "I overheard you arranging a meeting with LuEllen today. Any gossip?"

I smiled and told her about the clipping I had found and the fact that LuEllen was juror number nine.

"She claims she was pushed down a flight of stairs?"

"Yeah, the newspapers say she was in the stairwell of an office tower when she tripped and fell. LuEllen says someone pushed her and implied that it was because she was going to vote guilty."

"But that's jury tampering, not to mention attempted murder."

"Who and why is what comes to my mind."

"The why is easy. Terry walks free versus another trial, so she has a lot to gain."

"But she couldn't have orchestrated LuEllen's fall or somehow listened in or bugged the jurors to see which way they were leaning. She was in custody," I said.

"Exactly. So she must have had an accomplice."

"Either that or LuEllen is lying."

On my way back to Ryan's I stopped in at the lab and picked up Paulie. She moved around a lot in the cage as I took her to my car, but she didn't meow. My plan was to leave the cage open on my front porch with enough food for a day and see how she adapted. I couldn't do it on Ryan's porch or she'd adapt to the wrong house. I hoped the smell of the fire wouldn't drive her away. As I looked in the rearview mirror and saw Paulie fast asleep I wondered about Duncan's comment that she wasn't good in cars.

I drove straight to my house and was glad the porch light was on. I wrestled the cage out of the car and took it to the porch. Then I got two bowls, and filled one with food and the other with water from the garden tap. I placed them down carefully next to the cage and then opened the door. Paulie stayed inside. After waiting twenty minutes I left her there, hoping she could find a way to feel she belonged. She'd lived in the wild for more than a year. I figured that giving her her freedom, along with plenty of food, would win her over in time.

The next day was the day Patrick had his interview, and Rose woke me at 6:00 a.m. Full udders wait for no one! I was glad. It meant something else to think about besides Patrick. Maybe he wouldn't get the job, maybe he'd blow the interview. I hated wishing for something negative to happen, knowing how much he seemed to want it. As I pulled on some jeans and a T-shirt I had bought the day before I looked longingly at the bed.

Once I'd splashed half a lake on my face I began to feel better. I poked my nose around Ryan and Rose's bedroom door to check on Ryan. He was just a lump on the bed, still asleep, so I headed down for some of Rose's bacon and eggs and then went out to the barn. I looked for Paulie and thought I saw her disappear behind the barn, but it could have been one of our other barn cats. I began fitting the teat cups to the first cow. Mac arrived shortly after my third cow and waved. I waved back and we did our work in companionable silence for as long as it took.

Once I was finished I headed over to my house to reassess the damage. It was pretty intimidating, but when I ran a finger across one of the walls it left a nice slash. Nothing a good scrubbing couldn't fix, but it was everywhere. Not so bad upstairs as downstairs, but the coat of soot was tenacious. The kitchen, on the other hand, was a disaster. It would need to be gutted and rebuilt, something I fervently hoped the insurance company would pay for. I just didn't have that kind of cash lying around and the thought of taking out a loan that would take me years to pay down left me cold.

I collected some of my clothes and went back to find Ryan sitting in the living room, eating a big hunk of bread. I went over and threw my arms around him, whispered thank you in his ear, and gave him a big kiss on the cheek.

He returned my hug and said, "I don't know what I'd do if I ever lost you, Cordi."

I hugged him harder to let him know I felt the same way. He started to cough so I had to let him go, but he flapped his hand to make me stay. When the coughing was over he asked me my side of the fire story.

I filled him in on everything he'd missed. When I was finished he said, "So you really believe someone is still after you?"

"Yes."

"Does anybody else?"

"No. Although Duncan and Martha are not as adamantly opposed as they were."

"Watch your back, eh?"

I would have hugged him again for his implied support of me, but he was coughing again so I merely nodded and went in search of a phone. I hired a cleaning company to come in for two days, or however long it took to clean my house, and then I called a carpenter who said she could come right away and give me an estimate. I jumped at the offer. By the time she was finished it looked as though my bank balance was going to be a whole lot lighter. And that didn't even start to address what I'd lost in the shed.

I went back to Ryan's and faxed the quote to the insurance company, including what I'd lost in the shed, and then put it out of my mind. I hauled out the boxes Derek had given me that I'd brought home for weekend work and dumped them on the front porch, sat down on the floor, and began to go through them amidst several visits from the kids.

I was going through more of the newspaper clippings when my eye was caught by a photograph of Owen and Terry. They'd been caught unawares, Owen's face ugly and clean-shaven but recognizably Owen, and Terry unmistakably beautiful, the contrast between the two painful.

My eyes drifted to the caption below and screeched to a halt. "Terry Ballantyne Spencer and Owen Ballantyne in Happier Days" I sat back in my chair and eyed the photograph more carefully, but there was no resemblance between the two, so how exactly were they related?

At that moment the phone rang in the hall and Rose answered it. I could hear her voice rise up an octave — it must have been someone she knew — then she called out my name. I frowned, but got up and went inside. Rose mouthed at me "Patrick," and I felt my heart drop and lift at the same time. Weird sensation.

I answered the phone with a chirpy hi.

"How are you doing?"

I brought him up-to-date on everything right up to the fire, which elicited all sorts of questions, the last of which was why I hadn't phoned. I told him I'd tried but he interrupted me to ask for the tenth time if I was okay and should he come home? I studiously avoided asking about his interview and waited for him to say something.

When he didn't I finally blurted out, "How was the interview?" I was hoping for a pause but instead I got an immediate reaction.

"Good. They liked me. I just have to wait for them to interview the rest of the candidates."

"That's good Patrick," I said, but my heart wasn't in it and he knew it.

"Look, Cordi, we've been …"

I interrupted him. "I don't want to talk about it on the phone okay? It's so impersonal. When you get home."

We talked about a few more things, and some X-rated stuff I was glad Rose wasn't around to hear, then we rang off.

I stared at the phone in my hand and then dialed 411 and asked for directory assistance for Owen Ballantyne.

I drove in to work and spent some time catching up, reading research papers that I'd been putting off. Then I called Owen. I was really apprehensive because he was monotonally monosyllabic on the phone. I really had no idea what I was up against and I hadn't actually talked to him much, except on the plane. I wished now that I had so I'd have some idea how he'd react to me and to what I had to say. He had told me to meet him at a motorcycle shop on Bank Street in Ottawa. He gave me the address and nothing else, no cross street, nothing. But in the end it was easy to find.

I pulled up in front of a small shop with a big BMW in the window and Ballantyne Bikes emblazoned above the door. I shouldn't have been surprised, but I was. I had just assumed that he worked full-time for Terry. But why would Terry's job require a full-time assistant? I opened the door and was assaulted by the smell of oil and gas. There was a man behind the counter and I told him Owen was expecting me.

He opened a door behind him and yelled, "Owen. A lady to see you." He turned back to me and said, "Take a seat. He shouldn't be too long."

I had just sat down when he came out, wiping his hands with a blue rag.

"Ms O'Callaghan," he said and offered his hand. He led me back into an office with a tiny window looking out onto a brick house next door. His walls were covered with pictures of bikes of every description and it suddenly occurred to me that my brother had probably been here, being the bike enthusiast he was. Owen sat down behind an old wooden desk and waved me to a chair on the other side.

"Well?" he asked.

"I read about you in the paper."

"And?" He was giving nothing away.

"I know you were related to Terry in some way. Brother? Cousin? Husband?"

He touched the fingertips of both hands together. "And what does that have to do with your visit?" No sign of sorrow.

"Sandy doesn't think that Sally killed Terry."

"That would be the natural reaction of a friend," he said.

"Aren't you interested in who killed Terry?"

"I accept the police's verdict on that. They are professionals, you know."

I decided to try something else to shake him out of his complacency. Pure guesswork, but what the hey. I had a one in three chance of getting it right. "It must have been tough being Terry's brother."

Something flashed in his eyes but the rest of him stayed still. "You're not being very subtle, Ms O'Callaghan." He paused. "I am not unaware of the fact that she was very beautiful and I am definitely not. Our parents were very successful at distinguishing between the two."

Bingo! "So Terry got their attention and you did not."

"You're being redundant," he said.

And, I thought, you're being very uptight. Instead I said, "Why did you put up with the way your sister treated you? You're very successful here." I waved my arm around the room.

He smiled at that. "Do you have brothers or sisters?"

"One brother."

"Is he older or younger?"

"Older by one minute."

He laughed. "You can't know the power an older sister can hold over you, especially one as beautiful as Terry."

"Did she leave you anything in her will?"

"You are very transparent aren't you?"

I squirmed in my chair hoping he'd answer the question anyway.

"It's no secret. She left me nothing."

Dead end — or was it? "I would have thought a sister would leave something to her brother, especially if she had no other family."

He laughed. "You're looking for a motive aren't you? You think maybe I killed my own sister?" He laughed again.

I was feeling very uncomfortable, realizing I'd lost control of the interview. So I said, "Did you know that the jury for your sister's trial was tampered with?"

He looked up and smiled again. "You've got to be kidding."

I told him about LuEllen.

"Rotten luck to be called to jury duty, do your duty, and then get pole axed — if, of course, that is what happened. You do seem to have a penchant for the melodramatic."

I looked at him and wondered if he was thinking about my claims on the ship of being almost murdered. "When did your sister first sleepwalk?" I asked.

He hesitated. "The first time I remember I was only five years old. So she would have been nine. We shared a bedroom. She had the top bunk and in the middle of the night she got out of bed and stepped on me as she climbed down. I asked her what she was doing, but she didn't answer me. I heard her go downstairs and I followed her, I can't remember why. Maybe I was afraid she'd steal the last piece of cake or colour in my colouring book, because she did things like that a lot. It doesn't matter." He paused.

"I followed her into the kitchen and watched as she opened the refrigerator door and pulled out the Cool

Whip and began spraying the kitchen with it. I asked her what she was doing, but her eyes were glazed over and she didn't seem to see me. I was really upset because I knew I'd be blamed for it. I grabbed her by the arm, but she lashed out and hit me. I held back and watched as she opened a kitchen drawer, took out a knife, and gripped it in her fist. By then I was hiding under the kitchen table. She was like an automaton and I was really scared. I don't know why I didn't yell out. My parents used that against me later.

"She took the knife and walked over to a poster that my parents really liked and began to stab it methodically. When she was through with that she continued through the kitchen, stabbing everything in sight. Then she just stopped. She dropped the knife and I watched as she walked back upstairs. I heard our bedroom door closing behind her. That's what woke my parents. They found me cowering under the kitchen table.

"They wouldn't believe me when I said it was Terry. Even when faced with irrefutable evidence they refused to believe their darling Terry could have done those things, even though they eventually witnessed them themselves — until the trial that is."

"Why was the trial different?"

"Because there were experts explaining that she was a sleepwalker. Our parents could have helped way back when, but they didn't. Didn't even bother to take Terry to a doctor. They thought it was some dirty little secret and that she would grow out of it. When she was old enough she finally sought help."

"It doesn't seem to have helped her," I said.

"Oh, you're good at the monumental understatement aren't you?" He laughed a bitter laugh. "I'm not an insensitive brother, you know. We may have had our differences but she was my sister and I loved her. The only person I've ever loved."

"But you just said you got blamed for all her night wanderings, and other stuff too, I'm sure."

"Doesn't matter. She was my sister. I'd do anything for her."

"Including finding her killer?"

He rubbed his forehead. "Ms O'Callaghan, if you can't remember that the police already know who killed my sister then this interview is over."

And with that he stood up and showed me the door.

Chapter Nineteen

I spent the rest of my lunch break looking at more newspaper clippings and court documents, and putting off calling Elizabeth because she sort of intimidated me. When I ran out of clippings from one box I grabbed the phone and called her. She wasn't too happy about meeting me, but at least she agreed to it. I was feeling guilty about leaving work, but I figured I could work at home and catch up on my reading.

She worked somewhere near Stittsville, southwest of Ottawa, so it was a bit of a hike for me to get there. She'd told me to meet her at a little airport where she worked. I got lost. I always do in the territory southwest of Ottawa. As I finally swung down the roadway to the airport I could see a row of little planes sitting jauntily just off the runway. I parked my car with all the other cars in the parking lot and went inside. She had told me to ask for her at the flight instruction school, which was at the south end of the terminal. I had wondered about that, but she hadn't given me time to ask.

I found the building and went inside, which was just a big open area. There was one corner office with windows looking in on the open space and windows looking out onto the runway. It was little more than a shed, but it had all the high tech gear needed to train new flyers, or it sure looked like it anyway, plus there was a little plane parked inside getting worked on. It reminded me of Owen's shop, just with different machines.

I told the girl at the desk just inside the doorway that Elizabeth Goodal was expecting me. She pressed a buzzer and told me to have a seat. I went over to the lone chair and looked down at the magazines on the table, *Aviation Weekly*, *Private Flyer*, *Plane Mechanics*, and decided to spend my time looking at all the pictures on the wall. They were all of planes with people smiling proudly in front of them. There was a framed certificate that announced that Elizabeth Goodal was an authorized flight instructor.

"Dr. O'Callaghan."

I turned and there was Elizabeth, with a quick dry smile and one hand offered in greeting, the other holding a wrench.

I gripped her hand and smiled. "Please, call me Cordi."

She nodded and said, "I'm afraid you'll have to forgive me. I have to take up the plane for a test drive before my next lesson at 4:00. We'll have to postpone our meeting — unless you want to come with me?"

Was that allowed? I wondered. Taking a test drive with a passenger? But it was only the briefest of thoughts, and even though I couldn't tell whether she really meant it or was just being polite, I said yes.

She turned abruptly and went out the door I had just come in, leading me down a row of planes to a little one that said Cessna on. It looked like an origami plane, light as paper and about as strong. I had never been in a small plane before and this one was tiny, just a two-seater. It sported a nice coral blue streak, running from its nose to the beginning of its tail, and its two side wheels looked as though they were covered in plastic booties while the front wheel was naked. Elizabeth indicated the side she wanted me to take and I ducked under the wing and got into the aircraft.

Both of us had a set of controls, but she seemed to have more buttons or something on hers, probably to override a kamikaze student. She went through a standard check of all the controls. I was amazed at how easily the plane responded to her hands and how lightly and quickly we taxied out to the runway.

There was a hell of a difference between the little Cessna and a much bigger, more ponderous plane. You got the feeling this little guy could stop and turn on a dime. I had a few misgivings as the engine revved up for the takeoff, mostly because it seemed so noisy, but then we were away, riding on the wind like a butterfly. I hadn't thought about that aspect before we were airborne. I could feel my stomach begin to lurch as if we were at sea. I took a couple of deep breaths and concentrated on what I wanted to find out from Elizabeth. I didn't have much to go on, just the overheard conversation on board the ship. I figured I could use that to my advantage.

We were up high enough now that I could see the Ottawa River, and as I craned my neck I could see the Eardley Escarpment.

She glanced at me and said, "My students always like to fly over where they live. You live nearby, right? Do you want to fly over?"

I almost said no, just out of reflex, but what harm could it do? I said, "Yes," and some time later there it was, the farmhouse and the barn, and the long lazy road.

As she straightened out the controls and flew overhead she said, "Why are you investigating Terry's death?"

"Because I don't think Sally killed her."

"She was there, she had means and motive. What more can you want?"

"For it to be in character."

"She was very distraught over Arthur ditching her for Terry. Or at least, it looked as though he and Terry had hooked up. She just broke. That's all. She just broke. And then she killed herself."

There was something in her voice that didn't ring true. I turned to look at her but she was concentrating on flying the plane. I took a chance, not knowing where it would take me. "I overheard you and Peter talking on the ship."

She quickly looked at me and then just as quickly looked away. "Are you in the habit of listening to other people's conversations?"

"I couldn't help it. You had me trapped in a lifeboat."

She didn't respond and I watched the light dawn on what conversation I had overheard.

I continued, "You said 'She can't just take my man away from me.'"

I saw Elizabeth tighten her grip on the controls.

"Did you mean Terry? Was Terry the woman who took your man?"

"Yes, you could say she stole my man."

I was watching her closely and she kind of crumpled in her seat, but then she suddenly sniffed loudly and sat up saying, "Do you smell something burning?" in a tone of voice that put the fear of god in me.

I sniffed. "No."

"Take your controls."

I was confused and looked at her questioningly.

"Now!" she said, and I grabbed the controls.

"What's wrong?" I asked, trying to stifle my fear. But she wasn't in the mood to answer questions. She gave me a crash course in flying a Cessna. The word "crash" reverberated through my head like a death knell.

"Just fly her in circles until I'm okay."

"What do you mean? What's wrong?" I asked again.

"Hopefully nothing," she said and lapsed into silence.

I gripped the controls like a mad woman and then gripped them even harder when I saw that she had let go of hers. I kept looking over at her but she was just staring ahead. I wondered if she was having a heart attack and nearly had one myself. Maybe she just had the stomach flu. That calmed me down.

The plane was actually quite easy to fly. After a few minutes I was getting the hang of it when suddenly she yelled out and I saw her begin to convulse. It was a tiny plane and there was nowhere for her to go, but I had no way to keep her from hurting herself or hitting the controls. She was belted in, but her arms were jerking around.

I gripped the controls and tried to remember everything she said. Just fly in lazy circles until she's okay. Right. I could do this.

Suddenly there was a dizzying dip as the plane veered left and started descending on the Ottawa River. I pulled up on the controls but nothing happened. I looked over and saw that she had slumped forward and her body was wedging the controls on a course with death. I reached over and with all my energy hauled her back in her seat. She slumped over toward the door. I grabbed the controls. The plane was hurtling out of control, and I had no idea if I had passed the point of no return or was about to stall or what. I pulled up hard on the controls and time stood still. I could see the blue sky and the sun, and the earth below. I was overdosing on adrenaline as the earth slowly receded and I brought the plane back onto an even keel. I felt sick and looked over at Elizabeth, who lay flaccid. But her eyes were open. How long did it take to recover from a seizure? I looked at the control panel. There must be a gas gauge somewhere. I finally found it — there wasn't much left in the tank.

What was I going to do? I was afraid to touch any of the buttons on the dash in case one of them was the nosedive button. Keep flying in circles and drop out of the sky, or try to land and kill myself? I didn't seem to have much choice and the next twenty minutes passed by so slowly I was sure my hair had gone grey. With the gas almost on empty and my adrenalin overflowing I heard her moan. I wanted to shake her out of her stupour; we weren't going to make it if she didn't wake up.

Another agonizing five minutes passed. Suddenly she said, "How much gas?"

I told her. She tried to sit up and take the controls but she was still too out of it. "Where are we?"

I looked out the window and could see the Ottawa River right close by and the farmhouse. I'd done a pretty good job of circling, I thought, trying to calm myself down. I told her where we were.

"Too far to go back. We have to land now."

I liked the sound of the "we," but when I glanced over at her she was definitely not all there yet.

"Tell me where we can land this near your home. We're out of time."

I felt my heart leap. I told her about our driveway, how long it was, how wide.

"We're landing there. Now," she said, with some of her spunk returning.

She had me fly over once to check on the road and then she walked me through the approach. I froze and we lost the approach and had to try again. This time I didn't freeze but as we wobbled our way down to the road I couldn't keep the wingtips even. It looked like we were going to land left wing first, but she grabbed her controls and took it the rest of the way. It was an ugly, bumpy landing because she was still quite groggy. We bounced up and down a couple of times before landing, slewed along the road and came to a stop next to the field full of our cows, who had run away and then turned back to look at us. It didn't seem right that they didn't even moo. They just chewed their cuds and silently stared at us. We, who had almost died.

Chapter Twenty

I sat slumped forward in the seat feeling as if every ounce of my fear had drained out of me, leaving me feeling empty and unreal. With some difficulty I pulled the great weight of my head up and turned to look at Elizabeth. She was sitting with her head thrown back against the seat and her eyes closed.

"Please don't tell anyone I have epilepsy," she said so softly I barely heard her.

What the hell was I supposed to say to that? After all, she'd nearly killed me. What about her students? I was saved from having to say anything by Ryan bellowing to us from the front porch. By the sound of things he was feeling a lot better. I looked up and saw him coming down the porch steps with Rose hard on his heels. I opened the little door and ducked out under the wing to the ground and started walking toward Ryan.

I hadn't gone very far when he stopped dead and said, "Cordi?"

It was an hour later, after Elizabeth had been picked up by a relative and told us someone would pick up the plane the next day, that Ryan finally turned to me saying, "Spill it."

"You mean you don't believe the 'We ran out of gas' explanation?"

"Well, actually, I do. I heard the plane sputtering overhead, after it must have buzzed us a dozen times — I felt like a fish in a bowl."

"So?" I wasn't making it easy for him. I guess Elizabeth had got to me a little, because I didn't feel much like talking.

"So she sure wasn't looking very well and that landing was the pits."

I told Ryan all about the seizure and how she'd been out of it for maybe twenty minutes as I'd done what she told me and circled.

"How the hell does she have a license to pilot a plane?"

"Good question."

"Maybe she just developed epilepsy. Maybe that was her first seizure?"

"She knew exactly what was about to happen and what she had to do about it."

"Okay, so it's her second or third. Maybe she hasn't seen a doctor yet."

"Because she knows it will end her career." I turned to Ryan, at the same time exclaiming "Jesus!" Which, of course, imparted no information whatsoever.

He waited patiently.

"When I gave one of my lectures on the ship Elizabeth asked about the best way to murder someone."

"What are you getting at, Cordi?"

"Suppose Terry knew about Elizabeth's epilepsy."

"What? And then Elizabeth killed her because of that?"

"Possibly."

"But why wouldn't Terry tell the authorities about it? It's the only ethical thing to do."

"Maybe she didn't have time. Maybe Elizabeth had a seizure that Terry witnessed one night on the ship. Or maybe she was blackmailing her."

Ryan scratched his chin and shook his head. I hated when he did that.

"What?" I asked.

"She just doesn't seem like the type, that's all. There's something else there, Cordi."

"That's totally subjective, Ryan. You saw her when she was recovering from an epileptic seizure. She's bound to look vulnerable then. You don't even know her."

"Yeah, sure," he said, but I knew he didn't really mean that.

After eating dinner and helping Rose clean up I went back outside to check on the plane. It had ended up slightly to one side of the road and looked incongruous as a backdrop for our cattle. I opened the little passenger door and looked inside. I didn't know what I was looking for but I figured it was worth a try. I sat myself down in the driver's seat and scanned the controls. They looked as incomprehensible as they had when we came in for a landing.

There was a small storage compartment for manuals and what not, and I took them out and leafed through them. I was about to put them all back when one of the manuals flipped open and a card fell out. I opened it. Inside was a note that said:

> Flying on the wings of our love. May we
> never touch down.
> Love forever, M.

I flipped it over but there was nothing on the other side. I looked more carefully at the card, which was dated eight years ago. About the time she said her husband had died.

I carefully replaced the card and rummaged through the rest of the tiny cockpit. When I was finished I went over to my place to check on Paulie. I set out some more food for her then sat on the porch and waited. This time she came silently out of the night, nimbly jumping up onto the porch and heading straight for the food. I wondered if she would be so hungry if her belly was full of barn mice. She ate her food without taking her eyes off me, but she ate it all and then sat back on her haunches looking at me.

"Hey ya, Puss," I said and held out my hand to her. But she just sat there and stared at me and I finally wearied of it and went back to Ryan's and hit the sack.

On the way in to work the next day I called Martha and asked if she'd arrange meetings with Arthur and Jason for me. I'd been putting off talking to Arthur, figuring he wouldn't want to talk about the woman he jilted.

But maybe he'd like to not have her suicide hanging over his head if I could prove she didn't kill herself.

My office was empty when I got there and the latest copy of *Animal Behaviour* was on my desk. I picked it up and started flipping through it. When I heard Martha arriving five minutes later with an armload of birdfeed I called to her from my office. "Did you know that the Moray eel has a second set of jaws in its throat?"

Martha grunted so I went on. "It grabs its prey with its first set of teeth and then the second jaw comes up out of the throat, nabs the victim, and pulls it down."

I thought Martha would be impressed but she didn't say anything. I came out of the office to find out why. She was sitting at her desk staring into the computer as if there was a hidden room in it where she could hide.

"Hi," I said.

She looked up at me and I could tell by her face what she was about to say next.

"I'm taking the job, Cordi." As simple as that.

I took a big breath and congratulated her. She gave me my messages and some research papers my students had dropped off, then quietly left. I sat down at my desk feeling lonely and deserted. Sure, I'd still see her a lot, but it wouldn't be the same. And suddenly I understood why we had both wanted me to leave her apartment. It was a distancing thing, a way to make it easier on both of us. I chased those thoughts out of my head and checked my messages. Martha had located Arthur and he could see me that evening at the Orynx Theatre, but it would have to be during rehearsal. Jason she'd booked to come to my office the next day.

The day went by quickly and I almost didn't leave myself enough time to get to the theatre. It was an old cinderblock that had been spruced up with a maroon marquee and awnings. I circled around looking for parking and finally had to park with half my car in a no park zone and half in a park zone. Was I legal or illegal? I trusted the green hornet would ask the same question and give me the benefit of the doubt. The front doors of the theatre were locked. I looked up at the marquee. The play was called *Bullied* but no one was billed as being in it. I walked around to the side of the building and saw a door propped ajar by a Pepsi can.

I opened it and walked into darkness. I had to stop and let my eyes adjust. I could hear someone yelling somewhere off to the right. I followed my ears and broke out into the auditorium, right at the stage. Most of the seats were empty so I walked down the aisle a few rows and slipped into a seat. There were four actors on stage, but none of them was Arthur. As I sat and watched them bitching about some poor co-worker who was socially challenged, Arthur came on and proceeded to act like a very convincing nerd. The four co-workers immediately stopped talking but one of them mimicked Arthur's strange lopsided walk from behind his back. In perfect timing Arthur slowly turned, catching the mimic red-handed. The stage grew still, the discomfort of the four bullies palpable, until, from beneath his coat, Arthur suddenly drew out a gun and swung it past the heads of each of his tormentors in a graceful arc, saying, "You're history, dudes."

"Jesus, Arthur. Where on earth did that line come from anyway?" yelled the voice of a man seated in the front row. "Stop trying to be a playwright and be an actor. It has to be subtle, Arthur, subtle. You want to feel the menace more than see it.

"Okay, that's enough for now. Take a break."

I saw Arthur come down off the stage and talk heatedly to the director. I waited until he was finished and then stood up so that he would notice me. When I saw him peering into the seats the way a man would peer at the sun I walked down the aisle and he finally caught sight of me.

"Cordi, is it?"

"Hello, Arthur," I said and we shook hands rather formally, as if we'd never met before. But I guess we really hadn't. I'd never actually talked to him. Up close his white hair was spectacular, thick and as white as snow.

"Your secretary said you wanted to talk to me about Sally." His words were clipped. Martha would have been furious at being called a secretary.

I waited, expecting him to say that Sally was none of my business. But instead he said nothing. He walked over to the stage and leaned against it. There were people on stage moving some of the set back and forth. It was quite distracting.

"I wanted to know how long you and Sally had been together before you broke it off." Sandy had already told me, but I figured it was a pretty benign question to start off with.

He pulled on his earlobe and said, "The cops wanted to know that too." He laughed, but there was no mirth there. "I guess at first everyone thought that I killed her — drove her to suicide by being a callous lover."

"Or she might have killed Terry because Terry had stolen you. And she couldn't live without you or with what she'd done...."

"That's what the cops think now, as I am sure you are aware." He spat out the words. "Sally could never, ever kill another human being." The last word got caught in his throat and he turned his face away from me for a moment.

I was confused. Or maybe he was just acting, pretending he still cared for the woman he'd dumped.

"Look. She was a good woman. She didn't deserve to die like that. So why are you asking me these questions?"

"Sandy asked me to look into Terry's death and find out who really killed her."

His face softened at that. "But why would you want to involve yourself?"

I thought about the creature who was stalking me since almost the first time I stepped on the ship and I figured it might not be wise to wave that around as a reason.

"It's a job," I said. But that sounded callous. "I've helped in another murder investigation and I agree with Sandy that Sally is an unlikely murderer."

"Unlikely? Don't you mean impossible? She was the kindest, most caring, most lovable person I've ever met."

I found those words somewhat suspect coming from him, and before I could catch the words they slipped out. "Then why did you break up with her?"

He yanked on his earlobe some more and looked at me as if he were weighing his options. "I didn't."

I thought I hadn't heard him correctly because of the racket on the stage, but then he said it again. I was speechless. He looked at me and laughed that mirthless laugh. "It was all an act. I tried to tell Sandy, but she was so furious she wouldn't listen to me. Practically barred me from the funeral. Said I was a vulture." He swung his arms out to include the theatre and then fell silent.

"The breakup wasn't …"

"Real. It wasn't real." He raised his voice. "I loved her. I loved her so much I'd have done anything for her. And she loved me."

"So what I overheard on the plane — that was just part of the act."

He nodded.

"And what you took from her bag?"

He smiled at that. "You weren't exactly unobtrusive about eavesdropping on us. I thought it would add a little spice to our scenario. I took her cell phone."

I pretended I hadn't heard the dig, which I deserved, and said instead, "So you knew all along that she was acting a part?" Just as Sandy had said, which made sense of course, since he'd been going out with her for a year and she certainly hadn't been acting the mouse for a year.

He nodded again.

"Why? Why was she doing it?"

"I don't know. She just asked me to go along with her being an introvert to her creative writing friends and everyone on board, and then she asked me to jilt her — to play it like any part. So I did, because I loved her and because it was fun acting the part in a real life situation outside the theatre."

"Without knowing why."

"No, not exactly. She said she had a recall audition after the trip for a part she really wanted and she thought we could have a lot of fun with it aboard the ship. I thought at the time that it was rather good of them to wait for the audition until the trip was over, but I figured they really wanted her. She also said I wasn't to tell anyone that the breakup wasn't real. Not even Sandy." He hesitated and I held my breath, afraid of scaring him off. "I don't think the breakup was part of the recall script."

"What do you mean?"

"Sally and I were having dinner just before the plane left and she asked me to jilt her. She said she was afraid it would be too difficult to play the depressed mouse without a jolt from her real life to carry her through."

"So she needed something real, to make her feel sad."

"Except it wasn't real, but she could imagine how she would feel if I left her and her acting took it from there."

"She must have been very passionate about her work." What an understatement.

I waited, but Arthur just stared ahead at the stage.

"What about Terry?" I said. "Were you pretending to be her lover?"

"Yeah, but that was the most difficult part because she wanted none of that. But Sally thought it would be a hoot. The closest we ever got to looking like lovers was when I flung my arm around her shoulders. I could feel her stiffen under my touch, but at least she didn't fling me off. But I got the message. Unfortunately, it gave the police a motive for me. I dump the old girlfriend, who won't leave me alone, but the new girlfriend doesn't want me and in a furious rage I kill both of them."

"But surely you've told them the real story?"

"Yeah. They said they'd take it under consideration, but between you and me I think they thought I was just lying, making up a good story to save my skin. It is a crazy thing to do. But actors can do some crazy things."

"Like being a peeping Tom?"

Arthur looked confused for a moment and then smiled ruefully. "I was worried about her."

"Sally?" I asked, remembering his piercing stare at Terry.

"Yeah, Sally. I was pretty sure she was hiding something from me, but I didn't know what. I was checking up on her and pretending to be a besotted lover as far as Terry was concerned. I was just trying to get some answers, that's all. There's no harm in that."

"You didn't like Terry, did you?"

He hesitated and then made up his mind. "No, I didn't. Sally had told me enough about her that I instinctively reacted against her."

"Well, it looks like you're off the hook now anyway. The police aren't interested in you anymore."

"Yeah," said Arthur, but he didn't look too relieved about it.

"When you realized Sally was dead what did you think?"

"Besides being devastated? I thought that she'd been playing the part of a suicidal person and that somebody had taken advantage of that to make it look like she killed Terry and then killed herself." He paused. "She was just trying to save someone who was already dead."

"You mean someone framed Sally?"

Arthur nodded. "They planted the suicide note to make it look as though Sally had killed herself after killing Terry because of me." He was about to say something more when we were interrupted.

"Alright, people," the shrill voice cut through our conversation. "Time's up. Break's over."

Arthur turned and shook my hand. "If I can do anything else...." he said and then turned and walked away.

Chapter Twenty-One

W hen I got to my office the next day I saw an unfamiliar pair of legs stretching out from behind the door, which was hiding the rest of the body. Martha was nowhere in sight and I thought it awfully brazen of whoever it was to waltz into my office and sit down like that. I walked in.

He was out of uniform and the authority that went with it seemed to have vanished and been replaced by a carefree, slightly chaotic man. Captain Jason Poole. I'd forgotten that I'd asked Martha to set up a meeting. My mind was mush these days. He quickly rose to his feet and held out his hand. His other was gripping a familiar pink raincoat. Martha's. She must have left it on the ship.

He followed my eyes and laughed. "The girl at head office asked if I'd drop it off for Ms Bathgate, since I was heading this way anyway."

I nodded, both at what he was saying and at the chair he had commandeered, then sat down behind my desk. We did the usual inane bantering, talked about the weather and how *The Farmer's Almanac* was predicting a mild winter, talked about the ship and how it would soon be on its way to its wintering grounds in South America and the Antarctic.

Suddenly he said, "I heard you're looking into Terry's murder. I was just interested in what you had found, particularly since the police say it was Sally."

Why would he be interested? I wondered. But I was grateful that he'd started this line of conversation.

"Did you know Sally?" I asked.

"No, never met her before."

"Then why are you interested?"

"Because of Terry."

"Terry?" I asked, bewildered. "But you said you hated her."

"I never said I hated her."

"But the polar bear incident...."

"Was stupid and I could have wrung her neck, but that doesn't mean I hated her."

"What does it mean?" I asked, remembering him hunched over and crying on the bridge when he thought no one was there. He didn't answer so I continued, "How well did you know her?"

He leaned forward in his chair and said nothing.

"You were crying over her, weren't you?"

"What makes you think that?"

"Because I saw you. Because it wasn't Sally you were crying over and there were only two people who died."

He laughed then and I waited. "We do have outside communication you know. Ship-to-shore. It could have been bad news. My mother could have fallen ill."

I took a chance. "It wasn't that though, was it?"

"No, it wasn't."

"So why were you crying over someone you seemed to hate?"

"Because I loved her once." He looked out the window. He seemed to see something there that interested him because he stared at it for a long time. I resisted the urge to turn around and get a better view.

"I met her five years ago. She took my breath away. We lived together until six months ago, when I came home after a trip abroad to find all her things gone and a terse little note that simply said, 'Bye Forever.'"

"You both seemed to be very bitter about it," I said, then added, "I mean, neither of you seemed to like each other on the ship. It was quite palpable."

"That often happens when relationships go sour."

"Sour enough to kill for?"

He laughed. "I had no need to kill her. She wasn't part of my life anymore — just a memory, that's all."

Before I could say anything else he pointedly changed the subject and gestured at a picture of a cardinal on my wall. It was one that Ryan had taken but there were other, better, ones in two folders behind him. I debated on whether to point them out to him but in the end the pride I had for my brother won the day.

"My brother's a professional photographer," I said. "The green file folder behind you? Take a look inside. Forget the red one. It's older work."

I saw a strange look cross Jason's face as he turned to retrieve the folder, his hand reaching out, hesitating, and then grabbing the red folder.

I couldn't help myself; I gasped.

He jerked around to face me, the fear evident in his face. Dear god, a colour-blind captain.

I was speechless and so was he. Could someone be so passionate about their job that they'd endanger an entire ship?

I pictured one of his ships in the shipping lanes on an inky black night. The only thing telling him whether a ship was coming at him or moving away from him was the red port light and the green starboard light. Radar would help him, but not instantaneously. How had he passed the eyesight tests?

He finally said, "I was in an accident eight months ago in the U.S. that damaged my optic nerve and left me colour-blind."

"Surely the doctor …"

"I lied about my profession. It was easy to do. No questions asked and I didn't go blabbing it. They didn't know me from Adam. What can I say? I love my job. I don't know how I'd survive without it."

"But all your passengers …" I was feeling like a broken record, what with Elizabeth's epilepsy and now colour-blindness.

"Why do you think I stick to the Arctic and the Antarctic?"

"Yes, but you'd still run into traffic."

"My second mate covers for me. It works well."

"Why would he do that?"

"He owed me a big favour. I saved his daughter's life."

"Did Terry know?"

He didn't say anything, but then he didn't have to. It was written all over his face. And I remembered how Terry had told him to take care of his eyes, that day on the bridge. Her tone of voice had not been solicitous, more like malicious.

"That gives you a motive for murder, doesn't it?" I said.

He scraped back his chair and cleared his throat. "I can see you haven't got anywhere on this case if you're looking at me as a murderer. I'm sure there are plenty of others with better motives than mine."

He stood up but I stayed seated. "Such as?"

He brushed some lint off his pants. "Owen, for starters."

"He's her brother, for god's sake. Why would he want her dead?"

"I heard they were fighting over their parents' estate. They went down in a plane crash about three months ago. Money can turn blood to water, even with the best of us, and Terry was no princess."

"Owen told me he stood to gain nothing from her death."

Jason raised his eyebrows and shrugged.

"They were fighting and still working together?"

"Yeah. Weird, eh? They seemed to feed off each other. There was a need there that wasn't altogether healthy. She didn't treat her brother very well, which was surprising considering without him her writing career would've been dead in the water."

I looked at him curiously. "That sounds somewhat extreme since he was really just a glorified gofer."

"Ah, but no, he wasn't."

"What is he then?"

"Her ghostwriter."

I took a deep breath and said nothing, hoping he'd fill in the silence, which he did. "The book she wrote about her trial and being in jail. It was all Owen. I overheard them arguing about it one day. She was mad as hell because he was demanding money. I don't know if he was blackmailing her or what, but they were always fighting about something. I don't know why they put up with each other."

"What about all the courses she teaches, the novels she's written. He doesn't help there surely?"

"No, I don't think he does. I'm not sure how she's managed it, but what she writes now is good and different. I've read her work and while Owen may have ghostwritten the non-fiction book, he sure as hell didn't ghostwrite the others."

"Why are you so sure?"

He shrugged. "I'm not. She must have just reached that point we all long for that breaks us through to another level."

He was looking out the window again and this time I turned and looked too. There was a spider in the corner weaving its web, hoping to snare itself a meal on the fifth floor. How the hell had it climbed so far and why did it think my window was a good place?

I turned back to Jason. "Why did you really come today? You didn't have to agree to a meeting."

He stood there biting his upper lip, chewing it half to death before he let it go. "Because I thought you should know that I don't think Terry was who she seemed."

I waited.

"She was a schemer and there was a side to her that scared me."

"The sleepwalking side?"

He nodded. "When she went off her medication she'd walk and sometimes she would get violent and throw things around the room." He sighed again. "It was an animal violence that scared me. But you know what scared me more?"

I shook my head.

"I don't think Michael is the only one she murdered."

A few days later I was taking a break from work and going through the stuff that Derek had sent. There was an amazing amount of press coverage and lots of pictures of the murdered Michael. Turns out he had had a wife, Beth Grady, but there was almost no mention of her and no photos. I wondered why. I made a mental note to get Derek to find out more about her.

I picked up another clipping; a photo of a group of people outside the courtroom. My eye was drawn to a dark-haired, good-looking man, clean-shaven and hovering on the edge of the picture as if he was waiting for something. I looked more closely. He seemed familiar. I groped around for a pen on my chaotic desk and slowly scribbled in a beard and mustache. I leaned back in my chair, looking at the photo, and put my legs up on my desk. Couldn't be, I thought. I read through the clippings and then found the spot in Terry's book about the first man on the scene being a good friend of Michael's. Only she had used the name Lex. I knew him as Peter. I let the photo drop and looked out the window at a little chickadee that had sought shelter on my window ledge.

I was lost in thought when I heard a female voice outside my door. Before I could get my feet onto the ground, in walked Martha. "How's it going?" she asked as if there was nothing wrong.

"Okay."

"Cordi, you're as transparent as cellophane."

"I just don't like to lose you, that's all."

But it wasn't all. Having to go through finding somebody new was proving more difficult than I thought, and not just because many of the candidates weren't good enough, but because the three of us couldn't agree on any who were. Martha's last day was fast approaching and I was beginning to panic.

Martha moved some file folders off my only chair and changed the subject. "What's the latest on Sally?"

"I talked to Owen and Jason." I brought her up-to-date and then showed her the picture that now sported a beard and mustache.

"Peter," she said. "He's a wily rogue, that guy. Wouldn't surprise me if he killed Terry. He found Michael's body after all."

The newspaper clipping and Terry's book had told about Peter being the first on the scene in glorious, gory detail, but I wasn't sure what Martha thought that had to do with Terry and Sally.

"And why would he kill Terry?" I asked.

"Because she knew about the gyrfalcon eggs."

"What are you talking about, Martha?"

"You said yourself he was up in the Arctic studying gyrfalcons. Their eggs are worth a fortune in Saudi Arabia. What better cover for a poacher than a real ornithologist from Carleton University."

I remembered the paper Peter had been reading on the plane and wondered. Martha's suggestion had made me think twice, and after she left I sat staring at the telephone for a long time before putting a call through to Peter. He wasn't there, but he called me back an hour later and we arranged to meet at his office the next day. I think he said yes more out of curiosity than any interest in Sally, but I may have been wrong. But gyrfalcons? I wasn't so sure about that. I was more sure about his confirmed connection to Terry's innocent murder.

I managed to put the next day to good use, writing up a whole slew of new lab experiments for my animal behaviour course and helping one of my undergrads with some rarefied statistical analysis of his data. Peter had suggested 3:00 as the only time he had free, which was lousy for me because it meant I would be smack in the middle of traffic on the way home.

Carleton University is on the way to the airport. I was lucky to find a parking spot on a little dead end street nearby. It took me ten minutes to wind my way through to the Tory Building. I somehow got turned around and came at it from behind. I didn't actually see it until someone pointed it out to me, because the back side is obscured by a small pine forest. I walked up countless stairs and entered the metallic looking building at the third floor. There was a great mosaic of a fantastical scene that looked like a landscape of silhouetted E.T.s, or maybe iPods.

I walked up to the fourth floor and opened the door to the hall. The absence of any scent at all told me there were no labs on this floor, only offices. All the doors were either bright orange or royal blue, and the floor was tiled in pale yellow punctuated randomly by different sized squares and rectangles of multiple colours. I walked down the hall to Peter's office. Plastered on the door was an enormous poster of a magnificent cliff face with a lone bird circling above. I was looking more closely to see if it was a gyrfalcon when the door suddenly opened and I was face to face with Peter. Except it wasn't Peter. It was the clean-shaven man in the clipping.

I think my mouth was wide open because he looked at me quizzically. "Haven't you seen a man shave his beard before?" he asked, clearly enjoying my discomfiture.

For lack of any other lifeline I offered my hand and he took it. "You look completely different," I said.

"I hope that's a compliment," he replied.

I nodded like an idiot. He led me into his office and waved me to the only other chair in the room. It was a small office, though not as small as mine if you didn't count my equally tiny outer office. I noticed his window looked out over a gravel-laden roof that hid the bottom three quarters of the pine forest from view.

I sat down and waited for him to sit behind a beautiful cherry desk. I was dying to look underneath to see how it was made, but restrained myself admirably.

"People can be fooled so easily by the addition or absence of a beard," I said. He smiled and I went for the jugular. "Isn't that what you did on the ship?"

He stared at me, the smile gone and replaced by — what? A look of determination? Of anger? "What do you mean?"

"You were part of Terry's trial, weren't you? In fact, you were the first on the scene."

He looked at me, unblinking, his face expressionless. I sat and waited.

"So?"

"Terry's book says Michael was a friend of yours, wasn't he?"

Peter said nothing.

"You wanted revenge on Terry, but you didn't know how to make it happen. So you grew your beard and you waited, for years you waited, and when you learned that Terry was going on an Arctic cruise you figured you'd struck gold. You could throw her overboard and no one would know."

I waited for him to say something but he didn't, so I continued. "But you couldn't wait, so you confronted her while she was in the bathtub. You had words and your anger got the best of you. You drowned her and then you had to get rid of her. You carried her out of the suite intending to throw her overboard, but you heard someone coming. You had to act. Carrying a dead naked woman would raise questions. You dumped her in the pool."

"Where's that leave Sally and the suicide note?" he asked.

It was awfully quiet in his office, not even the hum of air conditioning.

"You framed Sally."

"For what?"

"For Terry's murder. You realized what you had done wrong — that the bathtub water was fresh and the pool was salt. That the police would know. You came back and saw Sally trying to rescue Terry, but she failed. You found a note that Sally had written and you placed it where everyone would see it."

"What note could I possibly have found?"

I had been hoping he wouldn't ask this question as it was the only weak point in my scenario. There had to be something I was missing because it all worked, except for the note. I had no idea how he could have got a note written in Sally's handwriting. I was saved from having to answer by his phone, which started ringing. He was on for so long, talking about an order for some sort of software, that I started to get up but he waved a hand at me and I sat back.

"Sorry," he said. "I must say, you have a wild imagination, Cordi." He picked up a file folder and flipped through it without seeing it. "I didn't kill Terry and there are fifteen crew members who will vouch for that. I was on the bridge that night. Why don't you believe the cops? Sally killed Terry and then herself because she was so distraught about Arthur."

I wasn't getting anywhere with this line of thought, and I was a little surprised at myself for having confronted him like that without any evidence. But I was on a roll. I thought about Martha and her theory about poaching gyrfalcon eggs.

"Maybe it had nothing to do with Terry and her trial," I said. "Maybe it had everything to do with gyrfalcon eggs and Terry finding out."

Peter's eyes widened and then he began to laugh. Wrong tactic. Nobody could fake a belly laugh like that, especially when it infected his eyes.

"You do realize, Cordi, that these questions you are asking me are tantamount to harassment?"

I didn't answer, hoping he'd forget what he'd just said.

"I did not murder Terry because she was blackmailing me over the poaching of gyrfalcon eggs. I am not, never have, and never will poach gyrfalcon eggs. Got it?"

I got it. But I still had stuff to ask him and as he began to get out of his chair to escort me out of his life I asked, "Can you tell me anything about Terry's trial? Anything not in the papers?"

He didn't say anything, but sat back down again with a thump.

"Was she guilty?"

The slamming down of the fist on the desk came so fast that I was totally unprepared and airlifted off my seat like a hovercraft. "As far as I'm concerned, and there are lots of people like me, she was guilty as hell."

"Why do you think that?" He looked like a man who had said more than he wanted to.

"No. Sorry. I can't answer any more questions," he said rather too quickly. He pushed back his chair. "If you still think Terry was murdered I'd advise you to stop thinking it was me and look somewhere else."

"Where?"

"There were about eighty tourists on board that ship and a slew of crew," said Peter as he rose from his chair. "Try some of them."

Chapter Twenty-Two

The next two days I had to buckle down and do some work at the university. I was teaching a comparative anatomy lab where the students dissected three different animal species to learn the differences and similarities of their anatomy. It was smelly work because of the formaldehyde, and if you didn't use gloves your hands wrinkled up, but it was satisfying too because it was all so elegant — the way we're all put together, the similar skeletal comparisons, the muscles we have in common with other vertebrates. Of course, we weren't dissecting human cadavers, but the comparisons were there.

Before I knew it, Patrick was coming home. We hadn't talked about his job in any of our phone conversations, but I wasn't going to let that spoil our reunion. I hovered around the arrivals gate like a bird caught in a thermal. Then there he was. I flew into his arms even before he could put his luggage down. It was so good to be hugged, even with his hands full of other stuff, and even with the job hanging over our heads.

Patrick was ravenous so we drove down to the Rover's Return Pub on Richmond and ordered up a mess of food. While we were waiting for it to arrive he told me everything about his trip — except his job. I decided not to point that detail out to him. Instead I told him all about my suspicions concerning Terry's and Sally's deaths and what had happened to me since we last talked. When I was done he looked at me, the worry lines digging into his face.

"So why aren't you being chased anymore?"

"I think that whoever it is has the luxury of biding their time for some reason. So it can't be time sensitive. That explains the perfect failure rate. They're waiting for an opportunity to present itself that will make it look like an accident. But I can't figure out what's driving them."

"So what you're saying is that you don't think they've given up?"

I looked at Patrick and grimaced. "Yeah, I guess."

We sat in silence for a long time before Patrick finally said, "You know, I got a phone call from Duncan the other day."

That wasn't what I was expecting. "In London?" I asked, surprised.

He nodded. "He and Martha are really worried about you. So am I."

"Is this all about my near misses, because if it is …"

"No, it's not. At least, not directly. I think we all believe something happened to you here and on the ship." I could hear the "but" lurking in his voice.

"You had a bad winter last year, Cordi. Martha says there were a bunch of days when she had to cover for you. She almost ran out of excuses."

"I was sick." I paused. "The university has a good sick leave policy. I just took advantage of it. There just weren't quite enough days to cover me completely," I finished in a voice that signalled the end of the conversation.

But Patrick barrelled on anyway. "I just thought it was the flu or a cold and you told me to stay away so I wouldn't catch it — you were very persuasive. I came anyway, but you were somewhere I couldn't go. You don't want to go through another winter like that."

I had to laugh. Not because the things he was saying weren't true, because they were. It was because I felt on top of the world and light years from feeling depressed. But if I was really truthful with myself it was because I was afraid to go and get help. Go figure. I wimped out and changed the subject. I'm very good at that. "Arthur is an actor too."

By the look on Patrick's face he wasn't too keen on changing the subject, but I told him what Arthur had said.

"Sally sounds like a woman who took her job too seriously," was all he said, and then added, "How long had the writing group been meeting?"

"Martha says about eight weeks."

"I presume she was acting her part at all the writing lessons and not just on board the ship?"

"Yes. Otherwise the writing group would have thought she had a split personality, shy and meek on the boat, outgoing and vivacious in Ottawa."

"Does it take that long to be recalled for an audition? Eight weeks?"

I stared at Patrick and tried not to look shocked. I was annoyed that I hadn't seen it. How had I missed it? Arthur had even alluded to it. I nodded slowly, pretending to look wise. "She lied to him. It wasn't a recall audition at all," I finally said.

"Either that, or he lied to you."

Lots of people seemed to be lying. I chewed that over for a minute and then told him about what Jason had told me.

"So Owen is a ghostwriter. How odd is that?" he said.

"It's what he said about Michael not being the only one that sent shivers down my spine."

"Did he mean she's killed others in her sleep?"

"No. He didn't say that, but he intimated that there were others."

"Did he offer any proof?"

"No. Nothing."

"So maybe he doesn't know what he's talking about."

"But where would he come up with that kind of statement? It wouldn't just crop up out of thin air. Something had to trigger it."

"Maybe he just couldn't stand Terry and is spreading malicious gossip."

We sat in companionable silence for a while, eating our fish and chips. I took a sip of the Keith's beer I'd ordered and broke the silence. "There's something weird about the whole thing."

Patrick raised his marvelous eyebrows at me.

"Four people on that ship had something to do with Terry's trial. Owen is her brother, LuEllen was a juror until her timely accident, and Peter found Michael."

"That's only three."

"Terry."

"Too much of a coincidence?"

"Maybe not. Terry and Owen travelled everywhere together, and Peter had been hired to work on the ship as a naturalist ornithologist, so that just leaves the coincidence of LuEllen ending up on the same ship as the others."

"Said that way, it's feasible."

"But they all have good reasons for wanting Terry dead. She murdered Peter's best friend. LuEllen nearly died, maybe because she was on the jury; she thinks someone pushed her. And Owen? Jason says they were fighting over their parents' estate, although Owen says he stood to gain nothing from Terry's death, so someone's lying."

"Where does Jason fit into all this?"

"He's colour-blind and Terry knew."

Patrick choked on a piece of fish.

"Colour-blind? Shit. He could be lying over the parents' estate to take the heat off him."

"But why lie? It's so easy to check that," I said, thinking of Derek.

"Well, one of them is lying," said Patrick.

I made a mental note to ask Derek.

"And then there's Elizabeth." I sighed. "She has no connection to the trial as far as I can find, but she's a flight instructor and she has epilepsy. And Terry might have known."

"So any of them could have done it?"

"Looks that way."

We lapsed into silence and when I next looked up he was looking at me with such sadness in his eyes. I could sense a farewell coming. "I'm sorry, Cordi. I have to take the job. They offered it to me today and it's a big step up for me. I leave a week Thursday." He looked as miserable as I felt. He reached out and took my hand.

I didn't trust my voice so I just nodded. It was a big step up for him.

"You can come over and visit and I'll come back as often as I can."

"For how long?"

"For how long what?"

"For how long could we keep that up?"

We looked at each other and I wondered how two people in love can unintentionally hurt each other so much.

"Come with me then," he said softly.

"My job," I said. His job. Our jobs. It didn't seem right that a job could ever dent something as amazing as love. But it could. And it did.

The week passed quickly despite my battered heart. I was skimming through the newspapers again looking for something, anything at all, to distract me when I came across the article about Michael and his wife. I picked up the phone and called Derek. His secretary put me on hold for a long time and I almost hung up.

When he finally picked up the phone and heard who was calling we chit-chatted for a bit, then I asked him to look into Owen and the fight over the family estate.

"Don't need to," he said. "There was mention of it at the time Terry died. There was no fight that I know of. Just the usual red tape that goes along with family inheritances — probating the will, paying off debts, that sort of thing."

"Did Terry leave it all to her brother?"

"I'd have to look into that, but if there was no will and he's her only relative it would all go to him."

I thanked him and then said, "Did you find out anything about Michael Grady's wife, Beth Grady?"

"You mean Elizabeth Goodal?"

My heart stopped for a moment.

"You still there?" Derek asked.

I managed to get out the words "Go on," as my mind whirled around in circles like a dog chasing its tail.

The card on the plane, signed by M — Michael.

"She wasn't with him on the trip when he died. She kept a very low profile at the trial — as in zero. She didn't attend. Wouldn't talk to the press. Just holed up in her house until it was all over. Then she took back her maiden name and moved to a small condo in downtown Ottawa."

I rang off and hunted around for Elizabeth's number. She didn't answer, but someone else did; she told me to just drop on by when she heard I was a friend of Elizabeth's. I struggled over whether I should take this stranger's advice and just show up. Elizabeth had come across as being quite a formal kind of person and she was likely to be very chilly over the fact that I had informed the authorities about her epilepsy. But how could I not? I still felt badly — it was her career after all.

It didn't take too long for me to make up my mind. Too many unanswered questions and my curiosity was killing me. Now five people aboard that ship had something to do with Michael and Terry.

Elizabeth lived in a condo right on Prince Arthur, where it overlooked the canal. Her place was in the basement, next to the laundry room, and I wondered how she had afforded the cruise if this is where she had to live. I double-checked the number and then rapped quickly before I could back out.

The door was flung open by a big, bouncy teenaged redhead with an enormous smile that was contagious. I introduced myself and she yelled back into the room, "Mum! She's here." She enlarged her smile and said, "She'll be right out. I have to go. See ya." And I was left standing alone in the doorway of a woman I wasn't sure would want to see me, especially after what I had to say.

Eventually she did come, but not before I'd thought about leaving a dozen times. She looked at me the way a stranger would and then slowly it dawned on her that she knew me.

"Hello," she said. "Cody is it?"

"Cordi." She nodded coldly and waited for me to say something. I blurted it out like a six-year-old who couldn't wait to tell a secret. "I wanted to talk to you about your late husband, Michael Grady."

She didn't look stunned. She didn't even look surprised. She just looked resigned. "Haven't you done enough damage already?"

But she asked me in and led me down a nondescript, narrow hallway and out into a brightly lit room overlooking the Rideau Canal. But it wasn't the canal or the spectacular view that stunned me, it was what was in the room. Birdhouses, birdhouse wallpaper, birds swooping from the ceiling on gossamer strands, glass birds, porcelain birds, straw birds, plastic birds, bejewelled birds, wire birds, terra cotta birds, bronze birds, cloth birds, leather birds, wooden birds, matchstick birds, pewter birds, all adorning every available surface and space on the walls.

I tried not to stare with my mouth open, but it was very hard and I don't think I succeeded because I could see she was enjoying my astonishment. But she didn't say anything, just sat down in a plush birdie covered chair and indicated that I should sit on the sofa littered with pillows covered in birds. I'll say one thing for her: not a single bird, painting, pillow, or sculpture was kitsch. They were all tasteful works of art. So much for being poor, I thought, as I spied what looked like an original Bateman of a raven looking particularly miserable in a forest. She asked me if I would like some lemonade and I almost said no, but the way she said it made me feel that it was somehow important for her to do something so I said yes.

While she disappeared into the kitchen I looked around some more. It wasn't all birds — there were two bookend giraffes standing on a side table with a single volume of *Birds of the World*. And the table that separated me from a huge comfy chair that was obviously the one she used was covered in rags and newspapers and a tin of Brasso. When I looked closely I saw there was a tiny burnished bronze elephant that shone with such warmth that it almost seemed alive. It was gleaming from its recent polishing, but the broken tusk left no doubt as to where I'd seen it before. Had she taken it from Terry's room? And if so, why? As I reached out to pick it up she came into the room with a tray and two tall glasses of pink lemonade. I had never understood the pink part of lemonade. Lemons are yellow.

She looked at me, her gaze unflinching, and I got the impression that she wanted me to ask the right questions so she could control the answers. But I was wrong. She took the offensive. "How did you find out he was my husband?" Her voice was calm and almost matter of fact.

"The newspapers …"

"Never used my maiden name."

"I did some searching. It's not too difficult tracking a person if you know where to look. You leave a trail." It wasn't really a lie. After all, I had tracked down Derek, which was the first step, and that hadn't been too difficult.

She placed the tray down on the table in front of me and then sat in the comfy chair. She hadn't taken her eyes off me since entering the living room. It made me feel like a cat on the prowl, and I guess I was because I went for the jugular. "Why were so many people associated with your husband's trial all in the same writing group?"

She was unprepared for that and she reached over and picked up the little elephant, stroking it with her fingers.

"Peter. LuEllen. Terry. Owen. You," I said. "All together on a cruise ship."

"How much do you know?"

"I know that Peter found Michael and was his best friend. I know that LuEllen was a juror who had a rather timely accident. And I know that Terry and Owen were siblings."

"I see," she said and gave me nothing more.

I decided to wait her out. I could hear her kitchen clock thumping through the seconds and somewhere on Prince Arthur a motorcycle was exploring the speed of sound. I saw a magnificent blue jay swoop down to the birdfeeder outside her window, scaring the little warblers away. I started checking out the various bird mobiles hanging from the ceiling and was just switching to the rather lovely wallpaper liner when she leaned forward, replaced the elephant on the table, and finally spoke. "Michael and I had been married ten years when he met Terry."

Her voice was noncommittal, but I wondered what it had to do with my statement. I decided to go with the flow.

"She was teaching a creative writing course and Michael had always dreamed of becoming a writer, so he took the course and he wrote a novel."

"Was it good?" I asked.

She looked right through me and I almost turned to look behind myself. "I don't know. I know he was hugely excited about it, but he never let me read his stuff, not until it was finished. It was all handwritten — he said he loved the heft of the pen and the scratchy sound of the ink staining the paper with his thoughts. I thought he was nuts to have only one copy. But, of course, he let Terry read it. He said she was going to help him get it published."

"What happened to it?"

"I'm not sure. I never found it among his belongings."

"How did the two of them wind up in the same campground when the murder took place?"

"I'm sure you've read the book, but Terry was scavenging around for ideas — she wasn't a well-known author back then — and Michael had told her that he and a group of zoology students were going to set up camp for thirty days and study a range of topics that I don't remember — obviously one of them was birds. Anyway, she somehow managed to wrangle an invitation from him. He wasn't too happy about it, but she had told him she would send his manuscript to an agent and he was gaga over that." She reached for her lemonade, which by now had lost its sweat and ice to the warmth in the room. "That's where she murdered him."

The word murder made me look at her. That and the venom in her voice. "She was acquitted," I said.

"She was brilliant. The sleepwalking defence was sheer genius. The perfect murder. Kill someone in your sleep, plead guilty to the murder, and then use a sleepwalking defence."

"So you think she acted out the whole thing?"

"I don't think, I know."

"You have proof?"

She glared at me. "I don't need proof. I just know."

She had picked up the little elephant again and was rubbing it back and forth in her fingers. I nodded at it and said, "I saw one just like that in Terry's room the night after she died."

Elizabeth stopped rubbing the little elephant and held it between her thumb and forefinger.

"Martha and I bumped into you in the hallway that night. Is that what you were doing? Stealing it?"

Her eyes flashed. "It wasn't hers, it was Michael's.

He kept it as a sort of talisman. Took it with him wherever he went. It went missing the night he died. I was just reclaiming what was rightfully mine." She carefully put the little elephant in her pocket, but left her hand there as if reluctant to part from it.

"You're saying that Terry stole it?"

"That's exactly what I'm saying."

"But why?"

"Because she murdered him and wanted a memento, or she murdered him and just liked the elephant. I don't know why. What does it matter? She did it."

"It matters to you," I said quietly.

She exploded out of her chair so quickly I dropped my empty lemonade glass. "Of course it matters to me. The bitch murders my husband and gets off scot-free? How would you feel?"

"Angry enough to murder?"

Her icy look told me I was making no friends here and she didn't sit down, signalling the end of the conversation.

But I still had my first unanswered question searching for an answer. I still wanted to know why so many people from the trial had inexplicably taken up creative writing as taught by Terry. I asked her again but she was having none of it.

She waited for me to extricate myself from the sofa, then escorted me to the door. I guess she had second thoughts, or didn't want to be rude and not answer my question because she said, "You'd have to ask them why they took her course."

Nothing like passing the buck.

"And by the way, your nice little phone call has me grounded unless a doctor will give me the all clear." And with that she quietly closed the door in my face.

Chapter Twenty-Three

By the time I got back to work I was busting a gut to talk to Martha and get her ideas on what I had learned. I raced into my office but she wasn't there. I went in search of her in my labs and those of the other two profs. She wasn't anywhere. Then I remembered — she was working full-time for Dean for a week trial period, her decision not his. Dean had hired a temp for us. I debated precisely two seconds about interrupting her in the rarefied environment of the Dean's office and then zoomed down the three flights to his floor. His office was huge and I found Martha pulling files, presumably in preparation for one of his classes.

When she saw me she grinned and started to say "Hi, Cor …" when she suddenly stopped and looked quickly over to the door leading to Dean Dean's office and lowered her voice. "Boss likes it quiet."

I looked at Martha in surprise. How the hell was she

ever supposed to keep quiet? Instead of asking her I said, "Where's your milking stool?"

Again, she looked over at Dean's door and whispered, "He doesn't like it. Says it's very unsophisticated."

I noticed she wasn't looking at me when she talked, which is totally unlike Martha. "You okay here?" I asked.

"Yeah, sure," she said without much enthusiasm, which for Martha was difficult to do.

"Can we talk?"

I could tell she was torn. Her face was having a roller coaster ride with her emotions.

"About the murders?" I said.

Her face brightened and then fell flat.

"Look, this is obviously not a good time. Come up when you have a free moment." She grimaced and I said, "Oh, come on, you must get free time?"

"Not like you guys give me," she said. "And I have to ask permission to leave. I'll come up as soon as I can."

The door to Dean's office opened and he came out and said, "What's all the talking out here? I can't get anything done."

He stopped when he saw me. "Cordi, hello." He didn't wait for me to answer. "If you don't mind, I need Martha to be doing her job and you are obviously a distraction. If you have obtained whatever you needed from her I would appreciate it if you let her get on with her work."

Martha made a face at me from behind his back and I smiled at Dean and said, "I was just getting some invaluable advice from her. I'm sure you don't mind her helping out an old friend."

I waved at both of them and left the office, feeling as though I had just been bitten. I didn't know Dean well enough to know if this was his normal behaviour or the behaviour of a person worried about losing a new employee back to an assistant professor before he'd even hired her.

I went back to my office and killed a couple of hours working on a research project, then made another appointment to see Tracey. Judging from her behaviour she was hiding something and I wanted to know what it was. How I was going to do that I didn't know, but it would come when I needed it.

It was after 4:00 when Martha finally appeared, looking tired and harried. She plunked down in my chair and we eyed each other in silence.

"It's a promotion," she said uncertainly.

"Yup."

"He's just a little eccentric."

"Yup."

"It'll get better."

I didn't answer and she looked away.

"Elizabeth is Michael's wife." I threw it at her like a curve ball — to get her attention — and it worked.

She jerked her head back and stared at me. "That's an awful lot of people in the writing course or on the ship who had something to do with Terry's sleepwalking murder."

"Exactly what I thought."

"What did she say when you asked her about it?"

"She clammed up."

I told Martha all I had learned since we last talked.

"So they all have motives."

"That's right. LuEllen was nearly killed and badly disfigured, so you could imagine her anger and need for revenge; Elizabeth lost a husband she loved dearly; and Peter lost a best friend. Owen potentially stands to gain from his sister's death. Who have I missed of the writing group?"

"Tracey. She was so humiliated by Terry that either she or her firecracker husband killed Terry out of fury."

"Yeah, that's possible, but not likely. I mean, who kills over a bunch of lousy writing?"

"I don't know. Humiliation is a pretty strong emotion. And her husband said her writing was supremely important to her. She's also the only one of the writing group with no known connection to Michael's murder. Besides Sally."

"And Peter and Jason are the only ones who are not part of the writing group but have reason to have killed her."

"What about me and Duncan? We're part of the writer's group."

I looked at her and laughed. "Friendship has its perks," I whispered. "You are not official suspects."

"Official?"

"Oh for heaven's sake, you know what I mean."

"Well that leaves only four — LuEllen, Elizabeth, Tracey, and Owen — who were part of the writing group in some capacity and who were on board."

"Exactly. I think you should get them all together for a meeting on the pretense of having a little bit of a reunion. All the members of the writing group, plus

Peter, Jason, and Sandy. I don't think we have any other suspects, do we?"

"What about Arthur?"

"Right. Arthur. He seems genuinely to have been in love with Sally so murdering her seems unrealistic. And he has no connection to the trial. He doesn't seem to have a motive that I can see."

Martha was looking at me in a strange way.

"What?" I asked.

"I should call it?" said Martha, my comment suddenly sinking in.

"It's only logical. You're a member of the writing group."

"And you were on the ship."

"Aw, but you were both."

"But my apartment is too small." She had a point, but maybe being in close quarters would loosen people up.

"No one will drive all the way out to my place."

I could tell that she thought I had a point. "Alright. I'll call and set it up for Wednesday after work." She made a face that left me in no doubt that she really didn't want to do this. "What're you hoping will happen at this meeting, Cordi?"

"Oh, I don't know. Maybe we'll catch us a murderer."

After Martha left I looked through the second box that Derek had sent. Half an hour later I came across a clipping about Terry Ballantyne and a Heather Dunne McNeil. I studied the picture of the woman whose middle name was the same as Tracey's. They didn't look at all alike and I wondered how they were related. Heather had been killed in a speedboat accident. The driver had been Terry.

∞∞∞∞∞∞∞∞∞∞

Two days later I found myself standing in front of a small, pale green bungalow with pale yellow shutters and some straggly cedar trees rounded to look like cones. Tracey had told me that George would be at work, but I still glanced around nervously as I walked up the front walk. The door was shiny jet-black with a big brass knocker. I raised it and let it thud onto the metal thud maker then listened as the sound reverberated around the neighbourhood.

Tracey opened the door just as I was beginning to feel impatient. She was wearing a bilious green sweater that made her look quite sickly. She asked me in and then took me through a dark living room furnished, as far as I could tell, with navy blue and black furniture, to a little sunroom off the back of the house. Compared to the darkness of the rest of the house this little room felt like a floodlight. It was pretty nondescript, with a green plastic table and four molded plastic chairs in matching colours.

She offered me some water and while she was getting it I prowled around. There wasn't much there, just a bookshelf with a few photos on it. I went to take a closer look. There were a couple of George, and of George and Tracey, and there was one of a younger Tracey with Heather. I picked it up to look more closely and nearly jumped a mile when I heard Tracey say, in a quiet, gentle voice, "Please put it down."

I felt embarrassed, quickly replaced it and muttered sorry. She handed me my glass of water and then we both sat at opposite ends of the little table.

"How were you and Heather related?" I asked.

She looked at me over the rim of her glass and sighed. "We were sisters."

"I'm sorry about the accident," I mumbled. What else do you say in answer to that?

"They were drunk. Roaring down the canal. Didn't even see her in her little scull. At least, that's what the police said."

"Terry was on board wasn't she? In fact, wasn't she driving?"

She gazed out the window at the little garden out back and nodded, as if in a dream. "Everybody said what a horrible accident it was."

I took advantage of that and said, "But you never believed that, did you?"

She refocused her eyes on me and for a moment didn't seem to register who I was. When she did her eyes widened. "Please don't tell George. He'll be so mad that I've spoken to you."

"Why did you take her course?"

Tracey looked at me and then looked down at her shoes.

"You must have been very angry at Terry."

Tracey looked up at me again, her face suffused with anger. "There isn't a word for what I felt about her." She hesitated, fighting some inner demons. "I could have killed her," she said suddenly and then clamped her hand over her mouth. "But I didn't. I didn't kill her."

∞∞∞∞∞∞∞∞∞∞∞

When I drove home after work the lazy summer sun was burnishing the surface of the Ottawa River. When I turned down our road I could see the rows of August-tall corn. Ryan and I used to play hide-and-seek in there when we were kids. It was like our very own private *Jack and the Beanstalk*, the dark green corn stalks towering over our heads, blocking out the sun as we ran and ran and ran. The first time we ever did it we got lost and Dad had to yell us out by letting us follow his voice. After that he taught us about the direction of the sun. But we still got lost lots of times because the cornrows are so close together.

The red light was on over the barn so I continued on to my place. The workmen had made a lot of progress and as I walked inside the acrid smell of smoke had receded to just a whiff. I'd be able to move back in soon.

I walked out onto my front porch and stared out at the fields of corn and at the cows grazing in nearby fields. It felt good to live here. I didn't want to go to England. I belonged here. I sat down on my porch chair and must have fallen asleep because the next thing I knew it was dark and something was rubbing against my leg. I sat up suddenly and Paulie bolted, but not completely. She stopped at the top of the stairs and looked back at me.

"Hey ya, Paulie," I said, reaching out my hand. The cat stared at me and I reached out for her, a tableau of indecision and hope, and the hope won. Paulie slowly and carefully retraced her steps until her head was just under my hand. She reached up and butted my palm. I began to scratch her ears.

"Friends?" I asked and she answered with a purr. I left her shortly after and headed back to Ryan's. I was going to be happy to be back in my own place. As much as Ryan and his family mean to me I missed my own home. When I walked into the house there was no sign of Rose or the kids. I had just gone into the kitchen and got myself a glass of wine when the phone rang. I debated answering but finally did because it might be for me. It was.

"Hey, Cordi," said Patrick, his voice sounding strained. "How are you doing?"

Since I wasn't doing very well at all as far as he was concerned I just mumbled a "Hi."

"No one stalking you?" He forced out a laugh but it didn't work.

I replied bitterly, "No."

There was a pause and then he said, "I leave in four days. What about dinner tonight, tomorrow, and the night I leave?" We'd both been too busy to get together, but it was more than that, of course.

I said yes, but I wasn't looking forward to any of the dinners, not because I didn't love him but because I did. I'd already started to distance myself, out of an instinct for survival.

"What about tonight? Can you drive in, sleep over?"

I thought about it. I was really tempted, but Rose might need some help with the kids and Mac with the milking so I told him that. Pretty lame excuse since Ryan was pretty much up to par and Rose didn't really need my help with the kids. He wasn't very happy with it, but neither was I. After I hung up I had second thoughts and called him to say I'd be there in a couple of hours.

Chapter Twenty-Four

We ate a candlelit dinner with scalloped potatoes swimming in garlic and cream, Portobello mushrooms, and baked Atlantic salmon that Patrick had made. We toasted each other and he caught me up and we kissed inside the moonbeam that splashed across his floor. It felt like I was caught in a raging river, my senses magnified to catch every sound, every touch, every taste, every sight. His hand on my skin made my body feel feverish and my mind go to mush as we intertwined like honeysuckle and bindweed, lost in the beauty and the rhythm of love.

I hardly slept at all that night, thinking about him as he lay beside me, thinking about us, about the Atlantic Ocean and how big it is. The next morning Patrick was fast asleep when I had to leave, so I gave him a kiss on the nose and left a note on the kitchen table. When I got into work I caught sight of Martha as she scurried down the hall and almost yelled out to her, but the fact that she was scurrying made me stop. She never scurried. At lunch she dropped in to tell me that she had tracked everybody down and most of them were able to come. She was flustered because she wasn't going to have time to buy drinks and snacks, and could I do it for her? I told Martha that she could leave everything up to me and she turned to leave.

"You okay?" I asked, but she was gone before she could hear my question.

My graduate student and I spent the afternoon going over his thesis to see what he still needed to do before he had to defend it. I remembered my own defence — four male professors peppering me with questions. After it was over I was sure they had spent hours coming up with the most difficult ones they could find. I had come out feeling sure I'd flunked. But I'd passed with much praise. It made me realize that just because you believe something bad is going to happen that doesn't make it so. But it was unnerving to be so sure — I mean, where did that come from? As I said: unnerving.

I left work in plenty of time to get the food and drinks, sit in rush hour traffic, and get to Martha's twenty minutes before the writing group. I was getting nervous about how I was going to handle my questions and I sat in the car outside for five minutes, pulling myself together. I managed to juggle all the groceries and drinks so that I could take them all in one trip, except that I forgot about the door into the apartment building. I waited a bit, hoping someone would come and was just starting to bend down to put some of the groceries on the walkway when a man's voice said, "Here, I'll get the door for you."

I couldn't look over the paper grocery bags to see who it was but I was thankful. I felt my way up the step and through the door with my feet, while trying to pinpoint the voice, which was familiar.

"Taking the elevator?"

I mumbled "Yes," and he asked me if he could take some of my groceries. I wasn't so keen on giving them up to a strange man, especially a strange man I couldn't see, but as I shifted them in my arms one of them slipped and the stranger grabbed it before it hit the floor. At that moment I could see who it was: Jason. He broke out into a nice smile and said, "Cordi, how nice to see you."

I smiled back as we stepped into the elevator and he pressed twelve. By the time we got to Martha's apartment Jason miraculously had both shopping bags and the case of pop, and he made them look about as big as pincushions. I rapped on Martha's door and waited. And waited. We looked at each other and I rapped again. No answer.

"She must be stuck in traffic," I said.

Jason put down the groceries and we stood awkwardly in the hall until I said, "What exactly did you mean when you said there had been others; that Michael wasn't the only one?"

Jason sucked on his lip and stared at me.

I stared back.

"Just little things that only a lover would understand. Sometimes she'd be distraught for days on end for no apparent reason, and other times I'd catch her poring over the newspapers as if her life depended on it."

"Are you talking about Heather?" I asked.

"You know about her? Terry swore it was an accident, that the wheel had jerked suddenly and the boat had mowed Heather down. Owen said so too. I was there as well, but I didn't see anything until it was all over. But she was hiding something from me. I know that it had to do with Heather."

"What do you think happened?"

"I don't know, but I got the feeling there was more to Heather's death than Terry was letting on."

We were interrupted as first LuEllen, then Tracey and George (who hadn't been invited), Elizabeth, Sandy, and Peter all arrived. Arthur and Owen had had to beg off, but I'd follow up with them later.

By the time Martha arrived everyone was sitting on the floor nursing a beer and talking about all the good times on the ship. I had to endure joke after joke about being seasick and telling everyone that someone was out to kill me.

I was more than a little relieved to see Martha. I hadn't wanted to start asking questions in the hallway. We all trooped into her little apartment, which had been transformed into an apartment full of chairs and one sofa. There wasn't room for anything else and everyone stood awkwardly on the threshold wondering what to do. Martha made a big show about getting everyone to sit down and after some fairly complicated gymnastics everyone finally found a seat.

When I figured everyone was settled I moved to a position where I could see all of them and called their attention to me. I could tell by the way they looked at me that they were expecting a little speech about the trip, and maybe a tribute of some kind to Sally and Terry. But that's not what they got. Instead they got this:

"Arthur and Sandy tell me Sally was pretending to be someone she wasn't. I want to know why."

I looked at all their faces. No one said anything but there were a few shakes of the head.

"Cordi, where do you come up with these scenarios?" asked Elizabeth.

"The same place you do."

She looked confused. "Meaning what?" she asked.

"Meaning you've all been lying about something and I want to know what it is."

No one spoke. I tried again. "LuEllen." She jumped at her name. "Elizabeth." She looked straight at me. "Tracey." She avoided my gaze. "Peter." He tilted his head. "Jason." He returned my stare. "Owen and Arthur. Three of you are members of the writing club. At least five of you are connected to Michael's death in one way or another. And at least two of you are connected to the death of a woman on the Rideau Canal. Both deaths are connected to Terry. Coincidence? I don't think so. So what are you all hiding?"

Still no one spoke.

"I don't know what you were up to, but I believe Sally was an innocent woman and I don't think she deserves to go down in history as Terry's murderer." I stopped speaking and let the silence pull them out of their guilt.

Tracey was the first to break. "She was a monster!" she blurted. George tried to stop her but she shrugged him off and the surprised look on his face was comical. "She killed Heather in cold blood. Planned it perfectly."

"There's no proof of that," I said.

"Of course not. She was too good. She planned the perfect murders. Turned the steering wheel at the last moment, that's what I think. And my sister had been so excited because Terry was sure her book was going to be a bestseller."

"Heather was a writer?" I asked, surprised.

Tracey looked at me and then at the others as if looking for help. She bit her lip. "Yes."

It hit me as if I'd been punched in my neurons. "So she was working on a manuscript at the time of her death?"

"Yes."

"Was it good?"

"I don't know. I never had the chance to read it. Not that I could have. It was all handwritten and her handwriting was really bad. She was very private about her writing."

I looked over at Elizabeth and caught her eye. "Isn't that what Michael was like?

She nodded.

"Three manuscripts: Heather's, Michael's, and now Sally's, all handwritten by shy writers who happened to die either by Terry's hand or in her vicinity."

"Sally wasn't a recluse or a writer, she was just acting a part. But she wouldn't tell me why," said Sandy. "And she would never have handwritten a manuscript, so what the hell is going on?"

But I already knew. I looked around at the other faces. Most of them weren't looking at me. They were looking anywhere else. "Terry stole Michael and Heather's books."

You could have heard a dust mote fall. I looked around at my audience. Only a few people looked

stunned at my revelation. The rest shifted their eyes
downward in a gesture that unmistakably said, "We
already knew."

"She was stalking vulnerable writers and then murdering them for their books. Sally, Heather, and how
many others?" I raised my voice. "And what about
Sally? Why was she acting a part?"

I let the silence drag on forever, trying to goad someone into talking.

It worked. "We had a plan to take Terry down."
Elizabeth's quiet voice cut through the silence like a deafening gong. "She was out of control. Killing for the sake
of a book. We had no proof. That's what Sally was going
to get for us. It had to stop."

"So you hired her to play the part of a vulnerable
writer."

"We had to catch Terry red-handed. It was the only
way. Sally was our eyes and ears. We knew we'd hooked
Terry when, weeks before the cruise, Sally told us that
Terry was interested in her book and wanted to help her
sell it. She just had to promise to keep quiet about it and
not let anyone read it. She said someone could steal it
that way. So Sally went along with it."

"And it killed her," I said.

In the silence that followed I could hear the thud
shunt of the elevator. I was about to say something else
when Sandy broke in. "Did Sally know?" Her voice
wobbled on all three words as she directed her question
at Elizabeth.

"Know what?"

"That you were using her to nail the murderer?"

Elizabeth had the grace to look away as she shook her head and I noticed Tracey, LuEllen, and Peter were all looking away too.

"I think she suspected something near the end," said Elizabeth and her voice trailed off.

"You killed her," said Sandy in a quiet, dangerous voice.

"You have to believe us. It was never meant to happen," said Elizabeth.

"So you set Terry up. You set your trap and you waited for Terry to fall for it," I said.

Tracey began to cry. The others shuffled uncomfortably, but LuEllen stepped up to the plate. "Sally was never meant to die. We had a schedule. One of us followed her everywhere."

"Except that night."

"Except that night. She snuck out of her room and by the time we found her she was dead."

"We just wanted to catch Terry in the act," said Elizabeth. "We planned to stop her before she killed. We thought we'd thought of every possible scenario and we could protect her." She paused and I suddenly thought of the asinine question she had asked me that day on the ship. "It was a good plan," she continued, "and Sally was playing her part beautifully."

I marvelled at how the human mind could be so convoluted; all of this horror created by a need for revenge. They seemed such ordinary people, pushed over the brink by uncontrolled emotions.

"But why would a writer want to steal from another writer?" asked George.

"Because she couldn't write," I said.

Elizabeth shook her head. "But the lecture on the ship where she crucified Tracey's writing. She made it a lot better."

"But that's different," said Martha. "Lots of teachers are good at fixing a manuscript, but when it comes to writing a full length book of their own they just can't do it. Either they can't do dialogue, or they can't do prose, or they have no stamina, or their plots stink." She smiled at me as if to say, "See, I know more about this than you think."

"Okay," I said. "So Terry had to use Owen as her ghostwriter for her first non-fiction book. My bet is that when she remembered Michael's manuscript she decided to make use of it, since he was dead and Owen couldn't write fiction. After that she had to keep looking for more victims."

"She's only written two works of fiction and one non-fiction book in seven years," said LuEllen.

Which meant she'd had trouble finding her victims — unless she used a pseudonym. The thought made me shiver. I wished Owen was here. He'd be able to confirm all this.

"What about Sally's manuscript? Where did it come from?" I asked.

"We had her copy out a well-written, obscure book that Terry wouldn't recognize."

"Just like Michael and Heather — handwritten. How the hell did Terry find two dinosaurs who were good writers?"

"As Martha said, she could turn a lousy manuscript into something good, she only needed to find authors who hated to create by computer — there's lots of those around still."

"Why didn't Terry recognize you all?"

"She never saw LuEllen after the accident. I never attended Michael's trial and kept out of the newspapers as much as I could," said Elizabeth.

I looked at Tracey. She looked scared and George stepped in for her. "Tracey had a medical illness during the trial and never crossed paths with Terry." Then added, somewhat defensively, "Tracey's parents were there."

I looked at Peter and then realized I already knew the answer. He was a completely different man with a beard.

"And Heather? How did you find out about Heather?" I asked.

"We kept track of Terry," said Peter. "And when we found out about the boating accident we hired a private investigator who led us to Tracey. When we learned Heather was a writer and had been taking a course from Terry we began putting the pieces together. It just seemed like too much of a coincidence that one woman could end up being involved in the deaths of two people who happened to be her students. Three now, counting Sally."

"But she didn't murder Sally," I interrupted, deciding to put the record straight.

"That's not true. Sally could easily have been drowned by Terry, but someone saw and went to her cabin to argue it out," Peter said, staring at Jason. "Whoever did it drowned her in the tub and then dumped her body in the pool with Sally, hoping everyone would believe one had drowned trying to save the other. They obviously didn't know the pool was salt water."

As I digested this new bit of information Peter continued, "And imagine having the good fortune to have the only juror on your trial who's holding out for a guilty verdict mysteriously fall down a concrete staircase. It was all just too suspicious."

"And then she killed Sally to get sole possession of her book and made it look like suicide by forging a note." I didn't feel like pointing out that the note had not been forged. "Which begs the same old question: who killed Terry?"

I scanned their faces looking for, what? Guilt? It was there in spades. How could it not be when they had sent an innocent woman to her death with their harebrained plan? But I was looking for something more. "Every single one of you had a good reason for wanting Terry dead. Elizabeth, Tracey, and Peter wanted revenge for a lost lover, sister, and friend; LuEllen for what was done to her in Terry's name; Owen for Terry's share of their parents' estate; and Arthur because he was still in love with Sally and wanted revenge. Jason wanted her dead because she knew about his being colour-blind, an affliction that would end his career as a captain."

I looked at their blank faces as they all just stared at me. No denials, no admissions of guilt, no nothing. It was very unnerving.

My evening with Patrick went by in a whirl. We'd promised each other that we wouldn't talk business or London or anything ugly, so things had been good between us. He wanted me to stay the night but I didn't want to

— it was just too painful and, truth be told, I really had started to distance myself from him and I think he could feel it. Before I left he couldn't not ask me about the murder case, so I told him everything.

"So let me get this straight," he said when I'd finished. "Terry faked it and murdered Michael in cold blood for a non-fiction bestseller and then for his book."

I nodded. "Or she really did murder him while sleepwalking and then took advantage of the fallout. She gets a non-fiction bestseller out of the ordeal, hoodwinks her brother into ghostwriting it, and gets a bonus murder mystery. Perfect."

"Then, once she makes a name for herself she realizes she can't write the books so she stalks and kills Heather to get her next fix," said Patrick. "What about Owen? Was he simply blind to all this or did he help her? Do you think he knows?"

I told him what Duncan had said about Owen being a doormat. "I think Owen just blindly does what his sister tells him."

"Would that include murder?"

I shook my head, but it did make me wonder. "And then Terry falls for Sally. She could have killed Sally before being drowned herself." I told him about Peter's theory

We went over some more details and then I left him standing on the threshold hoping I'd change my mind. But I didn't. The instinct for self-preservation; that's all it was.

I left for work early the next morning and got in before anyone was around. I worked for a couple of hours and then at 9:00 I picked up my list of people to call. Owen was at the top. Shit. He was so hard to talk to and I had no idea how much he did or did not know, but I needed to find out whether Terry had used a pseudonym and whether Owen knew anything about his sister's double life. I'd have to be careful though. He was her brother, after all. He might not take too kindly to my questions.

I phoned him anyway and told him what I wanted to talk to him about.

"Terry?" he said, the exasperation in his voice travelling down the wires. "We've been through all that."

"I just need to ask...." I said.

"Look. You've caught me at a bad time."

"When would be a good time?"

"Next year?"

There was a long silence, which I succeeded in not breaking.

"Look, I'm taking up a couple from New Jersey this evening. There's room for you. We can talk while they ooh and ahh over the beauty of the Outaouais."

I was totally at a loss as to what the hell he was talking about. Where was up? "I'm not sure I follow you. Where are you taking this couple?"

"Up in a hot air balloon."

"You're a pilot?"

"Of course I am. You can't pilot those things without a pilot's license."

"Will we be able to talk?"

"I wouldn't be asking you if I didn't think we could. They'll be too busy clicking photos to care what we're talking about. Take it or leave it."

Sounded fair enough. We arranged a time to meet early that evening and I spent the rest of the day missing Martha, worrying about Patrick, and working on a research paper.

I arrived at the field in the late afternoon, following Owen's excellent directions to a field near Carleton University. That and the presence of a number of balloons gave it away. I was early so I stood and watched as Owen and his crew readied their balloon. They'd already spread it out on the ground close to the wicker basket, which had some sort of contraption attached to it that I figured must be the burners used to heat the air. Two people were attaching the basket to the balloon using carabiners that I hoped weren't as flimsy as they looked. A big burly guy then took a rope — or was it a line? — that was attached to the very top of the balloon and had some kind of wicker ring on the other end. He walked it straight back from the crown of the balloon and waited. Meanwhile, Owen had manhandled a big fan so that it was facing the little opening of the balloon that was being held open by two other crewmembers. I wondered how many crewmembers were normally needed to make this thing work. It was nowhere near as easy as I had thought it was. You earned your flight with these things.

I watched as the balloon began to move, the air from the fan swirling around inside and the gossamer red cloth billowing out. The burly man, now a long way out in the field, was holding the rope's ring, had planted his feet, and was attempting to keep the motion of the balloon to a minimum. Once the balloon was about two thirds full of cold air Owen started the burners and hot air began flowing into the balloon. Slowly, gracefully, it began to rise from the ground. Fire and fragility. The cloth so thin that it didn't look possible for it to lift the little wicker basket. I glanced at my watch then looked around and saw others like me, hovering in the wings, waiting for their rides or just watching.

Owen's balloon was now fully inflated with a line tethering it to the truck that I presumed was going to follow us by land. I started forward and stood close to the balloon while Owen did whatever he had to do to ready the balloon for takeoff — a slightly different set of rules from a plane but the same basic training. Two of the crew came over to the basket and leaned on it as human anchors. When Owen finally noticed me he gave me a smile and waved me over.

"The couple from New Jersey are a few minutes late. They should be here any minute. You can come aboard if you want."

The basket looked so flimsy! I'd never been near a hot air balloon, much less been in one. I climbed into the basket. It was smaller than I expected, perhaps because of the propane tanks, fuel lines, and navigation equipment, and everything was padded like an isolation cell. I looked up. The burners above my head were supported by a four posted metal frame and fired by propane. When I looked beyond them into the mesmerizing softness of the balloon it reminded me of all the tents I'd ever slept in. Of course, none were ever as big as this.

I dragged my eyes away from the balloon and watched the big burley guy coming in from the field. He handed Owen the rope and then became another human anchor. Owen was busy with the burners and absent-mindedly dropped the end of the ringed rope into the corner of the basket. I wondered if there were two kinds of balloonists, the way there are two kinds of sailors: those who secure or neatly stow all their ropes and those who don't. I watched as the balloon next to us took off and saw that they hadn't even bothered to bring their line in; it was dangling beneath the basket like a loose thread.

I took my camera out of my pocket and snapped a bunch of artsy-fartsy shots while I waited for Owen and the people from New Jersey. They were taking their own sweet time. I hoped they wouldn't be too talkative and make it hard for me to talk to Owen, but I didn't really have much to say.

I'd read all there was to know about the accident with Heather. Terry had been at the wheel and it had seemed pretty cut and dried. She hadn't seen her; the bow of the boat was riding high because of the weight of people in the back. But I knew that Owen knew more about Terry than he was letting on. He was her brother. He had to.

I was leaning on the basket, watching another balloon take off, when the balloon moved and I glanced back to see Owen fiddling with the burner. Suddenly he yelled "Hands off!" and let the tether line go. We immediately began to rise, our three human anchors fading from view. I instinctively stepped back from the edge but there wasn't really anywhere to go, the basket was so small.

"The New Jersey couple?" I said, as I tried to calm an uneasy feeling in the pit of my stomach.

"Couldn't make it. Just got the call. Might as well go anyway," he said.

I cautiously looked over the padded edge of the basket. We were already forty feet up. Too high to jump. But maybe I was jumping to conclusions.

"Pretty impressive, eh?" he said. "Look over there. The Parliament Buildings."

And there they were, stalwart stone edifices of another era, soaring towards us, the clock tower like a finger beckoning. We were low enough that I imagined I could see the eternal flame on Parliament Hill. I could clearly see the library at the back of Parliament, its many windows reflecting the sun as it sat perched on the cliff overlooking the Ottawa River. I wondered if we were actually allowed here. It seemed like such an easy thing to fly over and drop a bomb. Between blasts from the burner it was quiet, no rushing air because we were moving with the wind. I was mesmerized by what little lay between us and annihilation. A little wicker basket, like an oversized picnic basket, yards and yards of gossamer cloth that reminded me of a spinnaker, and the flames licking up into the balloon.

Owen brought the balloon down quite low as we cruised over Gatineau, then silently flew over the trees to Meech Lake. By now I trusted the little basket and was actually leaning up against it and watching the land fly by us. I could see little wavelets on the water but felt no wind on my own cheek. Weird. I had totally forgotten the reason for being there, I was so mesmerized by the whole experience. We were really close to Harrington Lake, the Prime Minister's summer retreat. I wondered if he was in residence and if there was a no-fly zone over his place — but how can you enforce that on a hot air balloon driven by the wind?

I suddenly remembered why I was there and turned to look at Owen. But as I began to ask him about Heather he handed me a paperback book. I looked at him questioningly.

"Look at it. It's an advance copy," he said. "I need you to know what a mess you've made of things for me."

I looked at him curiously and then took the book; *KillJoy* by Terry Spencer. I looked up at him, uncertain what he wanted me to do.

"Read the back."

The little blurb said it was a book about black market organs and then it quoted some of the book.

"Now read the first page," he said.

I opened the book and felt the skin crawl on the back of my neck as I read. "Drenched in oil and blinded by blood, she held her breath and jumped."

My heart did somersaults in my throat. Dear god, I was alone in a little basket way up in the sky, with the man who had been trying to kill me. Had it been Owen all along? Trying to safeguard his investment? In cahoots with his sister? Did he know it was a book that had already been published? Sweet revenge that.

"Is that why you tried to kill me?"

He smiled at me and said, "You ruined everything the minute you picked up the manuscript on the plane and I saw you reading the first page. Unfortunately, I couldn't know how much or even what pages you'd read." He reached out and took the book from me. "You know, you've been particularly difficult to kill. When I visited your cabin on the ship I was sure that I could knock you out and throw you overboard. And that polar bear was a gift that didn't quite work out."

"And the Zodiac?"

"You are so impressionable, but you were barking up the wrong tree when you thought someone had cut the ropes. They really were frayed."

"So you had no hand in the Zodiac fiasco?"

"I didn't," he said. "But Terry did."

I waited impatiently for him to continue.

"I'd told her about you reading the manuscript and she was livid, with me and with you. When she stood up in the Zodiac she was aiming directly for you."

"To knock me overboard," I said slowly.

Owen nodded.

"And what about the dog?" I said.

He smiled. "Everybody just thought you were nuts. I played into that and took advantage of circumstances."

"And the fire?"

"Yeah, well, that took a little more thought."

"I'm glad you're so lousy at murder," I said, keeping my distance, trying to formulate a plan, any plan at all. "Why did you stop trying?" I was playing for time.

"Because I could afford to wait for the perfect opportunity. I never had to be good. If it worked, it worked. If it didn't there was always another time. It just had to look like an accident and happen sometime before the book came out."

"But you told me you didn't stand to gain anything from Terry's death."

"The book contracts were in both our names and I earned every penny. She agreed to it before she started making money because she was so grateful that I ghost-wrote her book. She tried to renege but our agreement was solid."

"What happens to her share now?"

"It goes to her estate."

I kicked myself for not getting back to Derek but I hazarded a guess. "Which, since she has no will, will go to you."

He shrugged and waved the book in my face. "This book is due out in a month and it stands to make me a pretty penny now that she's well-known. This is just an advance copy. So you see, I can't have you bouncing around like an out of control bowling ball." He looked at the book in his hands and then dropped it on top of a packsack.

So he didn't know. That gave me some much-needed courage. "Your so-called book was already published in 1927," I said, then paused to look at him. "By an Archibald Graham. Sally just copied it to get you to show your hand."

His jaw had dropped and I knew I'd hit a very raw nerve. But he recovered his cool frighteningly quickly. "A doomed woman will say anything to save her skin."

He smiled as if he had some secret he wanted to tell me. And then, with no warning, he lunged at me. I didn't even have time to put up my hands as his body slammed into mine. As I felt myself going over the edge of the basket I saw the line snaking down from the crown of the balloon. I reached out and grabbed it just as Owen pitched me overboard. I went into a dizzying drop as I swung out and away from the basket, slipping a few feet down the rope. I managed to stop my fall with clenched hands and a prayer as the end of the rope fell out of the basket and tumbled past me. I looked up and saw the underside of the basket and the balloon soaring far above it.

Of all the thoughts that tumbled through my mind as I hung suspended, the last thing I expected was anger that I'd die without answers. I knew that I wouldn't be able to hang on for long. I tried to grab the rope with my legs, but it was swaying wildly and I couldn't get a grip. I had to get to the wicker ring and give my hands something more concrete to grasp. It would buy me time. I glanced down quickly and looked up again, my mind and my body fighting over control of me. There was only five feet of rope below me and I cautiously moved down, hand over hand, to grab hold of the ring with both hands. But the psychological loss of the extra length of rope was unnerving. Nothing stood between me and Mother Earth.

I glanced down again and sucked in my breath. We were awfully close to the trees. If Owen dropped much lower maybe I could let go and chance getting skewered. We seemed to be going quite fast though.

My body was starting to tell me that I couldn't hold on, that I had to let go and everything would be okay. My head was in a screaming match with my body. It horrified me that my body might win, no matter how good an argument my mind had.

At about that point my brain finally registered what was happening on the basket end of the rope. Why hadn't he cut me loose? Surely there was some way a pilot could secure an errant line he couldn't reach by hand? I tried to remember what had been in the basket, but my mind was too traumatized to concentrate. I looked down again and saw that the trees were closer, looming up like little pointy umbrellas, and suddenly I realized what he was doing. He was going to drag me through the trees until I let go. Nice and clean. Of course, he could just wait for me to fall, but maybe he was just impatient to be rid of me.

I was on the verge of panic and my arms were throbbing from holding on. The urge to let go was almost overwhelming. I looked up but he was busy doing something. We were dropping and suddenly the trees were right there. As they raked my legs I tried to climb back up the rope, but there wasn't a hope with the condition of my arms. I brought my legs up as the treetops bent past me.

Suddenly the trees gave way to a lake. I looked down at the water and found it hard to judge the distance. We were almost level with the trees on the shoreline so we couldn't be that far from the water. I weighed my chances. A fall from, say, thirty-five feet into water would be okay if I fell the right way. Those Olympic divers dive from heights like that, don't they? Of course, I wasn't an Olympic diver, but it seemed like a better bet than being slammed into a forest.

By now I was hanging at least twenty feet from the basket; plenty of space for him to smash me into the trees on the far side of the lake and still control the balloon. I clung to the rope, my body feeling numb and surreal

— my mind foggy and dozy. It happened suddenly. My mind and my body let go as one and I concentrated on making my entry to the water as straight as possible, my body rigid through fear, not design. I hit the water feet first, the impact took my breath away as I plummeted deep beneath the surface. I crawled my way back up, fighting for air and retching as I treaded water and watched the balloon languidly float over the trees and out of sight with Owen staring back at me.

I was in the middle of the lake. Fortunately, the weather was still warm so I didn't have any heavy clothes on. I kicked off my shoes and swam towards the nearest shore, confident that Owen would not be there to greet me.

I crawled out of the water and lay there for a while, thinking about nothing, looking up at the trees and listening to the birds twittering.

I didn't hear the man coming. All of a sudden he was just there, looking down at me, puzzled. I sat up and he immediately drew a gun on me. He couldn't have been more than twenty-five years old and since I was all out of adrenaline I eyeballed him with some curiosity, wondering if Owen had hired crew to follow my descent.

"Who are you and what are you doing here?" he asked gruffly.

I could have asked the same of him but I didn't. Instead I said, "I just fell out of a hot air balloon."

He looked skeptical and asked for my ID. That was a relief — he wouldn't ask for ID if he was one of Owen's minions. But that's when I got skeptical and asked who he was.

"I patrol the grounds for the Prime Minister." Harrington Lake. Of course; I'd landed in the Prime Minister's summer retreat.

I fished through my wet jeans pocket and handed him my wallet. He eyeballed it and then offered me a lift back to his station where he said he had to fill out a report.

I didn't get to meet the Prime Minister, but I guess I couldn't complain. After all, I was alive.

I told my story about Owen and the balloon to the security guards and again to the police. They were very polite and didn't question my sanity, but the cards were stacked against me since apparently no one had noticed the balloon with a person dangling from a rope flying over Harrington Lake. Something about a change of shift was mentioned. They told me they'd look into it and get back to me. The fact that someone had tried to kill me didn't seem to merit immediate attention. A bodyguard would have been nice.

I called Patrick and told him there was a change in plans and could I stay at his place? It was a mess of packed boxes, he said, but I could tell he was happy for my call. I didn't dare go home for a change of clothes for fear of Owen, but I did call Ryan and let him know the situation.

I arrived at Patrick's still wet and bedraggled. I showered and changed into some spare clothes with many caressing interruptions from Patrick and a backrub in the shower. It had been what I had wanted to avoid and not avoid. The last time. So final. The last time remembered as the last time, as it was happening, was worse than remembering the last time in retrospect. I told Patrick about the balloon incident and he was really upset.

He grabbed me by the arms in the bathroom and I winced. They still felt like pulled taffy wrapped in one big ache. He tightened his grip, staring straight into my eyes. "You can't keep putting yourself in danger like this; you're going to get killed. It's not worth it, Cordi."

But I actually thought it was very much worth it. Justice; plus, if I had to be truthful, it was a real adrenaline rush to be put in situations where I had to test my own strength and courage. And even more of a rush when it worked. I felt invincible, which probably wasn't a good thing — I thought of all the invincible people now lying six feet under. I changed the subject. "Patrick, Owen showed me the jacket cover from Terry's new book. He's obviously publishing it posthumously."

He waited for me to go on.

"The back cover has an excerpt from the book." I paused for effect. "Word for word, it's what I read on the plane."

I waited for his reaction but there was none.

"Don't you see? Terry stole Sally's book, although it wasn't actually Sally's. It was written by a guy in 1927. Anyway, the manuscript was handwritten by Sally and the suicide note was identical to a scene in the book."

Patrick whistled. "So you think that's why he was trying to kill you on the ship? Because you would know as soon as you saw the book that Terry had stolen the manuscript."

"And that I might recognize the suicide note."

"So now I'm leaning away from the murder-suicide theory."

"And leaning towards?"

"Double murder."

Chapter Twenty-Five

The next day I awoke with the stomach flu and spent the day in Patrick's bed, hoping he wouldn't catch it. I was well enough to go into work the following day, and left before Patrick woke up — was I a coward? You bet. All morning and afternoon I found it impossible to work, but of course I had to.

I kept thinking about Owen. I needed to find out more without getting killed. I couldn't just let him control my life and then waltz in and end it. On impulse I packed up my things and glanced at my watch: 5:30. I still had an hour before our dinner and three hours before Patrick had to be at the airport. I took the Parkway to Parkdale, then went along Carling, past the high school, to Bank. I drove to within a block of Owen's garage, not really knowing why I was going, just knowing that I had to — offence rather than defence.

I walked the rest of the way on the other side of the street and studied the building. It was a large factory-type place, extending back from the street about a hundred feet. I remembered that the offices were in the front, but I'd never seen what was in back. I had no plan and no certainty that looking around his place would bring me any kind of information or proof of his theft — like a pile of Terry's new books. The police would believe that. But I didn't want to be just a sitting duck.

The storefront looked closed. I crossed the street and walked toward the building, deciding to duck down the back lane and see if there was any way in from the back. I needn't have worried. The two large back doors were wide open. I looked around me and then inside the building. Seeing no one, I entered the building; a typical boxy warehouse with off-white siding on the outside and unfinished plywood on the inside. It was full of cars and motorcycles, seemingly parked at random throughout the one room space. I was sneaking in along the sidewall, behind a dark grey BMW, when I was suddenly jerked to a standstill. My heart thumped around my body for a while until I realized I'd just caught my jacket on a blue Subaru. I yanked it off and it tore, the rip sounding like a canon going off in a Quonset hut. I stopped dead in my tracks and waited, but there was no hue and cry. I picked my way down past a blue Camaro, a lemon yellow VW, and a really nice old BMW motorcycle in pristine condition, with the keys in the ignition. Suddenly I heard voices raised in anger coming from the doors I had just entered. I ducked down behind the VW to watch.

"You're Michael's wife? Jesus." The man looked about and then said, "Look, it was a tragic accident."

"How can you defend your sister? She was a cold-blooded murderer and you know it."

The man and a woman stood in the doorway and I had a clear view of both of them. One was Owen, hands in his pockets and scowling at Elizabeth, who was waving her arms about in anger.

"I don't know it," said Owen. "My sister walked in her sleep from the time she was five years old. All the experts agreed that it was a tragic accident. That's all. If you'd been at the trial you would have known that."

Elizabeth reached out and grabbed Owen by his shirt. "But you don't believe it, do you? You know what happened that night because you were there. She would have confided in you."

"Since you seem to know so much about her, what do you think happened?"

"I think you helped her fake it. The perfect murder. She did have a history of sleepwalking and the case in Ottawa where the guy killed one of his in-laws and got off on a sleepwalking plea set you both to thinking."

Owen laughed. "That makes me brilliant."

"No, that makes you a patsy."

Owen took one step closer to Elizabeth, his face unreadable. What the hell was Elizabeth trying to do?

"She told you what to do, didn't she? And you did it because baby brother has to follow big sister's instructions. She treated you like a dog and you weren't man enough to stand up to her."

"You can't be serious."

"You did everything for her, everything. I think you planned the murder and told her what to do."

Owen visibly squared his shoulders, and I was pretty sure I could see a smug looking smile on his face as a gun suddenly materialized in his left hand. Where the hell had that come from?

The two of them stood frozen and framed in the doorway and I crouched there, paralyzed, wondering what the hell I could do, wondering what Elizabeth would do, and wondering what Owen would do.

His voice was low and wistful. "No one ever understood that the brains behind Terry were mine and always had been. Until now." He looked at her. "Everyone ignores me. They say I'm a patsy, just like you did, but without me Terry would have been nothing." He waved the gun at Elizabeth. "Ugly little brother — that's what I was until Michael."

Elizabeth looked stunned. "You had her kill Michael."

Owen laughed. "Terry, kill Michael? Give me a break. Even in her sleep she couldn't have done that without my help." He paused. "It was so easy. She was just the instrument that I played. I was used to following her when she sleepwalked, so like every other time I kept close to her in case she did something stupid. When she picked up the knife I almost stopped her, but something told me to wait." He sighed. "When she got to Michael's tent I followed her in and watched in fascination as she raised the knife two-fisted over Michael's body. I'd heard about the case in Ottawa — the acquittal — and realized I was looking at exactly what Terry needed to kick-start her career. But the stupid idiot froze so I came up quietly behind her and took her hands gently in mine, and together we killed Michael."

"You killed Michael for a goddamned career boost?" cried Elizabeth, the anguish in her voice causing Owen to look at her.

He laughed. "For the sensational publicity of a trial and an acquittal to launch a book about her experience as an innocent murderer. It worked too. She made her name on that book, although even then I had to help her."

Elizabeth stood there speechless, her fists clenching and unclenching as she took in what Owen was saying. "And Michael's book...?"

"Was gravy ... I didn't even think about it until he was dead."

I heard Elizabeth moan. "You killed my husband for gravy?"

"You could put it that way. You have to realize it wasn't that easy. I had to make sure no one had read it. But Michael was very accommodating. He was so secretive about his writing and only handwrote everything."

"You fucking bastard." Her voice was so full of hatred that even Owen was aware of it and he backed up several paces to keep his distance from her.

"I don't think it's a good idea to talk like that to a man with a gun." Owen jerked the gun and stared at Elizabeth, who suddenly squared her shoulders and glared at Owen.

"The sleepwalking murderer was a sensation. She was in all the papers and then when she was acquitted there was the story about the trial, her time in jail, her emotional pain. And plenty of publishers were lining up to buy it. It was a bestseller and it got her career off on the right foot." He was *really* rubbing it in.

"And you ghostwrote it."

"I ghostwrote it. So you see who really was in control."

"You were always stepping in for her, weren't you Owen?" Elizabeth's voice was frightening. "Was Michael just the first of many? How many books has she published? How many pseudonyms? How many murdered writers?"

Owen didn't answer.

"You pushed LuEllen down the stairs after you found out she was going to vote guilty. Your plan didn't call for Terry ending up in jail for good, just long enough to get material for a book. A hung jury would have ended in another trial. You didn't want that. The first trial was risky enough as it was — you knew that some other sleep-walking defences had failed — and Terry had already been in jail long enough." Elizabeth paused and then said in a cold hard voice, "And what about Heather?"

"You don't seem to get the point, lady. I killed Heather. Terry didn't do it. It was easy to do. I just bumped into Terry and grabbed the wheel from her for a split second. I know she knew but she never said anything. She played the perfect innocent, because she was. Same as with Michael."

"All for the sake of finding book material for Terry."

Owen shrugged.

"Whose idea was it to use Michael and Heather's manuscripts?"

"Who do you think?" sneered Owen.

"Rather lucky to find two very private and eccentric writers who refused to use computers."

"Not as hard as you might think. And it's a big country. Terry gave a lot of classes."

"Risky. What if they'd made a photocopy or read part of their work to someone else?"

"Risk is part of life."

"So is anger. Do you realize Sally died for nothing? That she was acting a part in order to flush Terry out? Only it turned out to be you ..." She paused. "You didn't know that did you?"

Owen cleared his throat but said nothing.

"Did you know that her manuscript was bogus?"

Owen still didn't respond.

"How do you feel about Terry now? She made you kill an innocent woman for nothing. What does that feel like, I wonder?"

"You think I killed Sally?" He laughed, but the bravado was gone.

"Yes, and I think you killed your sister too. There were no heroics here, no Sally saving Terry. You drowned Terry in her bathtub because she'd used you one too many times. You felt trapped by her, but you were not strong enough to cut the ties. She controlled you like a puppet and you let her. And then you killed her."

Owen laughed. "She only used me because I let her. She didn't control me. I controlled her. I let her think she used me. I used her as a murder weapon for Michael, then I convinced her that Heather and the others would benefit her if they were dead. She owes her fame to me. As I said, I made it happen for her."

Others? But Elizabeth had moved on. "Why? Why would you kill for her?"

"She was my big sister."

"You mean you killed Michael because she was your big sister?" Elizabeth's voice was on the edge of control and beginning to slip over. "So what went wrong?" she whispered, visibly trying to pull herself together.

Owen bit his lip as if debating on whether to tell Elizabeth everything. If he did it was her death sentence. I sidled over toward the BMW.

He finally made up his mind. "She was in the tub when I came to her cabin. She wanted out. Couldn't stomach the bad stuff, she said. I couldn't make her understand that there was no way out, no turning back. She belittled me, told me I was incompetent and a leech living off her income. Then she actually had the nerve and the unmitigated stupidity to try and cut me off. She fired me. Her own brother. I lost it." He was brandishing his gun now.

"So you drowned her."

"Yeah. I drowned her. It was so easy. It only took a minute. I was so angry, after all I'd done for her. But then I had to carry her outside so I could dump her overboard and she looked so pathetic lying there naked so I wrapped her in a towel. But then I heard Sally coming and had to dump Terry in the pool. I left the towel to make people think she'd just come from the sauna."

"And Sally? What happened to Sally?"

"Sally was collateral damage. But not the way you think. How was I to know she'd play the stupid little hero? She jumped in to rescue Terry without taking any of her clothes off. She was struggling but I couldn't stick around, and it suddenly struck me as the perfect murder-suicide. Sally kills Terry because she is distraught over Terry and

Arthur becoming a couple, then she kills herself, leaving behind a suicide note."

"Why not just keep it simple? Sally tries to rescue a drowning Terry and fails. They both die."

Owen smiled. "That was my initial reaction, but when I put the towel over the railing I suddenly remembered that the pool water was salt water and that the autopsy would show fresh water in her lungs. The police would start to snoop so I gave them a murder suspect."

"But the suicide note?"

"Was from her handwritten manuscript. It was too bad to have to sacrifice it, but what a gift. Anyway, I felt I had no choice. Just as I have no choice now." He raised the gun and I kicked the BMW to life. Owen jerked his head in my direction as the engine roared and Elizabeth pounced. I could see her out of the corner of my eye, struggling with Owen's gun arm as I skidded ninety degrees and drove straight for them and the doors beyond. Elizabeth and Owen looked up, even as the gun skittered across the doorway with Owen in pursuit. I slowed long enough for Elizabeth to get on and then opened the throttle and drove out into the sunlight. I turned the wrong way and had to make a big circle to come round to the driveway leading out to the main street.

"Owen is getting into a car," yelled Elizabeth as we screamed out of the driveway, bumped down onto the road, and squealed around ninety degrees then headed down Bank toward the Queensway highway, taking the turn at Catherine Street almost too fast. We went up the on ramp and onto the highway as I tried to figure out just where to go.

"He's right on our tail," yelled Elizabeth.

I had pulled out to the outer lane when suddenly Owen was beside us, forcing me into the gutter rail. I slowed and he slowed. So I sped up. He sped up and was just in front of me when suddenly he opened his car door and hit the brakes. I braked and swerved looking for the lifesaving hole between his door and the gutter rail. And found it. Just. I squirted through, feeling like throwing up but knowing I couldn't. Elizabeth was hanging on to me and I whipped over three lanes of traffic, took the off ramp at Parkdale, and squealed through a red light and under the Queensway.

We caught the light at Carling and Elizabeth craned her neck. "I think I see him. Blue Camaro, four cars back."

We played cat and mouse along Carling until I did another fast two-lane switch and turned down towards Dows Lake.

"Still with us," yelled Elizabeth.

I took a right at the lake and once I entered the traffic circle I stayed in it, feeling a bit like a rolling stone going nowhere fast. But at least I could keep moving until we ran out of gas. On our third pass around, the blue Camaro came screaming in ahead of us and we followed Owen for three turns before he manoeuvred his car behind us. The bump almost wrenched the handlebars out of my hands and I fought for control as the bike skidded sideways. We came out of it just before I was about to give up and I gave the engine more gas. We were taking that roundabout way too fast, with Owen on our tail, when I saw a policeman enter the circle. I made up my mind. I went around once more, unable to see where the policeman had gone because of the mound of grass, trees, and shrubs in the centre. I flew by two exits before I saw him speeding away through the experimental farm in the heart of Ottawa. He was going pretty fast and I had to open the throttle to catch him. When I was right on his tail I waited until two oncoming cars were out of the way then I pulled out and roared past him. It didn't take long before I heard his siren and I pulled over, my body numb and wobbly. I was glad I had Elizabeth's legs to help stabilize the bike.

"Jesus. Where did you learn to drive like that?"

I watched as Owen cruised by, looking at us, and I wondered how this would all end.

"Ryan — my brother."

"Thank god for Ryan," said Elizabeth.

Chapter Twenty-Six

The policeman had been very patient as we told him the whole story about Terry and Owen and the writing group, but you could see the skepticism in his eyes as he wrote it all down, including my asking him to cross-check with the police on the balloon incident. He'd probably heard every story in the book from motorists anxious to avoid a ticket. But Elizabeth had been livid that he didn't seem to understand what we were saying. We were talking murder and attempted murder. She was flinging her arms all over the place and working up quite a sweat. The cop eventually calmed her down and as he took details from us she thrust her right hand in her pocket, pulled out the little elephant, and began fiddling with it.

We were caught speeding, without helmets, on a bike for which we could produce no registration. And my wallet was missing. It must have been forced out of my jacket pocket when it got caught on the Subaru fender.

The policeman impounded the bike and we spent several hours at the police station straightening things out. They said they'd look into my allegations concerning Owen. Elizabeth and I had to find our own way home. She was in such a strange and angry mood that I offered to share a cab, even though we lived in exactly the opposite direction, but she would have none of it.

It was just before 11:00 by the time I finally got to my car back at Owen's garage. As I was about to get in I looked up into the night sky and saw the blinking lights of a plane bound for who knew where. Patrick! I'd forgotten about Patrick in all the excitement.

I grabbed my cell phone, knowing it was useless, knowing he was gone, perhaps even on that plane overhead. But I dialed anyway because I needed something to do. The chirpy little female voice said he was unavailable. Unavailable. It sounded so final. I dragged myself out of self-pity, then got into the car and headed to a hotel. With Owen still on the loose there was no way I was going home. But on the way there my resolve broke. I didn't want to spend the night alone. I went to Martha's.

She opened her door to my knock, took one scandalized look at me and said, "Lord. What's happened to you?"

I collapsed on the sofa and told her everything, ending by saying, "So now he's going to find my wallet first thing in the morning. I'm screwed. He'll just tell the cops I stole his BMW and my wallet will be additional proof that I was there. And I have nothing against him, nothing I can prove."

"I don't like what you're thinking, Cordi."

"But you don't know what I'm thinking."

"I still don't like it."

I got up off the sofa and headed for the door.

"Where are you going?"

"To get my wallet. I can't go in the morning and risk his being there. I'll never get it back otherwise." And I thought of the poem in that wallet. Patrick had written it for me when we first met. That was worth a small fortune to me.

"But it'll be locked."

"Maybe I'll get lucky."

"But isn't going to his garage a little stupid?"

"At this hour? He doesn't sleep there. It's the perfect time to go."

I opened Martha's front door and stopped on the threshold — she bumped into me. "I'm coming with you. You're going to need a second pair of eyes, in case someone comes."

I started to object but she gently pushed me out the door and shut it behind her.

We drove to Bank Street and parked the car a good block away, then walked back on the far side of the street. We looked across at his garage. The front office was in darkness, except for a low energy nightlight that had a bluish tinge, making it look as though someone was watching TV. I couldn't see the back offices. I wondered if he had an alarm system. We crossed the road a few houses down and walked along the sidewalk to the laneway that Elizabeth and I had roared down on the BMW.

There were no windows along this side of the building. When we rounded the corner there was one outside light at the back, but unlike my last visit the large doors were shut. We snuck up and checked the doors. Locked with a double padlock. But there was a small side door and we sidled over to it. No alarm sticker on it. I reached out to grab the knob when Martha jerked my shirt and nearly gave me heart failure.

"Fingerprints!" she hissed, ignoring the fact that I had just planted them all over the double doors. I was about to make some caustic retort when I realized we didn't have the time. We were drenched in a spotlight in full view of anyone looking our way.

I wound my jacket around my hand and tried the knob. Locked. We went back down the side of the building, scanning for anything. I was about to give up when I saw a little window about five feet up off the ground. It looked as though it was slightly ajar but I couldn't be sure. I looked at Martha and she looked up at the window, shook her head.

"You're not that small, Cordi," she said. "Besides, how would you get up there?" She glanced at my face and shook her head again. "You never give up, do you?" she asked as she bent over and I clambered up onto her back.

I wasn't sure why the window was there, other than for ventilation, but it was unlocked. I pulled it open as wide as it would go and looked in. There was a platform running along the length of the building just under the window, so I began squirming my way inside. Once I got my head and shoulders through I knew I was home free. I moved along the walkway to the stairs, went to the back door and let Martha in.

There was a scuffling sound over by the door to the office and I nearly grabbed Martha and bolted. But as we listened there was no repetition of the noise, just a low humming sound from the eerie nightlights. The cars, so brightly coloured by day, were dark, empty shapes, their presence somehow sinister. Quietly, we moved down the row of cars to where I had caught my jacket. It was so dark that I had to get down on my hands and knees and do a sweep before I found it. Martha was jerking her head all over the place — on the lookout I guess.

When I finally stood up she said, "Find it?"

"Yes," I whispered.

"Now let's go."

But I wasn't paying attention. I was looking at the door that led to the front offices. It was slightly ajar. Had it been that way when we first came in? I couldn't remember. I remembered the scuffling sound and the thought thumped through my mind that maybe Owen was here, hiding, waiting for us. It was an unnerving thought. But then why would he be skulking around his own shop in the dark? He couldn't have known I'd be dumb enough to come back for my wallet or lucky enough to find a way in. My heartbeat slowed and I touched Martha on the sleeve and jerked my head in the direction of the door. "Maybe we can find something in Owen's office that will incriminate him."

Martha gave me a startled-all-to-hell look that nearly made me laugh. The look eased into full-blown resistance and then into restrained acquiescence.

"What, like a written notarized confession?" she whispered.

I ignored her and headed toward the door. It was so quiet and the lighting was so eerie that it made me feel like I was on the set of a horror movie. I peered through the door. There were more nightlights in the hall but there was no light spilling out of any of the office doors. No one was home. We still crept down the hall as if there was someone there and I snuck my head around Owen's office door. It too was dimly lit by nightlights, although his had a reddish tinge. As my eyes adjusted I jumped back into the hallway and Martha let out an involuntary grunt then looked horrified. I put my finger to my lips and looked again. Thank god he was a deep sleeper. Owen was sitting at his desk, his head and arms resting on top of it in an awkward fashion. But it was his right hand that caught and held my attention. The dim red light shone dully off the barrel of the gun that he gripped, the same gun I had seen him waving at Elizabeth. When I looked more closely I could see the pool of blood he was lying in.

"I think he's dead," I whispered at Martha, as I moved back into the corridor.

She made a funny face at me that could have meant anything from, "Let's get the hell out of here," to "This is the stupidest thing I've ever done."

We entered cautiously, one at a time.

"Jesus. Don't touch anything, Cordi," Martha whispered.

I looked at her as if to say "duh." I went over to the desk and checked his pulse — I had to touch at least that and shook my head at Martha. He was still warm and it made me shiver. I glanced at the desk. There was a note, somewhat blood spattered, but I could make out enough of it to see it was a typewritten confession in the murders of Michael, Heather, and Terry. Sally didn't rate.

"He killed himself," said Martha as she hovered near the desk, one eye for Owen and one for the door.

"Looks like it."

"I don't get it," said Martha "Why would he kill himself if the only proof that existed was in his head."

"Maybe he couldn't stand what his sister had turned him into. A patsy. A murderer."

"But still, he loved her. Is that why he killed himself? Because he had killed someone he loved?"

It was pathetic really, a cold-blooded killer committing suicide. But then the value of a human life to a cold-blooded killer would be negligible, even his own life, it seemed.

As I reached out and picked up the phone with the hem of my shirt to dial 911, I saw something glinting in the purple broadloom just under the sofa. I bent down to take a look and caught my breath. A little bronze elephant with a broken tusk.

Martha's antenna went sky high when she heard me gasp and she zipped over to take a look.

"Elizabeth's been here. Tonight."

"How do you know?"

"Because two hours ago we were in a cop car and she was fiddling with her elephant."

"Do you think she tried to save him?" asked Martha as we looked at the typewritten note and the gun clenched in his right hand.

I had a flash back to the garage, Owen and Elizabeth and the gun. And suddenly I had a vision of Elizabeth's face as she learned what Owen had done, saw the anger and the revulsion, and the vengeance, saw Owen's hand gripping the gun — it had been in his left hand.

"Jesus," I said. "She didn't try to save him. She killed him."

"What?" said Martha.

"Owen was left handed."

The words were barely out of my mouth when there was a footfall in the corridor and suddenly Elizabeth blocked our way out with her body and a gun in her hand. Martha was standing next to her by the door and she waved her closer to me. "You're too smart for your own good, Cordi."

I'd always wondered about that expression until now. If I hadn't been so smart I wouldn't be about to die. Or maybe the word dumb works well too.

"What are you going to do? Kill us both?" I asked, as I judged the distance between us.

Elizabeth's gaze faltered.

"You're not the type, Elizabeth," I said.

"I killed Owen," she said between clenched teeth.

"But that was different. Your husband's death made it easy to want revenge."

She licked her lips and held the gun steady and I wondered if maybe I had underestimated her.

"We're just two people trying to solve the very crime you wanted avenged. You have no burning desire to kill us."

And into the silence that followed she said, "I have no desire to kill you." She looked beyond me, to Owen. "Unfortunately, I now have a need to kill you."

I should have seen that coming, but I definitely did not see what came next. A phone rang in the office across the hall, probably a wrong number, but for a split second Elizabeth turned her head away from us. In that splintered little moment Martha did the most amazing full-body tackle, catapulting Elizabeth against the wall. The gun slid across the floor and disappeared under the sofa.

"I got her! I got her!" Both Martha and Elizabeth were a tangle of arms and legs until finally Martha gained the upper hand and sat on the much lighter Elizabeth.

I stood there, opened mouthed, looking at the two of them, Elizabeth pinned down but still struggling and Martha, beaming at me. She turned around to check on her quarry and said, "For god's sake, she's turning blue. Get the gun, Cordi!"

Right! I thought, and went over to the sofa to fish around for the gun. But it was way under and I had to muscle the sofa out of the way to get it. I forced myself to pick it up as if I knew what I was doing, which I didn't. She would have had the safety off so I'd have to be super careful. I aimed it to the left and way above her head and Martha gave me a strange look and decided to stay sitting on Elizabeth, although she did shift her weight so Elizabeth could breathe.

I picked up the phone and dialed 911 with my free hand.

The police had arrived very quickly, but they took us down to the police station for the initial questioning. It was well past midnight before they were done with us (for the time being). As we drove back to Martha's we went over all the details of the evening again and again, until we were sick of them.

"Somehow it doesn't seem fair," said Martha finally. "On the one hand a truly cold-blooded killer never gets charged for his crimes, never gets what's coming to him, while his hot-blooded murderer will go to jail for a long time."

"Owen did die, Martha. That's a huge price to pay."

"Yeah, I guess it is. But that's not the way it's supposed to work. He should have been charged and tried and jailed for his crimes. Elizabeth shouldn't have had to take the law into her own hands and Sally should never have had to die."

We fell silent and watched the city roll by, the lights of Parkdale giving way to the lights of Wellington.

As we sat waiting for a red light Martha suddenly blurted out, "I hate my boss."

"I'm sure you'll get used to him," I said.

"He's a pompous ass."

"Well, that sounds like a bit of a hurdle, I admit."

"I'm coming back."

I played dumb but I was already starting to smile. "Where?"

"You know perfectly well where."

In the end I dropped Martha off and drove home for my first, somewhat foreshortened, night in my new home. The threat was gone and I wasn't adrift anymore. I needed to lick my wounds and figure out how to keep Patrick after what I'd done. He was somewhere over the Atlantic now — probably already in England — and I hadn't even said goodbye. How bad was that?

As I drove past the farmhouse, Barney, Ryan's new golden retriever, started making a ruckus and I floored it so he'd stop. He didn't. Instead he followed me down the lane barking his head off. When I turned down the drive to my cabin only my porch light and one living room light shone out at me in greeting. I pulled my car into the driveway and got out, breathing in the smell of fresh hay. It felt good to be free, to not have to look behind every door for a killer, to be able to venture into my home without any worry of an intruder bowling me over. Paulie jumped down from the porch and came over and rubbed up against me. I reached down and scratched her ears. I loved the purring sound she made, like a muted little engine softly whirring.

As I walked up the steps to the house, Paulie on my tail, a shadow flitted across the porch. I whirled. Old habits die hard. All I could see was a silhouette coming towards me from the direction of the farmhouse. "Hello?" I called out.

"Just me." Ryan's voice floated on the evening breeze and I realized how crazily I had hoped it would be Patrick. Ryan came up onto the porch and we sat side by side on the little bench I'd built the summer before, looking out into the darkness of the night.

"What are you doing up so late?" I asked him.

"I could ask the same question," he said softly.

He could always read my mind, my brother, and I knew he hadn't got up for the cows. I guess it was a brother-sister thing. So I told him everything that had just happened to me.

"Do you really think Elizabeth killed Owen?" he asked when I was through, and after he'd made enough brotherly comments to show me that someone cared what happened to me.

"Yes, I do, but we'll have to wait for the police to sort out who murdered whom. But off the record: Owen killed Michael in cold blood, using Terry as a murder weapon. Owen grabbed the wheel from Terry to kill Heather. He finally broke and killed Terry, but was tormented by it. Then Elizabeth, tormented by her need for vengeance, killed Owen and tried to make it look like suicide. And he just left Sally to die in the pool."

We sat in silence for a while, my mind squirming around like a two-year-old child.

"When did Patrick leave?"

"Probably when I was on the motorcycle."

"Shit. You didn't even get to say goodbye."

"No, I didn't."

He pulled me to him, gave me a hug. "He'll be back."

"Right. He'll be back," I said, but I wasn't sure I really believed that.

Also by
Suzanne Kingsmill

Forever Dead
978-1-550002-705-1
$11.99

The discovery of a bear-
ravaged body abandoned in the
wilderness, some killer rapids,
a fumigated lab, stolen research
disks, and a stalled career all
coalesce into the ripening
madness that hauls zoology
professor Cordi O'Callaghan
into some very wild, very dangerous places.

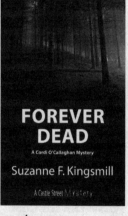

More Great
Castle Street Mysteries
from Dundurn

On the Head of a Pin
by Janet Kellough
978-1-55488-434-6
$11.99

Thaddeus Lewis, an itinerant
"saddlebag" preacher still
mourns the mysterious death
of his daughter Sarah as he
rides to his new posting in
Prince Edward County. When
a girl in Demorestville dies

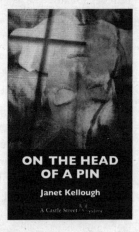

in a similar way, he realizes that the circumstances
point to murder. But in the turmoil following the
1837 Mackenzie Rebellion he can get no one to listen.
Convinced there is a serial killer loose in Upper Canada,
Lewis alone must track the culprit across a colony
convulsed by dissension, invasion, and fear. His only
clues are a Book of Proverbs and a small painted pin
left with the victims. And the list of suspects is growing
...

Blood and Groom
by Jill Edmondson
978-1-55488-430-8
$11.99

Someone in Toronto has
murdered nearly bankrupt
art dealer Christine Arvisais's
groom-to-be. Former rock
band singer and neophyte
private investigator Sascha
Jackson lands the case because
she's all Christine can afford.
The high society gal was jilted at the altar and she's the
prime suspect, not to mention Sascha's first major client.

In order to trap the murderer, Sascha enlists her ex-
boyfriend and former band mate to pose as her fiancé,
but will her ruse make her ex the next victim on the hit
list and lead to her own untimely demise?

Available at your favourite bookseller.

 DUNDURN PRESS
w w w . d u n d u r n . c o m

Tell us your story!
What did you think of this book?

Join the conversation at
www.definingcanada.ca/tell-your-story
by telling us what you think.